# Triangles

# Triangles

## Andrea Newman

MICHAEL JOSEPH
LONDON

MICHAEL JOSEPH LTD
Published by the Penguin Group
27 Wrights Lane, London W8 5TZ, England
Viking Penguin Inc., 40 West 23rd Street, New York, New York 10010, USA
Penguin Books Australia Ltd, Ringwood, Victoria, Australia
Penguin Books Canada Ltd, 2801 John Street, Markham, Ontario,
Canada L3R 1B4
Penguin Books (NZ) Ltd, 182–190 Wairau Road, Auckland 10, New Zealand

Penguin Books Ltd, Registered Offices: Harmondsworth, Middlesex, England

First published in Great Britain 1990

This collection Copyright © Andrea Newman 1990 and as follows:

Warmth 1973 (first published in *Cosmopolitan*); Poison 1982 (*Woman's Own*);
Secrets 1982 (*Woman's Own*); Counting the Cost 1984 (*Woman's Own*);
Finding a Voice 1984 (*Woman's Realm*); Fancy Seeing You 1985 (*Woman's Own*); A Long Way From Paradise 1985 (*Woman's Realm*); Jessica in Love
1986 (*Woman*); Christmas Magic 1986 (*Woman's Own*); The Consolation Prize
1987 (*Woman's Own*); Signs of the Times 1988 (*Woman's Own*); Casualties
1990; Luke's Women 1989 (*Living*); Memento Vitae 1990; Bliss on Wheels
1988 (*One to One*).

Filmset in 11/13pt Sabon by
Cambrian Typesetters, Frimley, Surrey
Made and printed in Great Britain by
Richard Clay (The Chaucer Press) Ltd., Bungay, Suffolk

A CIP catalogue record for this book is available from the British Library

ISBN 0 7181 3343 9

# Contents

# *Warmth*

They met at a party and he told her that he had been a virgin until he was twenty-nine. Several other people looked round in amazement, which her friends unkindly suggested later was probably the object of the exercise. But at the time she merely marvelled that anyone could admit such a thing in public, and thought him courageous.

He was then thirty-one. Of medium height, thick-set and dark with perfect features, he was probably the most beautiful man she had ever seen. She had several lovers and did not need a new one, but she took him home with her because of his beauty, as she might have bought a puppy or a picture. He made love quickly and clumsily, but with such warmth and enthusiasm that she was captivated against her will. In the night he woke her several times to make love again and was more demonstrative than anyone she had ever known, even her former husband. When he left for work in the morning he thanked her, which she found touching. 'Thank you for having me,' she said, her favourite old joke, and he replied gravely, 'Thank you for coming.'

They began to meet several times a week. He lived at home with his family whom he disliked but had not thought of leaving because they did his washing and put meals on the table. She tried to find out why he had made such a late start sexually, but he could not tell her and put it down vaguely to nerves. Also in his youth he had been seriously overweight. She could not imagine that he had ever been other than beautiful as he was now, so he showed her pictures to prove it.

He wanted to know about her other lovers and was pleased that she had them. Sex was so new and exciting to him, he said, that he wanted everyone to have as much of it as possible with any number of different partners. The concept of jealousy meant nothing to him. He did not intend to be faithful and did not expect fidelity from her. But he thought honesty was important. From time to time he mentioned various girls he had tried to sleep with but who had refused him.

In the summer they went away for a few days because he fancied himself in love with a girl in his office whom he wanted to leave her husband and live with him. The girl was not very interested and he thought a holiday might take his mind off her.

Despite this unflattering reason, the holiday was a success. The sun shone through the open roof of the car as they drove along. 'Come on, you golden beast,' he said. 'Shine on me, not on her.' He talked a lot about his work, which he enjoyed, and told her interminable stories about his childhood. When she was bored she had only to stare at his profile.

With him she felt the relaxation of youth: their jokes were repetitive, and very soon they had old favourites, always witty because well-beloved. They used catch-phrases that never failed to amuse and pulled faces and put on heavy accents. 'Ve have vays of making you laugh,' he would say in his stage German and she would collapse, knowing it was not really funny *again* but unable to resist it. Or he would imitate people in films or television for her entertainment, or mimic the speech of his colleagues at work. She found so much easy laughter very healing.

They ate huge meals and made love every night, every morning. He was always so affectionate that she felt she was floating in a warm bath, or painlessly connected to an electrical circuit, or elegantly wrapped in fur. Her other lovers had been sexy but cold, which ought to have been impossible but was only too easy: it meant that out of bed they did not like to be touched.

In the autumn he announced casually, 'I slept with a bird on Tuesday,' and described the details. It had not been very enjoyable and he wanted her to tell him why. What had he done wrong? She had never experienced jealousy before and found it uniquely painful. However, she tried to hide it as best she could because it was against his rules and she did not want to offend him. She reminded herself that he had warned her it would be like this, that sex was a novelty to him and he could not bear deceit. But she wished he had not told her. It always embarrassed her when he asked about her other lovers, although he did not mind at all.

He did not see the other girl again. They had had nothing to talk about, he said. She wondered what he meant. Sometimes she felt he did not know her at all. When she tried to tell him about her marriage he found it depressing. 'I don't like to hear about you being unhappy,' he said. If she talked about her work she could see his attention wandering. Her friends asked her if she thought she would become seriously involved with him and she said no, because he didn't have enough experience of life. She felt much older than he was, although they were the same age. He had all the charm and heartlessness of a child.

Gradually she taught him to make love expertly, until she thought she had never had a lover who suited her so well. But even more than that she enjoyed the pleasure she was able to give him. It was unique, he said.

He stayed at her flat several nights a week and every weekend. They went out to dinner or she cooked. They held hands in the cinema or watched television, curled up together like puppies. Between visits he would telephone her for no particular reason. Although she loved the calls, she always dreaded that he would mention another girl.

She would be unbearably tense until he referred to a boring evening at home or drinking with his friends, and then she had to disguise her relief. She tried to rationalise herself out of jealousy, but it was like toothache and would not be rationalised. It took over her head.

He began to talk about getting a flat of his own and she encouraged him. He was amazed.

'But why? You know it means I'll be more likely to sleep with other girls.'

She said, 'Yes, I know,' with an effort, 'but everyone should leave home and live alone some time.'

He took a flat but did not like it and was back with his family inside two weeks. 'I don't mind admitting I made a mistake,' he said.

At Christmas she thought she was pregnant and wanted to have it, which made her realise she had fallen in love with him. Another rule broken, for he had always said they must not become serious. He wanted her to have an abortion. He knew nothing about abortion and preferred not to be told; he thought it would be all right. Luckily she was not pregnant after all, but the incident unnerved her: she had not intended to get in so deep.

In February he had a short affair with his best friend's girl and was surprised that his best friend minded. He soon gave her up. 'Very dull and diluted compared to you,' he said. This time the jealous pain was much worse and against her better judgment she made several scenes which he disliked and she regretted. 'It's as if I'm eighteen,' he said. 'I want to try all the chocolates in the box.' She tried to keep calm and be fair, reminding herself that this was how she had felt when her marriage broke up. But she had kept each affair a secret from the other, if they were concurrent, to spare people's feelings. 'I never want to hurt you,' he said again and again, 'but I must be honest.' This made her feel it was her fault for being vulnerable.

He had changed his job to forget the married girl at work. In his new office he found another married girl and had a short affair with her. This girl she would have liked to kill.

He told her about the girl's contraceptive methods and her behaviour in bed. She tried not to listen but the subject had a terrible fascination. She lost control of herself and threw a glass across the room. It shattered a vase but remained intact itself, something she would have thought impossible had she not seen it happen. He was very upset by this display of violence but took her to bed and comforted her.

She asked him if he could keep it secret when he slept with other girls but he said that would be too difficult. If he had to be careful what he told her, it would spoil their relationship.

'I don't mind what you do,' he said. 'Why should you be jealous? So long as we're always honest with each other, that's the important thing. And you know I don't mean to hurt you.'

'No, but you do,' she answered.

'I'd hate to lose you,' he said. There was no answer to that, so they made love again and for a while she was happy.

She thought about it afterwards. It was true, he had never minded when she told him about other men, but now there was nothing to tell because she could no longer bear to sleep with anyone but him. Perhaps this was a burden to him. She wondered if she should invent other lovers to make him feel safe.

Her friends disliked him because he made her unhappy. 'You're mad to put up with it,' they said, flinching from her pain. 'But he makes me so happy as well,' she said. 'He makes me laugh and he's so warm and beautiful and sex with him is so marvellous.' She tried to explain, as much to convince herself as them. 'He's bound to want to sleep around, it's all so new to him, but maybe it's just a phase and if I'm patient he'll grow out of it.'

'Well, if he has to do it, at least he could keep quiet about it,' they said, angry on her behalf.

'I know,' she said, hating to hear her own thoughts expressed, 'but he's got this thing about honesty.'

She met his friends. Apparently they felt he was treating her badly too. But if anyone was unpleasant to him he did not mind. 'It's all attention,' he said.

He talked incessantly about himself, his past and his future. She listened, giving him even more attention than she had given her husband. It seemed a way of atoning. But they could not discuss anything controversial. 'I always feel you know more than me,' he said. 'You always win; you make me feel inferior.' At dinner parties he would change the subject after five minutes, just when she felt they were getting somewhere. 'I've got a butterfly mind,' he said cheerfully. Although she tried to accept that he preferred conversation to be superficial, she had to admit to herself that if she had not been in love with him she might have been bored. But they were so busy making love, eating and drinking, going for drives and laughing at each other's jokes that there was hardly time to notice. She reminded herself that nothing could ever be perfect: she had made the mistake before of expecting too much.

For six months he was very busy at work and she did not have to be jealous. Six months of warmth without pain: she absorbed it like a drug. 'I seem to have gone off other birds,' he said in a puzzled tone, as if he had lost interest in food. 'Never mind,' she said with an effort, 'I expect it'll come back.' He agreed. 'It's probably because I'm working so hard.' She took a chance and said, 'Of course, it can't be anything to do with me.' He laughed.

He began to talk about houses, children, dogs, all in a light-hearted, unspecific way, but often enough to give her hope that there was a future for them, although with her sober mind she knew it was insanity to think of such a thing. It was unlikely to happen and if it did it would not be ideal. But she was still under the physical spell she had created for herself. The power he was using over her was the power she had given him.

One time when he was very late and she had imagined him dead in a ditch, she let her panic and relief, combined with alcohol, allow her to commit the ultimate indiscretion of saying to him, 'I love you.' He had often told her he did not think he would ever be able to say that to anyone. 'But I suppose I love you more than anyone else,' he said, in bed and drunk. He went on about their being friends and fond of each other, which was not quite what she meant. 'I'll always want to sleep with you,' he said.

When she was ill he brought flowers and champagne, collected her medicine from the chemist, made funny faces to amuse her and cuddled her in bed until she felt better. 'I think you need me to look after you,' he said. He even emptied the bucket in which she'd been sick (before the champagne) and for this she was profoundly grateful. 'Well, you weren't very sick,' he said, 'or I couldn't have done it.'

They went abroad for two weeks and had a perfect holiday. Sun, food, wine, sex and laughter. It was hard to believe that anyone so demonstrative did not actually love her. The joy of sleeping with him every night made her a little dizzy, as if she had had too much sun.

After the holiday she had a doomed feeling, a premonition of disaster. They had reached their zenith: the rest could only be anti-climax. Everything continued as before but she could not repress her anxiety although she managed to hide it. It was so long since he had mentioned another girl. Had he learnt at last to deceive her? She did not want to know but the uncertainty nagged at her, poisoning everything. She had lived so long with the pain of being told: now that she had the relief of not knowing, she could not bear it.

In the autumn they went away for another week's holiday. It was not quite as perfect as before, although the sun shone, they ate lovely meals and made love every day or night. She could not have said what was wrong. She stared at his beauty, laughed at his jokes, curled up beside him in bed, and yet she felt there was a barrier that made a mockery of it all.

On the way back, at the airport, she suddenly asked if he had slept with anyone else recently. Yes, he said, twice. She felt the familiar constriction in her chest, the blackness, the heat, the demented sensation that made her understand what was meant by being beside yourself. She asked who it was and he told her. 'Was it a success?' she asked. 'That depends how you measure success,' he said.

She became quite dislodged from herself and made a scene in public, feeling that it was someone else who was behaving with such total loss of control. It was quite alarming, like being suddenly in the grip of a violent illness. He was embarrassed but held her hand all the way home as if to comfort her.

For two or three weeks they went on as if nothing had happened. Then one night he said he wanted to talk to her. 'I think we should meet less often,' he said. 'My feelings are not getting deeper. I don't think there's any future for us.' He told her he did not think he could ever love or marry anyone, or even live with them. 'It's been like one long honeymoon with you,' he said, 'but you have to come down to earth some time.' He began to cry and she had to comfort him: she held him while his body shook with sobs.

They went out to dinner. Once the shock had worn off and she had stopped fearing that she might be sick, she said she was willing to see him less often. He was pleased and grateful. 'I thought you'd throw me out,' he said. He became even more demonstrative, hugging her in the street. 'The trouble is,' he said, 'I find you so terribly attractive.' They spent the weekend together as usual making love, but she kept bursting into tears. 'Do you despise me?' she asked, and he said, 'No, I respect you more than ever.' The morning he left, she cried so much that her hairdresser took her out for a drink.

On Saturday he was back. 'I'm lonely and miserable too,' he said. 'It's not as if I'm leaving you for another girl.'

He behaved as affectionately as ever, confusing her, making her think she had imagined the whole thing. 'I'd like to die in bed with you,' he said one evening over dinner. But his visits grew less and less frequent. She never knew when he would phone and the uncertainty, after nearly two years of continuity, drove her crazy. She tried to be calm, just as she had tried not to be jealous, and with as little success. Her friends told her she should have given him up completely.

They spent Christmas together and opened their presents in bed. As usual, he had spent a lot of money on her. At New Year he was busy. The gaps between visits grew longer. She was supposed to be able to phone him, at work or at home, but did not feel she could. She imagined what he was doing. Her friends tried to console her but found her humiliation embarrassing. Some of them understood but others thought she should have had more pride. She tried to fix her mind on his faults. 'I never could talk to him about anything important,' she said. 'If it had lasted it would have been a disaster, I know that really.'

They met again and he was as amusing and demonstrative as ever. Encouraged by this, she invited him for the weekend. 'I can't,' he said. 'I'm seeing someone else regularly now.' She froze, hating him for not having, for never having had the grace to lie, to spare her feelings instead of his own. She asked, 'Does she know about me?' He said yes, and she lost control, hitting him and kicking him. Then she spent about five minutes telling him in precise detail all his faults. She dealt with his work, his family, his friends and his ego. He listened in silence, even nodding his head as if he agreed with her. Afterwards she could not remember what she had said but she knew she had covered it all. 'And I taught you everything you know,' she added, something she had always meant not to throw at him. He left in tears saying, 'I must go, I've been hurt.' Sobbing, she screamed at him, '*You*'ve been hurt? What about me?' He said, 'I know,' and left. In the morning he phoned to say they must meet and talk, but she knew it was over and he did not phone again.

It was almost a relief. At least there would be no more pain.

Later, talking to a friend, she said the worst part had been being in love with someone she did not respect. 'I suppose I wanted to fall in love and he was there,' she said.

Much later, talking to her favourite ex-lover who had returned, she told him what had happened. 'But think,' he said to console her, 'how boring it would have been if you'd kept him.'

'Boring but warm,' she said.

# *Poison*

Richard's best friend is called Nicky. They met at university and Richard was best man at Nicky's wedding. No doubt Nicky would be best man at our wedding, if we ever get married, but for one small snag: Nicky is a woman.

I wasn't jealous of Nicky at first. I was too busy falling in love with Richard and hearing all about his ex-wife Caroline. Nicky was just a name then; she was still living in California with her husband. If I was jealous of anyone, it was Caroline, for sharing all those years with Richard; but pretty soon I felt sorry for her instead. Poor Caroline: after all, she'd lost him, hadn't she?

I'd given up hope of meeting anyone like Richard; in fact I didn't believe men like him existed any more. Then one day he walked into the office, said he was looking for a two-roomed flat. He and his wife had just got divorced and they were selling the house and buying a flat each. I liked the matter-of-fact way he told me all that, although I was a stranger: I liked feeling he wanted to take me into his confidence. He didn't seem heartbroken, merely practical: it wasn't that he wanted me to feel sorry for him. But I did, of course.

I showed him all the flats we had on our books and he said any of them would do. He seemed remarkably uncaring where he lived. I urged him to wait, maybe pay a bit more, hold out for three rooms and a garden.

'If you're used to a house, you need extra space – and somewhere to sit in the sun, if we ever get any,' I said. He was a solicitor, so I thought he could afford it.

'You're delightfully bossy,' he said, making it sound like a compliment. 'Why don't we discuss my requirements over dinner?'

I don't remember what we ate that night. Richard said he couldn't bear people walking about above his head, so we agreed to look for a top-floor flat with roof terrace. I just kept gazing into his eyes and feeling dizzy.

He had strange-coloured eyes, sort of greeny brown, and a way of looking at you that made it hard for you to look away without seeming evasive. Rather like the way a cat stares at you: a challenge. He told lots of jokes against himself, laughing in a rueful way. When he smiled at me, I felt I was the most important person in the world. His hair was very short and curly, light brown, the sort you could wash and dry in ten minutes if you ran your fingers through it.

I was hopelessly in love.

'He sounds too good to be true,' my sister Kathy said when I told her about him. 'Thirty-two, divorced, solvent, sexy and *nice*. I simply don't believe it. Where's he been hiding? There has to be a catch.'

'Oh, don't, don't,' I moaned, drawing my knees up to my chin and rocking to and fro in her best bentwood chair.

'Did you sleep with him?'

'No.'

'Playing hard to get, eh? Very good.'

'He didn't give me the chance,' I wailed. 'He wouldn't come up for coffee. He just kissed my hand – my *hand*, imagine that – and drove off.' Leaving me chewing my knuckles with frustration.

'Clever chap.' She thought it over for a bit. 'You don't think he's gay, do you?'

'No, I do *not*.' I wanted to throw something at her

because she was saying all the things I'd thought. 'He told me I looked like the young Julie Christie.'

Kathy fell about with raucous laughter. 'That settles it,' she gasped, choking. 'He must be in love. And short-sighted as well.'

But the next time Richard took me out for dinner, he did come up for coffee and we fell into bed and it was wonderful. By then I knew all about Caroline and how she'd nearly driven him mad with her insane jealousy. She couldn't bear him to see his friends without her or even to work late, which was awkward as he did extra stuff in the evenings for the Citizens Advice Bureau and One Parent Families, which took up a lot of his spare time.

'Typical Aquarian,' said Kathy when I told her. 'All that social conscience and no time for his wife.'

'But she was having an affair all along,' I said triumph-antly. 'That's why they got divorced.'

After our first night together Richard made a date for the weekend before he left for work. No nonsense about phoning me later. That afternoon a huge bunch of flowers arrived at the office for me, with a note: 'Darling Alison, I thought I'd never be happy again. Thank you for proving me wrong.' It was as if he knew I was afraid he'd think me a tart and wanted to reassure me in advance. I burst into tears on the spot, and Ian, who was passing my desk at the time, said, 'Well, he's got style, I'll say that for him.'

'Oh, Ian,' I sobbed, 'I want you to meet him, I want your opinion, man to man. He's so wonderful.'

'Then you don't need my opinion, do you?' said Ian kindly, patting me on the head like an uncle. He'd been my first lover when I came to London and we were still good friends, which was just as well as we worked in the same office.

Richard and I started spending all our free time together. It was very exhausting. We were so busy making love and eating and looking at flats and telling each other our life stories that we got hardly any sleep and went around looking hollow-eyed but feeling unnaturally energetic, as if on a permanent high. Then a two-bedder with roof terrace came along and Richard said he wanted it. 'That is, if you do,' he said. 'I think we could be very happy here, don't you?' Three months later he moved in and I moved in with him. It was a great joke in the office that I'd found a new flat and a new man and still got my usual commission.

My parents were delighted, even though we were just living together. They thought it was only a matter of time before we got married and of course I was hoping that too. In any case they were sick of seeing me with married men and having me sobbing down the phone when each one went back to his wife. I hadn't enjoyed it much either, but I'd reached that stage, late twenties, when all the men I met seemed to be married. Until Richard. I felt so grateful to Caroline – if I'd met her I think I'd have gone down on my knees and thanked her for being such a jealous unfaithful cow. Something like that, anyway. Words to that effect.

Kathy and Ian were odd about Richard. They both claimed they liked him and they were happy for me, but Kathy said he was still too good to be true and Ian said he was used to getting his own way. Each remark sounded like a sinister warning, but when I complained to each about the other, I got the same response: 'Oh, it must be envy, pay no attention.' I pushed the thought away.

Nicky was still in America with her husband then. She was just a childish scrawl on an Air Mail envelope and Richard used to read out the funny bits. I thought it was nice that he shared her letters with me. I didn't mind her being a girl. I didn't mind anything in those early days: I knew we'd be happy for ever.

Then suddenly Nicky was getting divorced and coming home. Richard seemed very worried about her: apparently she was penniless. I didn't understand how; from what I'd heard of the Californian divorce laws, the wife got half of everything.

'True,' Richard said. 'But half of nothing is still nothing, even in California.' Apparently Nicky's ex-husband had gambled it all away.

Richard started getting the spare room ready for Nicky without even asking me. He tidied away all our suitcases under his desk and put my old duvet on the single bed.

'You don't mind, do you?' he asked, when he caught me inspecting his preparations. 'It's only for a few days, till she finds a flat.'

I hastily rearranged my expression. How could I say I minded Nicky in our spare room when only last week Ian had come to dinner, drunk too much and spent the night on our sofa because it was so near the office and saved him driving home? Richard hadn't minded that at all; in fact he thought it a great joke. Minding was something Caroline would have done.

'Of course I don't mind,' I said.

He kissed me and I felt rewarded. 'I'm longing for you two to meet,' he said. 'She's such fun – I just know you'll like her.'

It was a long drive to the airport so I had plenty of time to mull over that remark. Did he mean I wasn't fun and she wouldn't like me? Why was our relationship going to be so one-sided? Nicky was arriving at dawn and I could have stayed in bed, but I went along because I thought it looked more enthusiastic.

She was tiny. She wore blue jeans and a white T-shirt and no make-up, and she had very dark, very shiny hair that swung as she moved. It swung a lot as she hurled herself into Richard's arms and he actually lifted her off the ground.

'Oh, Ricky,' she announced to the airport at large, 'it's so great to see you.'

I could swear there were tears in her eyes, but she didn't let them fall, plucky little trooper that she was.

'This is Alison,' Richard said, when he finally put her down.

She looked at me for a moment and I was about to hold out my hand when she suddenly hugged me.

'I'm so happy about you two,' she declared. 'Ricky's had such a lousy time, he deserves a break.'

On the drive back I insisted she sat in the front seat. She didn't argue much. She and Richard kept up a continuous flow of chat about people they both knew and I didn't, including her ex-husband. Richard sounded as indignant about him as she was over Caroline.

Nicky defended him. 'He's changed a lot,' she said. 'It was really sad. By the time we split, he was so hooked on gambling, he'd have bet on his mother's life. I wanted him to get therapy, but it was too late, I guess.'

From my vantage point in the back seat I studied the cut of her hair and the peculiarities of her accent. You could still tell she was English, but only just. Why did I find the way she spoke so irritating? I had no reason to suppose it was an affectation.

When we got home, she admired everything extravagantly, denied having jet lag, talked a lot and fell asleep in mid-sentence. Richard carried her to bed and she was still there when we got back from work. She slept for fourteen hours. When she woke up she was bright as a button and clamouring to take us out for a meal. By the end of the week she had found a job in a travel agent's, rented a room and moved out, leaving a grateful note and a houseplant. The whole flat reeked of incense from the scent she used. Richard said yet again how nice she was and I agreed.

'You don't sound very sure,' he said, with that direct gaze of his. 'You do like her, don't you?'

'Yes, of course I do.' I was thinking how I would have to open all the windows and spray all the rooms with air freshener when Richard was out.

'I can't imagine anyone not liking Nicky,' he said.

I felt condemned.

'Invite her to supper,' Kathy suggested. 'Lay it on thick. Invite her so often even Richard gets tired of her.'

But I couldn't. I was so thankful Nicky had gone, I didn't want to see her again. Ever. I was sick of the sight of her dark shiny hair, and sick of the sound of her phoney accent, and most of all sick of the way Richard looked at her as if she was something special when they laughed about old friends. 'Sorry, Alison, this must be very boring for you.' Occasionally they'd remember I hadn't the faintest idea who they were discussing.

'But if she was a man, you wouldn't mind, would you?' Kathy said.

'No, of course not. Well, not much, anyway.'

'Then you've got to pretend.'

Easy for Kathy to give advice. She didn't have to answer the phone all the time.

'Hi, Alison, it's Nicky. How are you?'

'Fine.'

'Is Ricky there?'

'Yes. I'll get him for you.'

Their names were so silly, I twitched with irritation. Nobody else called Richard that. I longed to call her Nicola, but feared it might sound hostile, so I didn't call her anything. Hullo, you bitch, get out of my life, I wanted to scream. Instead I smiled at her a lot when Richard brought her home unexpectedly for drinks or dinner, the same way he brought friends who were men. Sometimes my face ached with smiling and I was so animated Richard thought I was drunk. Sometimes I was. I found it helped me be nice to her.

Kathy met her once, said she wasn't the two-headed monster I'd been describing. 'Her hair is maddening, I agree,' she said, 'but she's quite pleasant. Sort of ... ordinary.'

It wasn't a word I'd ever have thought of to describe Nicky. I felt I'd let my sister down: she sounded disappointed. Never one to mince words, she went on, 'You don't really think he's having it off with her, do you?'

'No. Not really. Only when I wake up at four in the morning. I'd believe anything then. But in a way that makes it worse. I've got no right to be jealous. Only ...

why does she have to be his best friend? Why does she have to be a woman?'

'Why does she have to *be* at all?' Kathy finished for me. 'Maybe Caroline had a point.'

I introduced Ian to Nicky in the hope they would fall in love, but he complained that she talked like Jackie Kennedy. 'That little-girl voice that forces you to listen.' And he was right, although I hadn't noticed. When she wasn't shrieking her head off at airports, she did have an unnaturally soft voice. 'Women like that are always very arrogant,' said Ian, as if he had met a lot of them.

Richard came home late with a pile of holiday brochures. 'I thought we could make plans,' he said, looking excited and pleased with himself. 'Get away for a week or two.' He started leafing through them.

I ought to have been thrilled: I'd been yearning for a holiday with him. But he hadn't phoned and supper was overcooked and I'd had a few drinks to stop me picturing him with Nicky. I picked up one of the brochures and saw the stamp of Nicky's agency on the back.

'Oh, you got them from Nicky, did you?' I said. It was an effort to use her name.

'Yes, of course. Might as well.' He didn't even look up. 'She'll organise it all for us, get the best deal.'

I tried to look through the brochure, but it didn't seem pretty any more. When he asked if I'd seen anything I fancied, I said no.

'I thought we could let Nicky stay here while we're away,' he went on. 'That room of hers is so depressing, poor Nicky.'

'Is that where you were?' I said. 'In her room?'

He looked up.

'Why don't we take her on holiday with us?' I said. 'Or better still, why don't you go off with her and I'll stay at home?'

He stared at me. 'What on earth's the matter with you?'

'You're late and dinner's ruined and you didn't bother

to phone, you were too busy having fun with dear little Nicky.' I heard myself sound like a nagging wife, my voice rising and shaking with rage, while my heart seemed to be giving a fair imitation of a pneumatic drill.

'I simply don't believe this,' he said, very cold. 'You're behaving exactly like Caroline.'

'Why not? That's how you're treating me. You do everything you can to make me jealous and then you blame me when I am. I'm sick to death of hearing about bloody Nicky. Why don't you live with *her* if she's so perfect?'

It was awful, like being two people. One of them was yelling abuse while the other one listened, appalled. I felt sick inside but I couldn't stop. Out it all poured, like a bilious flood. Finally there was silence, so I must have finished. It seemed a very long time before he put his arms round me.

'Darling,' he said, when I was quiet. 'Please listen to me. Nicky is a friend, no more, no less. She's a friend the way Bill and Steve and Martin and Peter are friends. Only she happens to be my best friend and she happens to be a woman. I've known her fourteen years. I do not fancy her and she does not fancy me. I couldn't even tell you the colour of her eyes and I don't remember her birthday. But I value her friendship and I have no intention of giving it up, even if it makes you hysterical. Now, that doesn't mean I don't love you, in fact I love you very much, but I can't accept that loving you rules out having friends of both sexes. I thought we got that clear at the start.'

For the first time I felt like one of Richard's clients. This was how he must sound, kind but firm, when he explained a legal point.

'If I don't mind you being friends with Ian,' he went on relentlessly, 'why do you mind me being friends with Nicky?'

Exactly. He'd got me there, neatly backed into a corner. I wished I'd never mentioned Ian but I'd been trying to prove how unlike Caroline I was.

'I don't know,' I said miserably. I felt ashamed of myself: I knew I was in the wrong. And yet, somehow, however obscurely, wasn't he a bit in the wrong as well, just a tiny bit? Well, if he was, I couldn't prove it. Maybe all my bad feelings were self-inflicted, like a psychosomatic illness.

'About tonight,' he said. 'I called at the shop for the brochures, then I drove her home and she asked me in for a drink. I tried to ring you, but her phone was out of order. We got talking about how she could get a mortgage on a studio flat and whether her parents could lend her the deposit. That's all.'

'Yes, I see,' I said. It was almost embarrassing to be so thoroughly reassured. It was like needing help because I had fallen down in the street. I was an object of mingled pity and scorn.

'Now,' he said, kissing the top of my head, 'shall we eat that burnt dinner and go to bed early?'

That should have been the end of it, and for a few weeks it was. Nicky's parents gave her five thousand pounds, Richard lent her another five, she got a mortgage for the rest and I showed her round several studio flats, though eventually she bought one from another agent. But we didn't book a holiday. Suddenly Richard was unexpectedly busy at the office. Maybe later in the year, he said.

I tried so hard I felt permanently exhausted, but I couldn't get the balance right. Either I was tight-lipped when he mentioned Nicky's name, or suspiciously radiant. Either I dragged her into the conversation at every opportunity or I never referred to her at all. If he said he'd seen her, I was resentful, whether I smiled or not; and if he didn't say he'd seen her, I was convinced he was seeing her on the sly. She became an obsession, and yet I knew, rationally, that she was no threat to me. But thinking about her poisoned my life. She cast a cold shadow, like somebody standing between me and the sun.

We had several more rows and Richard reassured me

each time. A pattern emerged: I would feel better for a few days, then, as if I had used up all the reassurance I had been given, I became frantic again. I was like a junkie needing a fix more and more often.

'You've got to stop it, Alison,' Ian said. 'You're going to drive him mad. I told you he was used to getting his own way. He won't put up with you behaving like this.'

But Richard did put up with it. He was patient and loving. I should have got better; instead I got worse. One day he even said, 'Look, d'you want me to stop seeing Nicky?'

I longed to say yes. 'No,' I said, 'because you'd resent it. You said you'd never give her up.'

He looked very tired. 'Maybe I've changed my mind.'

I didn't know whether to laugh or cry. 'It doesn't matter,' I said. 'I wouldn't believe you anyway.'

So – I'm packing. I've taken a day off work and when Richard comes home I'll be gone. I love him so much it hurts, but I can't cope any more. Perhaps he'll come after me. More likely he'll be relieved I've gone. Perhaps we stand a chance if we're not living together. Or we might meet other people. I don't know, I'm too tired to think. I'm giving up. I'm beaten. I haven't even got the energy to despise myself for running away.

I'm going away to stay with Kathy. She'll give me a hug and a large drink and say I told you so. 'I knew he was too good to be true.' That's what she'll say.

# *Secrets*

After she met Sean Reilly, Lynn spent a lot of time trying to work out when her marriage had started to go wrong. She puzzled over it, while she was ironing Matthew's shirts or getting the children's supper or weeding the garden. Not that she supposed it would help her if she knew the exact moment, but it seemed important to pin it down, rather like trying to remember where you had last seen a beloved object, now lost for ever.

They had been totally happy when they got married, that much was certain, despite the fact that she was pregnant and Matthew hadn't taken his final architectural exams. 'Getting off to a bad start,' her aunt called it, but they knew she was wrong and pitied her for being single. They couldn't understand how anyone could be nervous on their wedding day. Nerves surely implied doubts, whereas they were radiantly sure of themselves and each other. Most of their favourite pop songs at that time said something about being two against the world. Looking back now, she sometimes wondered if they had needed the illusion of a hostile world to make themselves feel invincible.

She couldn't recall a single argument during her healthy, interminable pregnancy in the cramped cold-water flat where they could hardly afford to run the metered gas fire and studied instead with blankets round their legs and overcoats blocking the draught under the door. In those days they went to bed early as much for warmth as to make love before they were too tired to enjoy it. Coming home from work or night-school, she used to pause on the landing to catch her breath before attempting the two final flights of stairs, or wedge herself into the loo, which was designed to be so space-saving that in the final month of pregnancy you could not actually close the door. Matthew, who said the designer should be bricked up inside it, was meanwhile standing guard outside or making occasional forays into the shared bathroom to light the geyser. He was justly proud of his expertise: the geyser was famous throughout the house. If provoked, or approached by an alien hand, it was known to retaliate by blasting the intruder across the room, and there were other tenants with singed eyebrows to prove it.

The slow painful hospital labour and forceps delivery were a shock. Previously convinced of her own health and vigour, positively smug about the ease with which all physical activities came to her, she felt her body had let her down for the first time. She was appalled to find herself repeatedly dissolving into tears, despite the euphoria she felt at the sight of her daughter. Post-natal depression was something which blighted other less fortunate women, something she had read about, pitied and forgotten, like plague in a distant country.

So was that the beginning, the first crack in the dream? Should they perhaps have stitched up her mind in hospital along with her body? But she recovered so quickly that she couldn't really believe it had happened to her. Matthew was understanding and supportive, changing nappies, sharing bottle feeds, getting up in the night. Through a mixture of saving and borrowing, they managed to move to an unfurnished ground-floor flat with garden, where she could hang washing on the line and leave Emma outside to breathe fresh air. Her friends said how lucky she was, and she agreed with them. Only – there was a difference. They were parents now, she and Matthew. Responsible people. Not lovers or newlyweds any more. She fancied he looked

different in some subtle way: older, more careworn. She
worried, and peered in the mirror to see if the same thing
had happened to her. Then she remembered when last she
had done that, after making love for the first time, and
laughed at herself for being so foolish. What was there to
fear, after all? It was all perfectly natural, a part of
growing up. She was on a par with her parents now, a
fully-fledged adult. But she missed the carefree romantic
days – and then she felt guilty for missing them. She felt a
part of herself and Matthew had died and she wept for the
loss, then blamed herself for weeping. In between all these
bouts of guilt and tears she was extremely happy, busy and
tired.

They decided to have a second baby two years later
because that seemed a sensible gap and both of them had
hated being only children. Lynn's friend Angie, also an
only child, said they were crazy because it was a great
thing to be. All that love and attention and a room of your
own. No problems about sharing your toys. A fine
preparation for life, she said, which was really about
grabbing as much as you could for yourself, although
nobody liked to admit it. Lynn privately thought Angie
might indeed be right, but it was more complicated than
that: she wanted an intentional baby this time instead of
an accident, however welcome. She wanted the experience
of deliberately choosing something as important as a child,
but she preferred to disguise this craving and present it as a
socially acceptable desire to make sure Emma wasn't
lonely.

Tom was surprisingly difficult to conceive: he took them
a year of what amounted in the end almost to hard work.
It was a strange sensation to be neither pregnant nor afraid
of pregnancy nor avoiding pregnancy. She had imagined
that trying to have a baby would be pure delight: instead it
soon became an anxiety. They were not making love for
fun any more: they had a serious purpose in view. The
longer it took to achieve that purpose, the less enjoyable

and the more dutiful it became. The joyous freedom she had imagined turned into a nagging worry. 'Have we managed it this time?' she thought, and each month was disappointed. 'Is there something wrong?' was the next thought, rapidly pushed away but constantly recurring. The more Matthew tried to reassure her, the more angry she became. She was amazed and disconcerted by her own sense of failure: it was savage and destructive. Then suddenly she was pregnant and all was well. The worries belonged to another life, another person.

This time she was very sick during the pregnancy but the birth was easy. Jokingly, she had promised Matthew a son, so she was triumphant. They had long ago agreed they could only afford two children, and everyone congratulated her on producing one of each sex. Life should have been idyllic, yet looking back now, she saw a great sense of unease and dismay. Matthew was less helpful with Tom than he had been with Emma.

'The novelty's worn off,' Lynn teased him, determined not to nag, but he didn't smile.

'I'm sorry,' he said. 'I know I'm not pulling my weight but I'm so worried.'

It took ages to get him to tell her what he was worried about. They sat up talking for hours, Lynn glazed with exhaustion from coping with Tom, a cheerful but frenetic baby who hardly seemed to need any sleep at all, and Emma, whose whole personality had changed under the weight of that terrible new experience jealousy, making her fretful and clinging, babyish and destructive by turns. Lynn felt (and tried to say) that she had never needed Matthew's help more, but here he was telling her that all he could think about was being passed over for promotion, not getting Greg's job, which had been almost promised to him before Greg left, and instead having to watch it being given to Peter, who had no original ideas, who was totally unimaginative, who had hardly been with the firm any time at all.

She agreed it was unfair but tried to suggest it also didn't matter as much as he thought because another chance of promotion was bound to come along; it was only a matter of being patient.

That apparently was the wrong thing to say. Matthew became very angry, telling her she didn't understand. If they thought so little of him, maybe it was time he looked for a job elsewhere. Unless, of course, his qualifications simply weren't good enough. He sounded very bitter when he said that.

'Don't be silly,' she said, 'of course they are.'

He looked at her as if it was all her fault and said grimly, 'How do you know? They'd better be, that's all, or we'll never be able to afford a house.'

She argued there was no urgent need for a house: it would be nice, of course, lovely, wonderful (when she saw from his face that nice was the wrong word) but it could wait, it was something to look forward to, and meanwhile the flat was perfectly all right.

No, it wasn't, he said furiously, it was too small, it was positively squalid, it was no place to bring up two children, and the people upstairs drove him mad with their heavy feet and loud music.

'I expect we drive them mad having rows and crying babies,' she said because she was so tired, before she realised he was in fact showing her the anger he dared not show his boss. 'You wanted Tom as much as I did,' she said, 'and the flat hasn't shrunk.'

At which point he yelled at her, 'God, you're so stupid, can't you understand how I feel if I can't even look after my own family properly?' Both children woke up and started to cry and the people upstairs banged on the floor.

For a long time after that, Lynn felt she had three children to look after instead of two. It was her task to boost Matthew's confidence so that he could keep on applying for jobs, going to interviews and tolerating rejection. It was uphill work because the more he lost faith in himself, the more she lost faith in him. She had never doubted his ability before and now he had put doubts in her mind. She was terrified. Suppose he was right to be unsure? Here they all were, all three of them, depending on him. What would happen if he really couldn't cope? They would have to stay in the flat for ever and it *was* too small and it *was* shabby and she couldn't imagine why she had ever defended it so staunchly because she *did* want a house. In fact there were times when she wanted a house more than anything else in the world. Matthew, by telling her it was important, had somehow made it become an obsession.

When Matthew wasn't behaving like a dependent child in constant need of reassurance, she felt he switched disconcertingly to the other extreme, becoming a critical parent, forever turning off lights, exclaiming over the phone bill and deploring the way she spent money. She didn't like Matthew as child or parent; she wanted her lover/friend/husband back again, but that person seemed gone for ever or at best glimpsed briefly and tantalisingly, like someone disappearing round a corner before you have time to attract their attention.

Her mother told her she should be glad Matthew was so responsible. Her friends told her that all marriages went through long dull patches and some never came out of them. Everyone seemed to think she had unreasonable expectations and it served her right if she was disappointed. Everyone except Angie, that is. Angie was getting divorced and going to live in the country. 'I'm bored,' Angie said, 'and boredom is bad for my health. I'm going to be a mistress again because that's what I'm good at.' Friends said Angie was only being flippant to cover up how deeply hurt she was. Others said bitterly it was all right for Angie, she didn't have any children. Lynn's mother said she had always known Angie was a bad influence. Lynn thought how much she was going to miss her.

Lynn and Matthew saved money. They stayed in and

watched television instead of hiring babysitters and going to the pictures. They got Chinese or Indian takeaways instead of going out to dinner. They didn't talk very much or make love very often because they were always so tired, and when they did make the effort (though she resented thinking of it like that) it was such a half-hearted performance she often felt they might as well not have bothered. Then she felt guilty. That was the one thing she still seemed to be good at. 'You're not guilty, you're angry,' said Angie, getting on the train to Somerset. 'Tell him.' Lynn agreed with her but she didn't tell him.

Matthew eventually got the job he wanted. They moved to Hounslow to be near his work. They bought a rather nasty little semi-detached house which was going cheap because it was near the motorway. She thought it was strange that he cared so much about good design for other people, yet didn't seem to mind living in a house like that. Or perhaps he did mind but was being brave about it. She felt she hardly knew what went on in his head any more and was afraid to ask in case he told her. If their marriage was in serious trouble, she thought, in a cold sweat of terror when she woke, as she regularly did, at two or four in the morning after dreaming of missed trains and lost suitcases, then she really didn't want to know.

They had been married eight years, both children were at school and Lynn had just managed to get a part-time job as an interviewer when she found she was pregnant again. At first she was incredulous; then she wept savage tears. She wanted to kill her doctor, who had insisted she came off the Pill for a rest and assured her that other methods of contraception were just as reliable if you were highly motivated. She told Matthew, who was equally appalled. They did not want another child, now or ever, much as they loved the two they had. It would mean going right back to the beginning again. They only had three bedrooms. She would have to give up her job, which had been so hard to find, before she had even started it. They had never been in such total agreement about anything: a new baby would be a disaster. Yet part of her resented the fact that he did not say, 'Don't worry, we'll manage somehow. It'll be all right.'

They discussed abortion and found they could not do it. They had no religious beliefs, they advocated abortion on demand as a matter of right for other people, but when it came to the point they found they were incapable of choosing it for themselves. Nightmare closed in. They were trapped.

Lynn tramped round houses and flats and high-rise blocks asking people questions about things they bought and the money they spent and the journeys they made. She filled in the answers on the questionnaires the agency had given her. Some of the answers were pre-coded and she only had to put a circle round a number, but if she got an unusual answer there was a space for 'Other: please specify'. There were not many unusual answers, but a lot of the people she interviewed wanted to tell her their troubles and if she stayed too long, being polite and sympathetic, she found that she ended up working for almost nothing. All the time she was praying to the God she did not believe in, to be merciful and let her have a miscarriage. And at three months He answered her prayers.

The shock and the relief were overwhelming, but instantly swamped by the sense of guilt. She and Matthew both felt like murderers. They had willed the baby to go and it had gone. Lynn was sure she felt worse than if she had actually had an abortion. Several of her friends had had abortions and seemed quite cheerful afterwards. She felt like a witch in a fairytale, who had put an evil spell on the unborn. She was certain she would be punished for it.

She couldn't discuss it with Matthew because they were fellow conspirators, driven apart by their shared guilt, like Macbeth and Lady Macbeth, whom she had once played in a school production. They didn't discuss it and they didn't make love. She wanted to talk to her friends but

feared they would think she was going mad. Only Angie
understood. Flippant Angie, the bad influence, now
earning a precarious living as a market gardener near
Taunton and revelling in her role as mistress to no less
than three men, who all claimed she was saving their
marriages. Angie took it in her stride. 'This is a crisis,' she
said firmly. 'You must see your doctor, talk to Matthew,
go to marriage guidance. Anything. You're not like me,
you take things to heart and you won't bounce back
without help. Please. I'm serious.' Lynn loved her for
saying it, but she didn't or couldn't take her advice.

So she was absolutely ready (although in no sense
prepared) for Sean Reilly when she met him a few weeks
later at London Airport. She was asking people a lot of
tedious questions about how often they flew and whether
it was business or pleasure and how they rated the facilities
on different airlines. Some of the passengers were only too
pleased to be interviewed; others were tired and cross and
jet-lagged. Sean Reilly impressed her at once with his air of
brisk efficiency blended with just enough charm not to
seem abrasive. He was darker than Matthew and a few
inches shorter, although heavier in build, and he had the
startling green eyes that sometimes go with Irish colouring.
She found herself thinking what an attractive man he was,
and that in itself gave her a shock, as if she had just woken
up after long hibernation. He carried hand luggage only
and described himself as a frequent traveller, working for a
merchant bank. He answered all the questions she had to
ask him as if they were of real interest (which was clearly
impossible) then when she had finished he gave her a quite
unnecessary smile and said, 'I've enjoyed talking to you. I
do hope we meet again.' To her own amazement she heard
herself say 'So do I.'

Mercifully he was out of sight before the full idiotic
schoolgirl blush engulfed her. The next few interviews
passed in a blur and she thought about him all the way
home on the tube. It was like meeting a film star

unexpectedly. She couldn't remember when last she had
felt so ridiculously joyful. Half a minute of harmless
flirtation, that was all it was, but it had transformed her
day.

When she got home, Matthew was already preparing
supper. He was better about cooking now that she had a
part-time job. He had fetched the children back from June-
next-door and they were watching their favourite television
programme.

'Hullo,' he said when she went into the kitchen, 'How
was your day?'

She hesitated for a split second and decided, for no good
reason, not to share her harmless secret with him. She
preferred to hug it to herself. 'Not bad,' she said, feeling a
great wave of deceitful glee. 'How was yours?'

He said it was okay; she poured herself a drink and went
into the other room to see the children. Their programme
was just finishing and she was only in time to catch the
credits. The name jumped out at her from the screen:
presented by Anne Reilly.

It was like learning a new word: there was an unwritten
law that you were bound to see it again three times within
a short space of time. She went on interviewing at London
Airport but didn't see Sean Reilly or indeed any other
attractive man. But the very next week there was a picture
of Anne Reilly in the paper, receiving some award for her
television programme, and an interview with her in which
it said she had a husband called Sean who was a merchant
banker. Lynn was thankful to be alone when she came
upon all this information, as she was sure the shock it gave
her would have been visible. Anne Reilly smiled up at her,
one hand ruffling her short dark shiny cap of hair, the
other clutching the award. She had a big wide smile and
slightly too large teeth that were none the less endearing.
She looked warm and friendly. You could see why all the
children in the country adored her. The interviewer praised
her successful career and her happy marriage. Anne Reilly

modestly put it all down to a mixture of hard work and luck. The interviewer unkindly pointed out that despite all this, she didn't have children of her own. Anne Reilly said that was the one great sorrow of her life and made the interviewer look like a heartless beast for mentioning it.

The day after that Lynn literally bumped into Sean Reilly at the airport as she was racing from loo to coffee lounge between interviews. 'We can't go on meeting like this,' he said laughing as he picked up her bag and scattered questionnaires. 'Come and have a drink with me, my flight's been delayed.'

It was out of the question, of course. She had work to do; she had children to collect. She was breathless with shock at colliding with him, but there was absolutely no point in their having a drink together.

'Thank you,' she said. 'That would be lovely.'

They sat in the bar and drank Martinis. She felt as if she were suddenly a character in an old film. She could not recall when she had last drunk a Martini or why it had suddenly become her favourite drink. His too, it appeared, or was he merely pretending? They talked about themselves: his green eyes staring at her made her feel mildly hypnotised. She could have told him anything. She felt she had known him all her life and yet he was still an exciting stranger who terrified her.

'I don't even know your name,' he said after the second Martini.

'Lynn Culver.' Her throat was dry despite the drink. 'And I should be working.' But already it didn't seem important any more.

'We can make it all up,' he said. 'I'll help you.'

'I saw your wife in the paper,' she said, 'getting her award.'

'Would you believe me,' he said, 'if I told you I've thought of nothing but you since we met?'

'No,' she said automatically, but she did believe him because she wanted to, and she smiled.

'If you gave me your telephone number,' he said, 'I could ring and invite you to lunch.'

She was overjoyed and confused; her heart seemed to do a disconcerting leap that made it hard for her to breathe. She muttered something about it all being impossible because of her husband and children; then she gave him her telephone number and watched him write it down in the back of his diary.

He rang a week later, when she had given up hope, despaired on the phone to Angie, cursed herself for being stupid and vain. He rang when she was loading the washing machine, prior to going to the supermarket. 'Hullo,' he said. 'Sean Reilly. D'you remember me?'

She said yes, she did, trembling.

'Lynn?' he said hesitatingly.

'Yes?'

'I wanted to ask you to lunch,' he said, 'but you sound so remote. Are you all right?'

'Yes, of course, I'm fine.' She heard her own voice, so cool, so detached, and marvelled that it could come out of her own throat.

'It's not the same at Heathrow without you,' he said. 'I wanted to ring before but I've been away, and when I got back they had a very inferior type of interviewer. Could I complain to someone, d'you think?'

She laughed. She assumed that was what she was meant to do. The tiny joke eased the tension and she suddenly felt relaxed with him again. 'Ah well,' she said, 'you see, I'm so expensive, they simply can't afford me all the time.' Which was one way of explaining that she was lucky to have a part-time job at all.

'I'm sure you must be very much in demand,' he said, 'but I do hope you can find time to have lunch with me one day next week. Would Tuesday or Friday be any good for you? Could you look at your diary?'

She glanced at the calendar where all the social
engagements, such as dentist and PTA, were scribbled.
Now was the moment to stop all this nonsense. They were
playing a silly game and they both knew it. Of course
lunch was innocuous in itself, but its implications were
not. She was flattered and that must be enough.

'I think Tuesday would be better for me,' she said, her
mind racing ahead. June-next-door could always collect
the children from school on a Tuesday if Lynn was delayed
at work, but she often went to see her mother on Fridays
and sometimes Matthew came home early for the weekend.

'Wonderful,' Sean Reilly said. 'How about the Savoy
Grill at twelve thirty?'

Angie fell about laughing down the phone when Lynn
told her that. 'He's certainly trying to impress you,' she
said.

'He said it was near his office,' Lynn added feebly, and
Angie laughed even more. 'And he gave me his office
number to ring if I got delayed. So I can always cancel.
That's what I should do really. The whole thing is
ridiculous. I know that.'

'If you cancel,' Angie said, 'I'll never speak to you again.
This is a chance in a lifetime to cheer yourself up. It's not
actually a crime, you know, to have lunch with a man who
isn't your husband.'

'But I've got nothing to wear,' Lynn heard herself say.

'That's better. You've got that red dress you wore to my
divorce.'

'But that was a birthday present from Matthew.'

'Well, it looked very nice in court. A blonde in a red
dress always looks sexy. Especially with legs like yours.
Even my solicitor was impressed and he's half dead. And
you must wear those silly shoes, the ones you got in Bally
sale.'

'But I can't walk in them.'

'Of course you can't, but you can totter very nicely. Just
travel in your wellies and change in the loo. I've heard

rumours that they actually let you sit down for lunch at the Savoy Grill. That's probably why it's so expensive. Now please may I go? There's a load of manure outside that's really demanding my attention.'

Lynn had the red dress cleaned, smuggled it in and out of the house like contraband. When she was alone, she practised walking in the silly shoes. They hurt so much that after a while her feet went numb, but they certainly did wonderful things for her legs, Angie was right about that. Then she suddenly wondered what all the fuss was about. Sean Reilly had already seen her at Heathrow in jeans and jersey, with no make-up.

Matthew had taken on a lot of freelance work so they could afford a proper holiday abroad. He spent most of the weekend at his drawing board which was set up in a corner of the living-room and she watched him covertly while she did the ironing. Through the window she could hear the delighted squeals of Emma and Tom visiting June-next-door, whose popularity had soared since she acquired a puppy. It was a typical family weekend.

Lynn tried to see the Matthew she had married, the young man now submerged under a load of domestic responsibility. She remembered thinking of him in her teens as a replacement for the teddy bear she had grown out of: all brown hair and brown eyes and cuddly warmth, always in touch with her moods, ready with understanding and comfort. Where had that image gone? Matthew looked much the same physically; he hadn't really aged any more than she had. But in some way he had turned in upon himself, become shut down, as if for protection. Had she burdened him so greatly with her pregnancies, her miscarriage, her need for financial support mixed with just the right amount of independence, her conflicting demands for sex and celibacy, conversation and silence? Had she, in short, been impossible? Or had he withdrawn from her for reasons of his own? Should they be discussing this very subject or was it safer to leave well alone?

'Coffee?' she said.

'Thanks.'

She unplugged the iron and went into the kitchen. While she was making the coffee she thought about Tuesday. She felt like a naughty child planning to play truant from school. She prayed that neither Matthew nor Tom nor Emma would go down with an infectious disease on Monday night. Where could she legitimately be going in the red dress at that hour on Tuesday morning? To an interview with another agency, she decided, in the hope of getting more and better paid work. But would even that worthy intention justify leaving the sick one on their bed of pain to be cared for by June-next-door or Rosemary-opposite?

She went back into the living-room with the coffee and Matthew took it out of her hand without looking up from his drawing. 'I think this might be good,' he said in tones of real enthusiasm. 'They're mad about roof terraces, these people, and they've got money to burn. I might have to go and stay with them again to get it all sorted out.' It was one of the features of his new job and his freelance work that he occasionally had to spend a night away from home.

'It looks terrific,' she said, although she had never really learnt to read plans properly, and he knew it, so he laughed, though not unkindly. She envied him work that could make him so visibly excited. She envied the clients with money to burn and wondered if they were at all like Sean and Anne Reilly. Then she reflected that envy was not an attractive quality and she should give it up. The children came back from playing with the puppy and Matthew stopped working and had a game with them while she prepared supper. She thought what a lucky woman she was and how grateful she ought to be for her good fortune.

God was indulgent to her and nobody fell ill on Monday night. She lay awake for hours, listening to Matthew's steady breathing and wondering how he could possibly fall asleep without noticing how tense she was beside him. She finally took a pill and had terrible dreams about buses going in wrong directions and herself getting off and waiting on the kerb for the next one but knowing it was already too late to reach her destination on time.

Tuesday dawned bright and sunny. Everyone was healthy and departed for work or school. Her hands shook as she did her make-up but she had an absurd sense of well-being. She was actually going to be allowed this enormous pointless treat, like a prisoner out on parole. No one was going to arrive and say her permit had been cancelled.

Sean Reilly was every bit as mesmerising as she remembered him. There had been an awful moment on the tube when she imagined he might have turned into some kind of odious conceited boring dwarf. He seemed impressed enough with the red dress and the silly shoes to gratify even Angie; he said, 'I was afraid you might cancel,' and when they were both looking at the menu, she noticed that his hands were ever so slightly shaking. She felt instantly better: excited but calm. A woman of the world at last – what a joke. It had only taken her twenty-eight years to achieve it.

The prices made her dizzy, but she ordered what she wanted, although by the time it arrived she could hardly taste it. They had had several drinks and discovered a shared passion for Humphrey Bogart. They spent much of the meal trying to out-do each other with their memories of his films, but all the time Sean Reilly was looking at her as if he was thinking of something much more intimate. She found herself wanting him in such a basic physical way that she developed the sort of pelvic ache she only dimly remembered from the early days with Matthew. She was ashamed, and she also did not care. She felt beautiful and desirable and strong. She felt alive again. Fun had been missing from her life but now she was having precisely that once again. A line from the Beatles came to her: 'Fun is the one thing money can't buy,' yet here was Sean Reilly's

money buying it for her. Then she remembered the line
came from a song called 'She's Leaving Home', and she
was suddenly frightened.

She had talked about Emma and Tom as well as
Humphrey Bogart. After lunch, Sean said he had an
appointment in Chiswick, so they could share a taxi and
she would be in time to collect her children from school. In
the taxi she found herself badly wanting him to kiss her,
but instead he held her hand and said, 'You've no idea how
much I envy you having children.' She was astonished but
before she could say anything he added, 'Anne doesn't
want them, you see.'

Lynn said, 'But in the paper –'

He said, 'Oh yes, she always says that to reporters, it
sounds a lot better, the big grief. I can't really blame her,
she's got a great career going – why should she give it up,
even for a year?'

'But you do blame her,' Lynn said, because his voice
made it clear and she already felt she knew him well
enough to say so.

'No,' he said, letting go of her hand. 'I blame myself for
not getting all that straight before we got married.' He got
out of the taxi and paid the driver to take her on to
Hounslow. 'I hope I see you again,' he said. 'You're very
special. May I phone you?'

She was home in time to change out of the red dress
before she had to explain it. She chewed mints so the
children wouldn't think she smelled of alcohol. Angie rang
up and chortled and said Sean was being very subtle and
clever with all this sad humility. 'A man of experience,' she
said. 'He's been over the jumps before. Still, he'd be no use
to you if he hadn't.' It was at times like this that Lynn
regretted having told Angie that Matthew had been her
first lover. Worse, that she had never kissed her previous
boyfriends without clenching her teeth. It made her feel so
old-fashioned, when the newspapers were telling her how
permissive everyone else was. And now here she was

feeling guilty for something she hadn't even done yet. The way the word *yet* popped into her mind was alarming. She suddenly understood something that as a schoolgirl she had always thought was stupid: that bit in the Bible about committing adultery in your heart. It sounded like grounds for divorce. It also reminded her of food getting spoilt in the shops, like tins of salmon that had to be sent back before they poisoned you.

That night Matthew made love to her for the first time in many weeks. She couldn't remember exactly how long it was but she knew she had thought resentfully that she might as well not bother taking the Pill, though she did. She had given up making the first move, however, because Matthew so often was not in the mood, and then she felt rejected and humiliated, which usually led to a row. It was simpler to ignore the whole issue, wait for him to be ready, and then go along with it, whether she was in the mood or not, because if she refused, then that too would lead to yet another row. She much preferred silence to rows. But that night it was all magical. She wondered if he had somehow picked up her mood of suppressed elation and that had made her subtly more attractive. Whatever the reason, Matthew made love to her that night and she fantasised about Sean Reilly.

After that it was only a matter of time. She went on meeting him for lunches in smaller and more intimate restaurants, or drinks in secluded pubs. She was always afraid of being seen by someone she knew, yet somehow also convinced she wouldn't be. Their relationship seemed to have a magical element, a sort of time warp, that rendered them almost invisible, although they were present in the same places and at the same hours as everyone else. They talked about their marriages and their childhoods. Sometimes they just looked at each other without saying anything for what seemed like long spells of time. They held hands under the table and they kissed in taxis. She felt young again.

Her job proved a help and a hindrance. It gave her a legitimate excuse to be out, but the time she spent with Sean meant she either had to skimp her work or earn less money. Sometimes they sat together making up the answers to her questionnaires and she discovered there were more varieties of guilt than the merely sexual. She had always prided herself on her honesty, and here she was, cheating her employer and deceiving her husband, and all for what? Technically, nothing.

They both longed to make love but he did nothing to persuade her. 'It's different for me,' he said. 'Anne and I don't sleep together any more, we're more like brother and sister. But you and Matthew still have a real marriage. I wouldn't like to do anything to harm that. So it has to be your decision. You know how much I want you – but only when you're ready. Maybe you never will be. I have to risk that. It won't change how I feel about you.'

Lynn didn't repeat much of that to Angie. She could already hear Angie saying, 'If you believe that, you'll believe anything,' and there was no way she could explain to Angie that she only had to look at Sean, hear his voice, to know he was telling the truth. 'Irish blarney,' Angie would say, in that jokey contemptuous way she had. 'We know all about *that*, now don't we?'

Matthew brought home holiday brochures and they discussed the relative merits of Italy and Yugoslavia. The children got excited: they had never been abroad. It was the same excitement Lynn remembered from her own childhood. What could this new strange experience possibly be like? But she noticed that Emma and Tom soon drifted back to the familiar delights of the television. She herself found it increasingly difficult to look at Anne Reilly's cheerful face without wishing her ill.

Matthew was friendly, busy, remote. They made love about once a month now, but without much enthusiasm, as if they were doing it for their health. He went away on business every two or three weeks and he sometimes brought her back a present. One night when she was nearly asleep he suddenly put his arms round her and said in a low voice, 'I'm sorry it's not all better. I'm sorry we never really talked about the baby and all that.' She was so startled that for a moment she couldn't reply; then she said, 'Never mind, it's all right,' and held his hand while she thought. Finally she added, feeling on some deep level that she still owed him her first loyalty, if only for this shared experience, 'Maybe we still can.' She waited for a reply but none came and she realised he must be asleep. She was angry, sad and relieved all at once, for the missed opportunity.

In some obscure way that was what made her go to Sean's hotel room the next afternoon, although she couldn't have explained it to anyone, not even Angie. It was as nearly spontaneous as anything could be after nearly four months of weekly meetings. She was having a drink with him at Heathrow where he had just arrived from Nice and was staying overnight to catch the morning flight to New York. It wasn't worth going home, he said: Anne was away researching a programme about zoos. Home, she had long ago discovered, was a flat in Bryanston Square and a cottage near Newbury, but she had refused to visit either, no matter how sure he was that Anne wouldn't be there. She felt it would be an invasion of territory, though she was intensely curious; she was also extremely afraid of getting caught.

But the airport, that awful crowded noisy neon place, seemed like home, their home, because they had met there. It seemed the most natural thing in the world to move on to the airport hotel, like going at the right moment from living-room to bedroom. They hung the 'PLEASE DO NOT DISTURB' notice on the door and turned to each other, looking and kissing, undressing and stroking. It could so easily have been a disappointment but it wasn't, because they had waited long enough but not too long. Through some divine skill or luck, they had judged the moment just right. She forgot all about Matthew and the children and work and guilt and Angie's jokes: she seemed to have deposited all those things with her clothes on the floor. She knew only that she and Sean were at last naked together on the bed and able to give each other unlimited pleasure, as if they had both been deprived for a long time. But it was more than that: it had all the excitement of strangers and the familiarity of friends. She felt abandoned, yet safe. She couldn't remember ever before having such a sensation of release.

When it was finally over and they couldn't come any more, they lay in a tousled, sweaty, untidy heap, with their bodies still entwined, gazing at each other so closely that their vision went slightly out of focus. She felt they had both been away on a long journey, together and yet separate. She heard the fatal words spoken: 'Lynn, I love you,' and her own voice answering: 'I love you too.' The solemnity of all this and its terrifying implications might have overwhelmed her but he had the instinct to turn the moment into something lighter, without taking anything away from it.

'Promise me,' he said, 'give me your solemn word of honour you'll never cut your hair,' and suddenly she was laughing.

Angie was shocked. Lynn could hear the good old-fashioned honest shock in her voice. She had never imagined herself capable of shocking Angie.

'You can't be serious,' Angie said. 'This whole thing is meant to be about sex and lunches and presents. Not love. For heaven's sake, you've got a husband and two children. That's what love is about. That's why it's not exciting.'

'I can't believe this is you talking,' Lynn said. 'You sound exactly like my mother. That's just what she'd say if she found out. Well, the last bit, anyway.'

'I feel like your mother.' Angie was almost shouting at

her. 'You do realise this is 1982 and people don't have to fall in love to justify falling into bed. Particularly not if they're married to other people. Particularly not if they're you.'

'I'm sorry,' Lynn said humbly. 'It just happened. I know it must sound crazy to you but –'

'Yes, you're right about that. You've lost your marbles.'

'But I feel so happy,' Lynn said, and almost laughed. She felt light-hearted and light-headed. 'Can't you be happy for me? There's no one else I can tell.'

After a long pause, Angie sighed heavily. 'Yes, of course I'm happy for you. In a way. I haven't heard you sound like this for about ten years. In another way I'd like to kill myself because it's all my fault you're in this mess. I was the damn fool who encouraged you.'

'I'd have done it anyway,' Lynn said.

'Maybe. All I can say in my own defence is, I never dreamed you'd be such an idiot as to fall in love.'

'But we both have. That's why it's so wonderful. I wish you wouldn't keep making it sound so one-sided.'

'Listen,' Angie said. 'I have three of them down here, right? They all say they love me but I know they don't and they know I know they don't. They love their wives. They fancy me, that's all. It's a game. It's all perfectly safe so long as you stick to the rules. But you, my poor sweet innocent child, are going to get badly hurt if you think for one minute –'

'This is different,' Lynn said firmly.

Angie let out a positive wail. 'God help us. Now I've heard everything.'

Sean borrowed the flat of a friend who lived in Chiswick. It was above an estate agent's, so Lynn could always say, if seen by neighbours, that she had been enquiring about property. She and Matthew had always hoped to live in Chiswick eventually, but it cost a lot more than Hounslow. She also could no longer actually imagine moving with Matthew to a new house anywhere.

Sean's friend was away a lot because he worked for an
airline, so they began to think of the flat as their own. They
gave each other presents that could be left there discreetly,
such as scent, scarves, records. They bought special
champagne glasses. They sent one another cards to the
same address, as if they were living together.

She began to feel she was two people. At home the calm
friendly busy person Matthew knew. She marvelled that
the explosive secret inside her did not leap out at him like a
live thing. She waited daily for him to say, 'Lynn, what's
happened? You look different,' but he never did. She
wasn't sure if she was relieved or disappointed.

At the flat she was the excitable crazy romantic person
Sean knew. The place was full of flowers and bottles of
wine. They were always meeting to make love and drink
champagne and talk, and they never had enough time for
any of it. They certainly never had time to quarrel or get
bored. One day she said that to him.

'We wouldn't anyway,' he said with perfect confidence.

'Yes, we would,' she said. 'Everyone does.' But she
didn't believe it.

'Not us,' he said.

She began to daydream about letting her two selves
merge. If she couldn't get back the excitement with
Matthew, could she find security with Sean? They joked
about running away together.

'Anne wouldn't mind too much, would she?' Lynn
asked. 'She's got her career. She could have an affair with
some television person, couldn't she, and let you go?'

'I've no idea,' he said. 'We don't talk very much. We
always seem to be having people to dinner.'

Lynn wondered where Anne found the energy for
entertaining after a long hard day in the studio. It was ages
since she and Matthew had had anyone to dinner, except
her mother from a sense of duty.

'Anyway,' she said, 'if we were together, the children
would drive you mad.'

'You know that's nonsense,' he said. 'I love children. But you couldn't take them away from Matthew. What's he done to deserve that?'

She was never quite sure how serious these conversations were. Were they planning a future together or playing parts, as they had at their first lunch, pretending to be characters out of Humphrey Bogart films? When she went home, the sheer solidity of Matthew and the children shook her, the noise they made, the demands on her time, attention and energy, the actual reality of them filling the house. And yet they did all that without seeing her, Lynn, the person, who was all that Sean saw. She found herself shaking her head as if trying to clear a moment of double vision.

She felt sorry for Matthew these days, as if he were an old friend who had fallen upon hard times. She felt his life was still black and white, whereas hers had launched itself into technicolour. She felt great affection and pity for him and wanted to cook him nourishing meals to make up for all the emotion she could not give him. She was startled to find that her mind wandered even from the children, so that they often said in that cross, forthright way they had, 'Mummy, you're not listening.' She no longer fantasised about Sean in bed but merely tried to avoid making love with Matthew, who seemed easily deterred.

Italy in August, the precious two weeks of blissful family foreign holiday they had all worked and saved for and looked forward to so avidly, now began to loom as an endurance test, an impossible amount of time to spend away from Sean. It would be their longest separation since they had met. In self defence they planned a weekend in Devon while Matthew was away on business. It was beginning to obsess them both that they had never actually spent a night together. Lynn begged Angie to provide her with an alibi.

'Matthew will be in Ireland looking at someone's house,' she said, 'and I'll get my mother to look after the

kids. Then I can pretend to be with you and you can ring
me at the hotel if there's a crisis.'

'God forbid,' Angie said automatically. 'And ask for
Mrs Reilly, I suppose.'

'Yes, of course.'

'You realise this is about as silly as us both dressing up
in our mothers' shoes when we were ten?'

'There's no one else I can ask,' Lynn said. 'And I can
come and see you and you can meet Sean.'

There was a long silence. 'Wouldn't it be simpler,' Angie
said, 'to make it another weekend and let Matthew look
after the children? Then you needn't involve your mother.'

'I know,' Lynn said, 'but I can't somehow. It doesn't feel
right.'

Angie actually laughed.

Matthew thought it was a splendid idea for her to visit
Angie while he was away. She was looking tired, he said,
and the change would do her good. Her mother was
thrilled at the prospect of having the children all to herself,
and they were only moderately put out at the prospect of
Lynn going away. She was surprised how easy it all was
and wished she had dared to try it before, often. Proverbs
such as nothing ventured, nothing gained, or seizing the
nettle danger drifted through her mind. But mostly she was
just bemused at the thought of two whole days and two
whole nights with Sean. He was visiting the West Country
on business and would meet her at Taunton to call on
Angie and drive to the hotel.

She was so happy. Afterwards that was what she
remembered most clearly. There was something very pure
about her happiness as she arrived at Paddington with her
luggage in good time to choose magazines to read on the
train. As an afterthought she bought the evening paper as
well. She was full of goodwill for the whole world; she
caught herself smiling at strangers.

As the train drew out she relaxed with a sensation of
carefree liberation. She was off on an adventure and no

one was angry with her, no one could stop her. She gazed out of the window for some time, savouring the feeling of floating in space with no duties, no anxiety. Then she decided to read: a further indulgence, a positive luxury. On impulse she opened the evening paper first.

She never read headlines if there was a picture, because her eyes were always drawn to the picture. This time it was a picture of Anne Reilly smiling with all her impressive teeth, and the caption said: 'Baby for TV Auntie'. She blinked as though someone had hit her in the face, and read it again. Anne Reilly went on smiling up at her with what seemed like a look of triumph and there was a short interview in which she said how it seemed too good to be true that she was pregnant after so many years of disappointment. The interviewer too appeared impressed, as if it were a miracle that Anne Reilly, having entertained millions of the nation's children for years on television, should finally face the prospect of entertaining one, all by itself, in her own home.

Lynn wasn't aware she was crying until she caught the woman opposite staring at her with a blurred face. She put on her dark glasses, which she had brought partly because it was sunny, partly because she wanted to look mysterious, and cried on and off for the rest of the two-hour journey. She hadn't cried so much since she was a child, deprived of some treat; then, she had cried herself to sleep. She wished she were in bed now: she would have liked to hide from the whole world.

He was waiting on the platform when she arrived at Taunton. He actually came running towards her as she got off the train. He looked so innocent, radiant; so pleased to see her, as if he had nothing to hide, nothing to fear. She held out the paper and watched his face change, to a look more of rage than guilt, though, she was surprised to see.

'Oh God,' he said. 'Damn it all. She said she wouldn't tell them for at least a month.'

'Them?'

'The bloody press. Of course I was going to tell you, I knew I had to, but I thought there was plenty of time. We've only just found out ourselves.'

Lynn put her suitcase down and sat on a bench. Her legs seemed to have gone very weak. He sat beside her and tried to hold her hand, but she pulled it away.

'Darling,' he said, 'I'm so sorry. I never meant it to happen like this. It's a hell of a shock, I know. It was for me too.'

'It must have been,' Lynn said, 'if you were like brother and sister.'

He flushed slightly. 'That was true at the time,' he said. 'Well, nearly. That was how it felt, anyway.'

Lynn said, 'I think you lied to me right from the start.'

'You're wrong.'

'You must have nearly died laughing at how gullible I was.'

'Stop it.' He shook her by the shoulders, quite roughly, and passers-by glanced at them. 'I never lied to you. I just left a few details out because I was so afraid of losing you. That's God's honest truth.'

Lynn pointed at the newspaper lying between them. 'That's quite a detail to leave out.'

'But I was going to tell you, only Annie jumped the gun. Look, when you think about it, when you get over the shock, there's no reason why it should make any difference to us at all.'

Lynn got up. She picked up her suitcase but left the newspaper lying on the seat. 'I'm going to get a taxi,' she said.

He got up too and followed her to the exit. 'But I've got the car.'

'I know that, but we're going in different directions. I'm going to stay with Angie.'

'Darling, please. It's a lovely hotel. We can sort out this whole mess, you must give me a chance.'

'There seem to be things I can't do,' Lynn said, 'and

sleeping with a man who has a pregnant wife is one of them.' She caught a look of genuine bafflement on his face and added, 'You see, I know how I'd feel if Matthew had done that to me. You're so vulnerable then, you feel so –'

She started to cry again.

He said, 'But I love you so much.'

She got into the taxi she could not afford and gave Angie's address. Her last sight of him reminded her of one of her own children about to say, 'But it's not fair . . .'

About halfway through the journey she noticed that he was following her taxi in his car. When they reached Angie's cottage, he paid the driver, who went off reluctantly, as if he would have preferred to stay and find out what happened next. Sean and Lynn struggled over her suitcase, which he was trying to put in his car. Angie came out and asked what the hell was going on. 'I want to stay with you,' Lynn sobbed. Angie threatened Sean briskly with the police, as if that was something she had to do every day, and he drove off.

Angie hugged her, took her inside, poured her drinks, made her eat, listened. She managed not to say 'I told you so.' By the end of the evening Lynn was so exhausted that she surprised herself by sleeping well.

In the morning Angie brought her breakfast in bed. 'Pity I don't have neighbours,' she said, 'they'd have loved all that last night. Better than the telly.' She sat on the edge of the bed and looked at Lynn closely. 'How d'you feel?'

'I don't know yet.'

'Well, you look as if you've been in a fight but you just won on points. If you want to cry any more and you're really going home tomorrow as planned, then try to get all the crying done by six o'clock tonight, or your eyes will never recover in time.'

Lynn smiled.

'I'm serious,' Angie said.

'I don't think I could cry any more. Not now, anyway.'

'Well, it's now or never,' Angie said. 'You absolutely mustn't let Matthew know about this. That's all that really matters.'

'Is it?' Lynn said, and started to cry again. 'I was thinking of leaving him.'

Angie put her arms round her. 'Not really you weren't,' she said. 'You were just a little crazy. We've all been like that once or twice. By the way, you'd better ring your mother. Tell her you tried to ring last night but the phone was out of order.'

'You think of everything,' Lynn said.

'It comes of getting caught out once too often.'

Angie's cottage was in an isolated spot, but they went for drives and spent a lot of the weekend walking in the countryside or along the beach. By the time Lynn went home even she felt she had talked out her problems to the point of exhaustion.

She had braced herself for the noise of the children and a grudging welcome followed by sulks because she had been away. She expected to answer her mother's questions about Angie's cottage and the error of her ways. Instead she found Matthew alone.

'Where is everyone?' she said. 'Why are you home early? Is there something wrong?' She was suddenly terrified: visions of accidents and hospitals, divine retribution, flew into her mind.

'The kids are with your mother,' he said. 'I told her you were staying on with Angie till tomorrow.'

'But why?'

'I've got to talk to you alone.'

That was it. Somehow he had found out. Now that it was all over, she was going to be punished for it.

'What's the matter?' she said. 'Are you all right?' He looked quite ill, as if he might be getting flu.

He poured two large drinks and handed her one. 'I have to tell you this while I've still got the courage. I'm being blackmailed.'

She said, '*What*?' and sat down rather suddenly while he paced up and down.

'There's this girl at work I've been seeing and when I tried to break it off she said she'd tell you. So I thought – I thought I'd better tell you first. In case she meant what she said.'

Lynn was silent, too astounded to speak. It wasn't possible. *Matthew*, who had always been so reliable . . . All this time and she had never even suspected . . .

'I don't know if you can ever forgive me,' he went on rapidly. 'It wasn't serious and I never stopped loving you. Only . . . we seemed to get so far apart after the baby and you didn't seem to want me and she did. I realise that's no excuse but –'

Lynn said, 'How long – ?'

'Nearly a year.'

A *year*. Longer than she and Sean had. She felt tears starting again.

He said humbly, 'D'you want me to go away?'

She shook her head. She wanted to hug him, he looked so guilty and sad. She wanted to comfort him and say, 'We're in the same boat,' and tell him everything so he could forgive her and they could start all over again, level. But what if he didn't forgive her? Never let Matthew know, Angie had said, and Angie was supposed to know about these things. What if Angie was right? All her instincts prompted her to confess, but her instincts had also got her into the affair with Sean. You could always tell a secret later, but once you'd told it you could never take it back unless you said you'd been lying before and then you might not be trusted again. She looked at Matthew and thought how much she had missed or forgotten about him that this other girl had seen and wanted.

'I think a lot of this has been my fault,' she said. 'Let's try again. Let's try harder this time. Both of us.'

He looked at her as if reprieved from a death sentence. 'You're so generous,' he said. 'That's so much more than I deserve.'

Next day the phone rang twice. Once it was Angie who
said Matthew was very clever and probably making the
whole thing up just to regain her interest because he had
felt she was slipping away. Very successful he'd been, too,
she said, but confession was still definitely out. The double
standard was alive and well, and it never did any harm to
be one up. Lynn didn't think Matthew was capable of such
a complicated double bluff; but then she hadn't thought
him capable of an affair either. He was obviously capable
of one or the other and she would probably never know
which. Angie said it didn't matter: either way, they would
have a better marriage. And one day Lynn might want to
see Sean Reilly again, or she might meet someone else.

'I don't think so,' Lynn said. 'I've learnt my lesson.'

'There's no such thing,' Angie said. 'You've had a lucky
escape, that's all. Quite different.'

The second call was from Sean. She listened to his voice
saying he still loved her and he wanted to see her again.
She put the phone down without answering. Her children
came back from school and switched on Anne Reilly's
programme. Matthew arrived home from work with roses.

# Counting the Cost

Lizzie was still in the bath when she heard Sam's key in the lock. 'I'm in here,' she called, and in he came, carrying his airline bag, from which with a conjuror's flourish he now produced not one but two bottles of champagne. 'My God,' she said, impressed. 'Are we going to get through all that?'

He was a great bear of a man, not tall but wide and solidly built, ideal for hugging. He had the sort of well-worn face that made you think he had led a life full of interesting excesses, and a smile that made you want to tell him your secrets. She should have been used to all this by now but, she was pleased to note, she wasn't.

'Well, one bottle's never quite enough, is it?' he said, putting them down. 'I think they're making them smaller these days. It's probably something to do with the Common Market.'

'Happy anniversary,' she said, as he leaned over the bath to kiss her. 'You're early. I meant to be all tarted up before you arrived.'

'I prefer you like this.' He sat on the edge of the bath. 'In fact I may join you in there in a minute.'

He looked tired. She said tenderly, 'Was it an awful trip?'

'No, just routine. I must be getting too old for all this dashing about. You look like Alice in Wonderland without your make-up.'

'I must have my hair cut,' she said.

'Not without my permission.'

She was a small woman, blonde, who had once been thin and still wasn't fat, but she fretted about the lines round her eyes and the size of her breasts and the stretch marks on her stomach. Only when he said she was beautiful, she believed him. The evening extended ahead of them, seemingly endless, like the start of the school holidays.

'You're not really worried about the job, are you?' she asked. 'They couldn't manage without you, you're like an ambassador.'

'More like a glorified salesman.'

'Well, you sold yourself to me all right.'

'Best deal I ever made,' he said seriously, kissing her again.

'Come on then,' she said. 'You're all talk. Get 'em off. Let's see a bit of action.'

He undressed slowly, making a production of it, while she watched and heckled. Finally he got in opposite her, making the water splash dangerously close to the edge.

'You look wonderful,' she said, hugging him. 'And you feel even better.'

'I'm putting on weight,' he said sadly, waiting for her to deny it.

'Aren't we all? Why d'you think there's so much foam in this bath? To hide the proof that when you're away, I eat biscuits.'

They tried to make love under water, but as usual the idea was more fun than the reality.

'We must be doing something wrong,' he said. 'It always seems to work in the movies.'

'They cheat,' she said. 'They cut and come again.'

He smiled. 'You really do make the most awful jokes.'

'I know. And they'll be even worse when I've had too much champagne.'

'We could make a start on that.'

They climbed out of the bath, shared a glass of warm

champagne, put the rest in the fridge and went to bed. 'This is all I could think about,' he said, 'while I was away. What it would be like to make love to you again.'

She always worried a little that it was too good to last, that next time some of the magic would be gone, but it was always better than she remembered, as if they simply could not get it wrong, no matter what they did. First there was the simple excitement of skin on skin, then all the various complicated games they played, watching one another for recognition of each move, smiling at the way it never failed, then the final shattering freedom of letting go and crashing out somewhere, quite apart from themselves, and coming back to earth warm, relaxed, dazed and somehow dislocated, as if from some tremendous journey.

'Wow,' he said. 'We're improving.'

'Not bad for only three years,' she said. 'In another twenty-three we might get it right.'

'Or even thirty-three,' he said. 'I certainly think we should persevere. The main thing is not to get discouraged.'

They lay quiet for a while, wrapped round each other, contemplating their good fortune. She began to think he might even be asleep when he suddenly said, 'Oh, Lizzie, what are we doing, why don't we just tell them? I want you with me all the time.'

She felt the thrill of terror, the temptation of the forbidden, impossible thing. 'But it wouldn't be like this,' she said. 'It'd be mortgages and fish fingers and socks.'

He sighed. 'That's what we always say. Maybe we're wrong. I'm not sure I care, anyway, I just want more of you.'

She sat up and looked at him, kissed him, traced his features with her forefinger. He looked younger after making love, as if orgasm, like death, had the power to rejuvenate, smoothing out the creases. 'You're getting the best of me,' she said gently.

'I know. But I want more time. Don't you?'

'Of course I do. I just can't imagine telling them –
hurting them. And I don't think you can, not really.'

He didn't answer.

'If you had to go home and tell Claire tonight,' she
persisted, using the name on purpose to shock him back to
reality, 'how would you feel?'

He closed his eyes.

'You see?' she said.

He shook his head. 'She'd get over it,' he said. 'As long
as she had the children and enough money. She'd be hurt
and angry at first but she *would* get over it. She'd probably
remarry.'

'The children wouldn't,' Lizzie said.

There was a long silence. 'I have this fantasy,' he said,
'that I tell Claire and you tell Roger, and they fall in love
with each other, so we've really done them a favour.'

'Oh, me too,' she said. 'That's what I think every night.'

'It happens, you know,' he said. 'I've read about it in
the papers.'

'That's why it makes headlines,' she said. 'Because it's so
rare.'

'All right, you've convinced me again.' He kissed her.
'Let's have some more champagne.'

'I love you for saying it, you know,' she said. 'If you
didn't, I would, and then you'd have to talk me out of it.'

They got up, put on bathrobes and went into the living-
room where she had lovingly prepared a feast: gazpacho;
salmon trout with salad, mayonnaise and new potatoes;
fresh mangos. He fetched the champagne, now beautifully
chilled, and they gave each other small gifts that would
pass almost unnoticed at home and have meaning only for
them, music they had made love to: Sinatra, Gilberto,
Miles Davis, Puccini. She lit candles and they started to
eat.

'Where are you meant to be?' he asked.

'At the NFT with Ginny seeing *Casablanca*. Then
supper.'

'Will he believe that, after all the times it's been on television?'

'He believes anything of Ginny because he thinks she's slightly mad. Actually she *has* gone to the NFT. She wanted to see it again on the big screen. So it's not really a lie at all.'

'Dear Ginny,' he said. 'Whatever would we do without her?'

'We don't have to,' she said. 'She loves going to the pictures and we do use our own sheets. What are sisters for?'

'We'll be sunk if she ever gets married again.'

'She'll have to marry Paul. Are you meant to be having dinner with him?'

'Yes, reporting on the trip. But I promised Claire I'd catch the last train.'

Suddenly it felt like the middle of August, the holidays half over, hurtling towards September and you did not know where they had gone. She shivered in the warm room.

'Why didn't you just say you were on a later flight?' she asked.

'I'm a bit superstitious about that. In case it crashes.'

'Oh, don't. How would I explain why I couldn't stop crying?'

'No, I meant in case the other one crashes. How would *I* explain being the only survivor?'

She laughed weakly. 'You might have to disappear and start a new life.'

'Would you come with me?'

She thought about it. 'I'd want to, but I'd be scared. When I left home tonight Roger was slumped in front of the television and the kids were thumping about upstairs. I kissed him on top of the head and told him supper was in the oven and he just grunted. When I get back he'll be in bed asleep.'

'Sounds just like me and Claire.'

'But that's exactly my point. It's marriage. We're all like that after fifteen years. And you and I would be too if we just . . . went off.'

'I don't believe that,' he said. 'I love your body and your cooking and your conversation. I want them every day, not once a week. I want to go to sleep and wake up with you there.'

'I'd be an awful disappointment,' she said. 'I'm very bad-tempered in the mornings and I grind my teeth at night.'

'Oh, darling,' he said, 'you're really scared, aren't you? Come here.'

They curled up on the sofa and she felt safe while he was holding her. The telephone rang, but they ignored it as they always did and let the machine answer.

'So we're not really trying to spare the others pain,' he said. 'We're protecting our investment.'

'Can't it be both? It's so good the way it is, why change anything? You can't afford two homes, you're at full stretch already. Can you imagine all the access visits, taking the kids to the zoo on Sundays and all that? Wouldn't we feel guilty? We might blame each other – and then what?'

'Why do you have to be so practical?'

'Because you're romantic – and I love you for it.'

She shut her eyes and tried to make time stop. She always knew the moment before he looked at the clock.

'Well, my love,' he said, looking at the clock, 'I'll have to be going.'

He got up and fetched his clothes from the bathroom. She watched him dress as attentively as she had watched him undress, but without the joyful anticipation; she saw the lover disappearing back into his suit and shirt and tie, becoming the business man again. Prince into Frog.

'Oh,' he said suddenly, 'I knew I'd forgotten something. Claire might ring you.'

'My God,' she said, 'whatever for?'

'It's all right,' he said. 'Calm down. She just said she might ask you and Roger to dinner.'

'But she hardly knows us. We were only neighbours, not friends.'

'I think she's feeling homesick for London even though it was her idea to move to the country. Don't look so worried. You can always make an excuse. I just thought I should warn you.'

'I don't think I could look her in the face,' she said. 'I like Claire. I wish I'd never met her.'

'But then we'd never have met either.'

'I know,' she said. 'There's no answer to it, is there?'

They kissed goodbye.

'Lunch on Tuesday?' she said.

'Next week is bad, it's the sales conference. I could maybe manage a drink after work on Thursday.'

'No good – PTA meeting.'

'Lunch on Friday somehow?'

'Lunch on Friday no matter what.'

They kissed goodbye again.

'Hurry, darling,' she said. 'You mustn't miss your train.'

'We didn't finish the second bottle,' he said.

'Never mind. Ginny will appreciate it.'

When he had gone she made herself deliberately very busy, so as not to feel alone. She washed up and tidied the flat and changed the sheets back again. She scribbled a note to Ginny; 'Thanks a million. There's a little something in the fridge for you. Lizzie.'

Leaving the flat was always painful and had to be done fast, slamming the door and locking up, putting the key back in its hiding place. She was grateful for the tube journey: she needed time to relapse into her other self. The guiltiest secret of all she still kept hidden, even from Sam, because it seemed like an insult. If there should be a divorce, even assuming the court gave her custody, as they probably would, what if the children chose to stay with Roger? They were old enough to choose. Sometimes she even had nightmares about it, though when she was awake she told herself not to be ridiculous.

When she got home she was relieved to see the house in darkness except for the hall light. It was reassuring to find everything as it should be. The hall light shone on the hall table, where the telephone sat; there were two phone numbers on the pad and two messages, which she stopped to read, almost needing her glasses for Roger's small, precise script.

'Lizzie – Claire Roberts rang. She and Sam want us to have dinner with them next Friday. I said you'd ring her back.'

And below, in handwriting even more cramped: 'St Thomas's Hospital rang. Apparently Ginny was knocked down by a car. She is all right but has concussion. They found our number in her diary. I have gone to bed early to give you time to think. Please try to come up with something convincing. I'm not sure I can bear the truth just yet – R.'

# Finding a Voice

The day started badly. Jenny on the phone at breakfast time, breathless and apologetic: 'Sorry, Mum, but is it all right if I come home next weekend instead of this one? Only I've got an essay to write and there's a party on Saturday that Tom wants to go to and . . .' Her voice trailed away. She waited to be understood and forgiven, told it didn't matter.

'That's fine, love. I don't mind,' Meg said firmly. 'I've got plenty to do.' She was absurdly disappointed but she hoped it didn't show. At all costs she must avoid sounding like her own mother, who always made her feel she had not done enough.

'Do something nice,' Jenny said. 'Don't just go and see Gran. Give yourself a treat.'

'Maybe I will.' The pips went. 'Shall I ring you back?'

'Well, I'm late for a lecture —'

They were cut off. Meg put the phone down, furious and miserable that there hadn't been time to make it feel all right. She resented being dependent on Jenny: it unbalanced their relationship. If Johnny had still been there, it would have been quite different; he'd have hugged her and it wouldn't have mattered, one weekend or the next, so what? They had each other.

She couldn't be bothered with breakfast after the phone call, so she set out for work instead, thinking she'd be early. But the bus didn't come for twenty minutes and the rain did; she ended up standing and swaying, jammed against a lot of strangers who smelled of damp raincoats, a smell that always reminded her of school cloakrooms.

Not the day to ask for a rise, she thought, arriving at work late and finding Mr Ferguson already there. He allowed himself the satisfaction of glancing at his watch but he didn't say anything sarcastic such as 'Afternoon'. That meant he was in a good mood. In fact he looked positively joyful, in so far as he could. Meg thought he resembled a bloodhound, and she wondered if people ever said to him as they did to her: 'Cheer up, it may never happen.' Greengrocers, being merry little souls, seemed to say it more often than other people, and she was heartily sick of smiling through clenched teeth or grimly replying: 'It already has.' She didn't suppose that Mr Ferguson went to greengrocers much; Mrs Ferguson probably did all that. And even if he did, there was something about him that would make anyone think twice before they told him to cheer up. Meg, being a woman, was fair game.

'It's sexual fascism, Mum,' Jenny always said. 'You should fight back. They're all male chauvinist pigs.'

'I wouldn't mind so much,' Meg explained patiently, 'if they only did it when I really feel depressed. But they do it when I'm quite cheerful as well. I can't help having a droopy face. It's not doing them any harm, after all.'

'You're too meek,' Jenny said with a mixture of sympathy and contempt. 'You should stand up for yourself.' But of course she had never had to before: there had always been Johnny to fight her battles for her.

It was all her mother's fault, Meg reflected, taking dictation faster and faster. Mr Ferguson was like a man inspired today, and she thought she knew why. Her mother, bringing her up to be polite to everyone, never to give offence. It was odd, when you thought about it, because her mother went around giving offence all over the place, although she called it speaking her mind. So why hadn't she brought Meg up to do the same?

'Don't be daft,' Jenny would say. 'There wouldn't have been room for both of you in the same house.'

Mr Ferguson went into overdrive around midday, then drew to a screeching halt about twelve fifteen. 'That should keep you going this afternoon,' he remarked with satisfaction. 'I'll be lunching with a client, back about four. But if my wife rings, better say I'm in a meeting. Too many expense account lunches and she thinks she doesn't have to cook.' He winked.

'Right.' Meg was pleased that her intuition was on target. Mr Ferguson had just told her, in code, that Corinna was in town and he would be spending the next four hours in bed. She could have done without the wink, though.

Corinna was an air stewardess with an American accent, although she came from Reading. She had shiny hair and shiny teeth and no one would ever tell her to cheer up because she was always smiling. Sometimes she called in the office to discuss her stocks and shares with Mr Ferguson. She liked Hermès scarves and Gucci bags and Ivoire by Balmain. Meg knew because she often had to buy these items gift-wrapped during her lunch hour, so that Mr Ferguson could present them to Corinna later. She also had to send flowers to Corinna in Reading and to Mrs Ferguson in Haywards Heath. Mrs Ferguson liked Hermès scarves and Gucci bags and Joy by Patou, but she only got them at Christmas and on her birthday, whereas Corinna got them all the time.

When Meg started typing, she noticed that the calendar said it was Friday the thirteenth. That explained everything, she thought. Not that she was superstitious, of course. Perhaps she *should* ask Mr Ferguson for a rise today: Corinna was sure to put him in a good mood. If you want me to tell lies and do your shopping, Mr Ferguson, Meg said to herself, you ought to pay me more. I'm valuable. I could ruin your life.

Around quarter to four, Mrs Ferguson phoned. Her

instinct was amazing. After weeks of not phoning, she always picked a Corinna-lunch day.

'I'm sorry, Mrs Ferguson,' Meg said smoothly, 'he's in a meeting. Can I get him to call you back?'

'No, thank you.' Mrs Ferguson sounded grim. 'I'm at Harrods.'

Oh God, Meg thought, as she put down the phone. The vengeance spree. On some unspoken level, Mrs Ferguson knew all about Corinna and would now go raving mad with her American Express card. When Mr Ferguson came back at ten to five, all rosy and replete, she reported the conversation, and he looked so stricken at the mention of Harrods that she hadn't the heart to discuss her salary. He repaid her by dictating another half-dozen letters and asking her to stay late to get them in the post. On a Friday. She ought to be angry; she *was* angry. But she did it.

'You're too soft, Mum,' she could hear Jenny saying. 'You should make a stand.' But she hadn't even been able to insist that Jenny tidied her room, so that it didn't look quite like a bomb-site; she had preferred to ignore it. And after all, what did it matter? The room was tidy now, because Jenny was gone.

'You spoil that girl, you know,' her mother said, disappointed that Jenny wasn't with Meg on her Saturday visit. 'You let her walk all over you.'

'She had an essay to write,' Meg said defensively.

Her mother snorted. 'More likely off somewhere with that boyfriend of hers, enjoying herself.'

Sometimes Meg almost hated her mother for voicing her own resentment. She also wondered why Jenny got blamed for being a bad daughter but she herself didn't get praised for being a good one.

'She was sorry not to see you,' she lied. 'And she sent her love. Now aren't you going to have a slice of this cake?'

Her mother peered at it and sighed. 'Chocolate,' she said. 'Why do you always make chocolate cake?'

'Because you said it was your favourite.' One day I shan't make any cake at all, Meg thought, and *then* you'll get a shock.

'It *is* my favourite, but that doesn't mean I want to eat it every week. Can't you be more imaginative? I'd like a surprise now and then. Anybody would.'

'Yes, of course. Fruit or sponge next time? Or ginger perhaps? Or walnut?'

Her mother stared. 'If I tell you that, it won't be a surprise, will it?'

Meg cut a slice of the offending cake, counted to ten and regaled her mother with an account of Mr Ferguson's love life. Anything to change the subject. She expected disapproval, but her mother expressed the view that since Mr Ferguson was paying the piper, he was entitled to call the tune.

'It's just a pity he doesn't pay this particular piper a bit more,' Meg said. She was pleased in a way that her mother could still surprise her, although Jenny would have complained about the old double standard rearing its ugly head, and how Gran would never approve of *Mrs* Ferguson behaving like that. What was more, Jenny would have got away with it. Sometimes, listening to them argue, Meg was amazed how alike they were. She felt like the filling in the sandwich, totally flattened, or a bone between two dogs, tugged this way and that. They thoroughly enjoyed their arguments, which they called discussions, and had a healthy respect for one another.

'Gran's impossible,' Jenny would say fondly.

'Jenny takes after me,' her mother boasted. 'She's got a mind of her own.'

God help me, Meg thought, if I tried to copy either of them. I'd soon be shouted down.

'I shouldn't fret about your salary if I were you,' her mother said. 'You're lucky to have a job at all the way things are these days. And you know you could always move in with me. It's ridiculous paying for two lots of everything when we're both on our own.'

Meg knew this was just her mother's way of saying she was lonely. Compassion mingled with panic: it was the obvious solution but it wouldn't work. Surely they both knew that? Guilt wriggled its way in next: am I a monster because I can't share a house with my mother? (Worse still, is this how Jenny feels about me?) Oh, but it's too soon, she told herself; I can't give up yet, I'm only forty-one. It can't be all over yet, surely.

'And it wouldn't be easy,' her mother added, 'finding another job at your age.'

'I must go,' Meg said, kissing her. 'See you next week.' She looked at the neat bungalow and the disciplined garden and knew she could never live there.

'You could stay the night,' her mother said. 'What's the point of rushing back to an empty house?'

When Meg took flowers to the cemetery on Sunday, she stared at Johnny's grave for a long time. 'It's all your fault,' she said to him. 'Why did you have to die? It's not fair, I can't manage without you.' She put the flowers in water, tidied the grave and said a prayer, accepting her anger as part of her love. It had been Jenny who released it, saying one day with eyes full of tears, 'Oh Mum, I'm so *cross* with Dad for dying.' Meg recognised her own feelings, long suppressed out of guilt. And when she read books and magazine articles about bereavement, later on, she discovered it was normal to be angry with someone for dying and leaving you, even though they could not help it. Only no one had told her and so she had tried not to be.

It was only three years. Some said it took five, others seven. A few said you never got over it, merely came to terms with it, whatever that might mean. She wasn't sure why she still prayed, because she was angry with God too. Why take Johnny away, when they were so happy, why not take one of the one-in-three couples who were busy getting divorced, and save them all the trouble and expense? People said it was a merciful release, when they knew Johnny had cancer, but why had God let Johnny get cancer in the first place? She had argued the point with the vicar, who had tried to explain but failed.

She pinned her hopes to Sunday evening: supper with Edward. She found the prospect very soothing. They took turns to cook and Edward always talked about his girlfriend Roz and how they couldn't get married because she had to stay with her invalid husband. Meg would listen and sympathise. Her mother said she ought to marry Edward but her mother didn't know about Roz. Besides, Meg didn't like the way Edward kissed her. He had only done it once, one Sunday night a year ago when he was rather drunk because he and Roz had decided yet again that they should do the decent thing and part for ever. Meg thought they had probably been watching *Brief Encounter*. Anyway, what alarmed her was the way Edward's lips came forward and his teeth disappeared as if retractable. It was like being kissed by a small hungry bird: she felt Edward was waiting for her to drop a worm into his open, pursed-up mouth. 'Oh Mum, how yukky,' Jenny said when Meg told her. Meg felt guilty about exposing Edward to Jenny, but she had to tell someone and there was no one else to tell. The bird image persisted after that, for Edward was tall and thin. If he had stood on one leg, he would have reminded her of a heron.

The kiss was never repeated, so she assumed Edward found it equally unsatisfactory. She was greatly relieved: she preferred to go on thinking of him as good old Edward who was like a brother to her, had once been Johnny's bank manager, and made an excellent goulash. She was particularly looking forward to seeing him tonight in the hope that he might allow her to talk about Mr Ferguson and her rise, Jenny's empty room, the problem of her mother. She felt if only he would listen to her for a while, she might get things clear in her head and make a few decisions. But Edward, stirring and tasting and flavouring something in a vast pot on the stove while she sat in the kitchen and watched him, wanted to talk about Roz. 'I don't know how to tell you this,' he said. 'It's rather delicate.'

Meg sipped her drink. Surely Roz couldn't be pregnant? It seemed unlike either of them to be careless after all these years. Then she noticed Edward's lips were quivering as if he were trying not to laugh.

'The thing is,' he said, 'oh dear, it's sad in a way so I shouldn't rejoice, only, well, the fact is Roz's husband has finally died and we're going to get married.'

Meg stared at him. She couldn't think of a thing to say.

'After a decent interval, of course,' he added.

'Congratulations,' Meg said faintly. She was surprised how angry she felt. Bang go my cosy Sunday evenings, she thought. Suddenly everyone (except her mother) was having more fun than she was: Jenny with Tom, Mr Ferguson with Corinna, and now Edward with Roz. None of it would have mattered if she could have shared it with Johnny. But if Johnny had still been alive, she wouldn't have been here in the first place.

She was still not used to the fact that unhappiness made you angry. Women were not supposed to be angry. They were supposed to be plucky, smiling creatures who went merrily on, no matter what happened, because others depended on them. In extreme cases, a little mild depression might be allowed from time to time. But anger was definitely out. Anger was unfeminine.

'I've asked Roz to join us,' Edward said. 'I knew you wouldn't mind.'

And what could she say to that? How astonished he would be if she screamed and yelled: I don't want to see bloody Roz, I don't like Roz, hell, if you're going to marry this wretched woman, surely you can give me your undivided attention for one evening, is that too much to ask? How lovely it would be to be two years old again permitted to have tantrums, to fall over and shriek and drum her heels on the floor.

'Of course I don't mind,' she said.

Roz duly arrived. She talked about her husband's last hours, which so reminded Meg of Johnny that she almost started to cry. Had Roz's husband known, Meg wondered, that Roz was only waiting for him to die?

'It was a merciful release,' Roz said. Edward held her hand and she smiled at him. Meg drank some more wine.

'Meg understands,' Edward said. 'It was the same thing with her husband.'

Roz beamed. 'Oh,' she breathed with relief, 'then you really know how I feel. You must go on coming round here, you know. We'll always be pleased to see you.'

'Thank you,' said Meg, 'but I think I should go home now. It's getting rather late.'

They offered to call her a taxi. Meg insisted that she did not want a taxi, she would catch the last bus, and in any case if she missed it, she could always pick up a taxi in the street.

'Oh, but you shouldn't be out alone at this time of night,' they said, as if they were her mother.

'Nonsense,' said Meg, smiling brightly. 'Nothing ever happened to anyone in the high street at half past eleven.'

Roz lifted the phone. 'It won't take a minute,' she said.

'Thank you for a lovely evening,' Meg said, and ran.

Outside in the street she breathed the cool air and tried to collect her thoughts. She hung about for a while but there weren't any taxis or buses around so she decided to take a short cut to the main road where she would have more choice.

The side street was small and quiet but well lit. She had often used it before. At first she was hardly aware of the man walking on the opposite pavement; her mind was full of Edward and Roz.

'Cheer up,' he suddenly called across to her.

She couldn't believe it. In daylight perhaps, she was fair game, a woman on her own looking miserable. But at quarter to twelve on a Sunday night under a street lamp,

how could he even see if she was looking depressed? And
what did it matter to him?

She glanced at him out of the corner of her eye without
turning her head. He was average height and build, grey-
haired. Very nondescript really, nothing to be afraid of.
But why couldn't he leave her alone?

'Shut up,' she called back, emboldened by Edward's
wine and the disappointment of the evening. She walked
on, pleased with herself for this display of spirit. In
daylight she would have just ignored him.

'Cheer up,' he called again a moment later.

Something in Meg simply snapped. The events of the
weekend, the pain of the last three years, the loss of Johnny
– all suddenly erupted into the first unpremeditated action
of her life.

'Shut up and fuck off,' she shouted very loudly indeed,
and to her own amazement raced across the road directly
at him, swinging her handbag. She was going to hit him.

But he ran. She had never seen anyone move so fast. One
moment he was there, the next he had disappeared back
into the building he had come from, like a rabbit down a
hole. Meg stood by the traffic lights breathing hard,
cheated of her prey, both relieved and disappointed, still
high on adrenalin and amazed at herself. A taxi drew up
alongside.

'Hop in, love,' the driver said admiringly and she did,
feeling she deserved a taxi now even if she could not afford it.

'Now that's a very useful lesson for you,' the cabbie
went on. 'Ninety-nine times out of a hundred a man will
run if a woman screams that loud. He's not expecting it,
you see. Gives him quite a shock.'

Meg dimly remembered something of the sort being said
on a TV programme about self-defence that she had
watched with Jenny, who claimed that she would always
opt for a crippling blow to the groin if anyone attacked
her. That would make them think twice, she said, before
they did it again.

Meg still didn't believe she had actually used that word. She had heard Johnny use it, of course, either lovingly in bed or furiously when he struck his thumb with a hammer; and she had heard Jenny shush her friends when they used it without thinking when Meg was in the next room. But to use it herself. To a perfect stranger. In the street. She was dizzy with astonishment.

'Trouble is,' she heard the cabbie say, 'a woman swearing always turns me on.'

There had been a time, probably until about ten minutes ago, when any sort of sexual remark from a taxidriver would have alarmed her greatly. But now, what did it matter? If she could frighten a man in the street, there were no limits to what she could do. She laughed.

'That's your problem,' she said.

Plans took shape in her mind with amazing speed. She would ask Mr Ferguson for a rise and if he refused she would leave. There would always be another job for someone like her. She would let Jenny's room to a student who would be away in the holidays when Jenny was home. Or she would find a residential job and let the whole house. Why not? She would join clubs and evening classes; she would meet men and stop being angry with Johnny. She would forget about Edward and Roz; she would visit her mother once a fortnight when they might both handle it better. She wished she could tell her mother what had happened, but her mother would be alarmed at the danger and appalled at the word. But she could tell Jenny, and Jenny would be proud of her.

'You know,' the cabbie said, when she paid him off, 'you're a very interesting woman.'

'Yes, I know,' she said.

# Fancy Seeing You

Geraldine had dyed her hair orange. It was so bright that it seemed to enter the room before she did. 'Lucy,' she exclaimed, holding out her arms. 'It's good to see you again.'

Lucy accepted a bunch of chrysanthemums from one of the extended arms and hugged Geraldine in return. She couldn't recall if they had been on hugging terms in the past, but it seemed to go with their reunion. 'I'm glad you could come,' she said, although with Geraldine barely inside the door she was already beginning to wonder if the visit was a good idea. Geraldine's voice was louder than she remembered; she seemed to be vibrating with energy; and the orange hair was a shock. If only her mother had asked her before giving Geraldine her phone number, Lucy thought, but that wasn't fair: she had been curious enough to invite Geraldine when she rang up. Anything for a change, a novelty, she had thought; anything was better than sitting here night after night, staring at her own four walls and feeling sorry for herself. She told herself sternly that the evening was going to be fun, but she wasn't convinced.

'What would you like to drink?' she asked. 'Wine or gin?'

'What are you having?' Geraldine lit a cigarette and looked around for an ashtray, which Lucy, having given up smoking, did not possess.

'Gin,' said Lucy, who had never understood why anyone's choice of drink should depend on what the other person was drinking.

'Gin would be very nice,' said Geraldine.

She was looking well, there was no doubt about that. Perhaps it was the blusher that gave her a healthy glow, or the pink eye-shadow; maybe they were one and the same. She looked somehow contemporary and made Lucy feel old. She poured a large gin for Geraldine and began to arrange the flowers. 'These are lovely,' she said. 'Thank you very much.'

Geraldine gestured absently. 'Oh, they're nothing, they come from my ma-in-law's garden. She can't do enough for me now Charlie's gone off, she's so grateful I still let her see the children. Cigarette?'

Lucy explained about having given up and Geraldine asked her if she minded other people smoking. Lucy hesitated, torn as always between honesty and tact.

'Not when I like them very much,' she said, giving Geraldine a soup bowl for her ash, some of which was already on the floor.

'If I can't smoke, then I can't go out at all,' Geraldine said cheerfully. 'I can only see people in my own home. How on earth did you manage to stop?'

Lucy didn't want to admit she had been so miserable it seemed the ideal time to stop. If you have lost your husband, then you don't mind losing cigarettes as well, just as if you are drowning you hardly notice if it comes on to rain. 'Oh, I don't know,' she said vaguely. 'I just did.'

'God, such willpower,' said Geraldine, puffing energetically. 'I simply couldn't. Not this year anyway. Not after all I've been through.' And she laughed.

'Come and sit down,' said Lucy, 'and tell me all about it.' She led the way from kitchen to living-room, wanting Geraldine to admire her Habitat lamps, her Peter Jones curtains, her junk shop table and chairs, the clever way she had made them enhance each other. At night she often sat admiring her room before she went to bed, thinking that here at least was something she could do well, create a home, even if no one wanted to share it with her. But Geraldine barely glanced at the room before she flung herself down with her drink and her cigarette and put her feet up on the coffee table.

'Well, at first I just never stopped crying,' she said. 'I must have cried every day for six months, I should think. Then one day I woke up and I actually felt happy again, for no reason.'

Lucy thought of an article she had read recently which claimed that emotionally healthy people, who comprised only one fifth of the population, grieved intensely for a short time, then recovered and got on with their lives. Geraldine must be very healthy, she thought.

'After all,' Geraldine said, 'to be miserable just because I've lost a man, that's crazy.' And she laughed again.

She had two distinct types of laugh: a small soft chuckle, the kind of sound a kitten might make if it could laugh, and a full-throated roar, the equivalent of laughter in the jungle from a big cat. Neither sounded as if she were really amused, rather concerned to prove her cheerfulness. As the conversation went on, Lucy noticed that Geraldine used the laughs quite often, after remarks that were not funny at all.

'So,' she said suddenly, 'what happened to the Italian then?'

Lucy, already feeling uneasy, thought this was a strange way to refer to her husband. 'Oh,' she said, 'we separated.'

'I know that,' said Geraldine. 'Your mother told me that. But what happened? I mean, with Charlie and me it was simple. Once I'd had the kids, it was all over. He just didn't want to know. Headaches at bedtime and all that. Now he's living with a bloke. Well, that says it all, don't you think?'

'I don't know,' Lucy said honestly. 'They might be just sharing a flat.'

Geraldine roared with jungle laughter. 'Come off it. How naïve can you be? Could I have another gin?'

'Oh yes, of course,' Lucy said, getting up. 'Sorry.'

'You still haven't told me what happened,' Geraldine shouted after her.

Alone in the kitchen, Lucy poured two more large gins. She felt her inside squirming with the need to be secretive. It was too humiliating to admit how making love for pleasure had turned into making love for a purpose and still produced nothing. How could she say to Geraldine, with her two fat children, that Luigi had ended up banging her head on the floor with frustration, until she was afraid to make love in case it ended in violence. Refusing to believe her doctor's report that there was nothing wrong with her, he also refused to go for investigation himself. In Italy he had made several girls pregnant, he now told her, so he knew there was nothing wrong with him. It must be Lucy. The doctors were fools. Perhaps she could have an operation.

'What happened to the girls?' Lucy had asked. It was the first time he had mentioned them and she wondered if he was lying.

'Oh,' he shrugged, 'some had babies, some had abortions.'

Lucy, shocked, asked how many there had been, but he didn't remember. She had felt suddenly out of her depth, in an alien country, although they were at home in London at the time. It had never occurred to her that her marriage depended on children because she had assumed that children would follow. But they had not, and now Luigi, who had been so loving that she had walked around with a permanent smile on her face, was blaming her.

'Why didn't you tell me about them?' she said.

'It was before we met. You don't tell me about everyone you loved before me.'

'Yes, I did,' Lucy said. But it was no good. Not sufficient that they made wonderful love, had enough money, both adored opera and pasta and sunshine. They must have a baby to prove all was well. Adoption was out of the question. Waiting and seeing would not do at all. They had done that already, for far too long.

'Perhaps we're allergic to each other,' she said one day in desperation. She meant in a chemical way, having heard something on the radio about antibodies, but he took it to mean they should get divorced. Even after she explained, the thought was still there and it was as if she had given him permission.

'Oh,' she said, going back into the living-room with the drinks, 'it burnt itself out.'

'What a shame,' said Geraldine. 'I thought Italians were supposed to be so passionate.'

'I've only known one,' said Lucy, 'and he was.'

'Well, I just don't understand it,' said Geraldine. 'There's Charlie living with a bloke and your Italian running out of steam. What's the matter with men these days? No stamina, that's their trouble.'

Lucy gulped down half her drink. 'We probably expect too much,' she said, although she did not believe it.

'Nonsense,' said Geraldine. 'My father still worships my mother, waits on her hand and foot, and they've been married thirty years. I think it's Women's Lib, you know. If we're not careful, we'll end up having to make do with each other.' And she laughed, the kitten chuckle.

'Isn't that a separate issue?' said Lucy faintly. She had a feeling that the evening was getting out of control, galloping away into the sunset and dragging her after it, her heel caught in its stirrup.

'How would I know? I lead such a sheltered life.' Geraldine narrowed her eyes, as if she were staring at Lucy from a long way off. 'Fancy seeing you,' she said, 'after all these years.'

'I think we should eat,' Lucy said. 'The lamb will be overdone.'

'It'll be mutton dressed as lamb.' Geraldine laughed, the

tiger's roar this time, and sank back into her seat. 'Can I do anything to help?'

Lucy brought in the lamb, the peas, the roast potatoes. She went back for the gravy and opened a bottle of wine. Perhaps they had had too much gin; maybe that was the trouble. Too much gin on an empty stomach. She was never sure if gin suited her but she liked it for a treat.

Geraldine ate ravenously but without praising the food. She drank rather fast, too. Lucy began to wonder if one bottle would be enough.

'Did he call you Lucia?' Geraldine asked suddenly.

Lucy's stomach lurched. 'What?'

'The Italian. Did he call you Lucia?'

'Oh. Yes. Yes, he did.' But it was too late. Tears scalded her face, tears she hadn't known were lying in wait for her. Geraldine watched for a moment, looking shocked and sympathetic. Lucy found to her own surprise that she didn't mind making this exhibition of herself, that there was a voluptuous sense of relief in tears, even if Geraldine had to witness them. Then Geraldine got up and came round the table. She hugged Lucy.

'Poor you,' she said. 'What a shame. Poor Lucia.'

It was comforting to be hugged, even by Geraldine, whom she did not know well and had not seen for ten years. Going to the same school on the same bus, always being the two last to be chosen for netball teams, having mothers who were friends: none of that made for intimacy, but it did establish a sort of comfortable familiarity. Cousins rather than sisters; friendship was something else. Then she became aware that Geraldine was kissing her on both cheeks and around the eyes, somehow drinking up her tears as fast as they appeared. In a way it was appropriate, and nice; in another, simultaneously, it felt incongruous and wrong. She drew back, on the pretext of wanting tissues from the box on the table, where they had been doubling as napkins. Geraldine went back to her seat and lit another cigarette.

'Bloody men,' she said.

Lucy blew her nose and started to mop her face. She felt shaken up and yet somehow calm as well, like someone who has just missed being run over by a bus. Now that the moment was past, she was not at all sure she hadn't imagined it.

'Whatever made you leave London?' Geraldine asked in a conversational tone.

'I felt like a change,' Lucy said, 'and I've always been fond of the sea.'

'But what d'you find to *do* down here?' Geraldine drummed her fingers on the table. 'I mean, it's fine for a weekend, like me now, visiting Charlie's ma once a year, but what do you do in the winter?'

'I haven't been here in the winter yet,' said Lucy, 'but I think it will be all right. I just wanted to live somewhere quiet for a change. And there was a job going.' She felt as if she were being auditioned: having failed to land a starring role, she might yet be offered something in the chorus.

'Well,' said Geraldine, standing up, 'there must be some night life in this godforsaken place. Come on. Let's go and find some men.'

Outside in the street it was cold: the wind whipped their faces and the sea made a reassuring noise. Lucy wondered what she was doing there when she longed, suddenly, to go to bed. It had seemed as if the only polite way to get Geraldine out of the flat was to go with her, but there had also been, left over from school, a feeling that Geraldine might be right to go looking for adventure, and Lucy would be feeble, a stick in the mud, if she refused. Geraldine had always known the best places to smoke undisturbed at break and the best dances for picking up boys. If anyone could find a nightclub at half past eleven in a seaside village, it was Geraldine.

I must be drunk, Lucy thought, as they approached the car. And if I am drunk, then so is Geraldine and she shouldn't be driving.

Geraldine drove fast and Lucy was frightened. She was glad seat belts were compulsory, so that Geraldine couldn't be offended when she put hers on so promptly.

'When Charlie went off,' Geraldine said, as if they had been talking about him, 'he came back one day to fetch some things when he thought I was out, only I wasn't out, I was hiding under the bed, and he cut up some of my clothes. Wasn't that amazing?'

'Weren't you terrified?' Lucy asked.

'Yes, of course. But flattered as well. I didn't know he had such strong feelings.'

Periodically she stopped, whenever she saw anyone, and asked if there was anywhere to go dancing. Most of the people merely looked surprised, but finally she found someone who assured her that Jack's Place, at the top of the hill this side of town but after the second lot of traffic lights, would be just what she was looking for, and she couldn't miss it because there was a red lamp in the window.

'Well,' said Geraldine, accelerating, 'that's appropriate, anyway.'

'I'm beginning to lose my nerve,' Lucy ventured. It seemed a daring confession and also a gross understatement.

'Don't be chicken,' said Geraldine, shooting a red light. 'Fortune favours the bold.'

Jack's Place, when they finally found it, looked anything but inviting. A red bulb glowed faintly in the doorway, and there were a few parked cars and motor bikes outside. In the lobby a bored girl looked at them curiously and picked her teeth.

'Are you members?' she asked.

Lucy felt panic, imagining huge entrance fees. Why am I so timid? she wondered. Is that why Luigi banged my head on the floor? Or am I timid because he did that?

'No,' said Geraldine, 'but we'd like —'

'Then you'll have to sign in,' said the bored girl, pushing the register at them.

Geraldine signed with a flourish. Lucy, peering over her shoulder, was startled to see the names Jane Smith and Natasha Rostova. Geraldine, catching her glance, winked at her. The past rushed back at Lucy: evenings at the local disco, with Geraldine pretending to be foreign.

'Come on,' said Geraldine, advancing. 'Into the valley of death rode the four hundred.'

Following the sound, they found themselves in a medium-sized room with a bar at one end and an electric organ at the other. There were a few couples at the bar and a crowd of young men doing nothing in particular and looking very unsettled. No other women in sight.

'What would you like?' Geraldine asked when they reached the bar.

'Oh – white wine,' said Lucy, thinking that most of all she would like to go home, and (second best) to die. Geraldine paid for the drinks, the couples moving out of her way and the young men crowding in. She picked up the two glasses and made for a corner table; Lucy followed. Coloured lights revolved and the organist worked himself up into a frenzy.

The corner table was a mistake. No sooner had they sat down than four or five young men joined them and they were boxed in. The young men came almost at a run, as if determined to be first in the queue for something in short supply.

'D'you come here often?' one asked, and his friend guffawed behind him. They were both very young and had the acne to prove it. Lucy felt a hundred years old. Never had the vision of an early night, alone, in a Viyella nightdress, with a mug of Horlicks seemed more attractive.

'*Niet*,' said Geraldine to the spotty youth, and turned to Lucy with a burst of pseudo Russian.

'You what?' the young man asked, not unreasonably.

Oh God, Lucy thought, realising she was meant to translate. 'She's over here on holiday,' she said.

'Where's she from then?' his friend asked, staring at Geraldine.

'*Russki, Russki*,' said Geraldine passionately.

'Go on,' said the first youth, his lip curling with scorn, 'you're having me on.'

'No, really, she's Russian,' said Lucy. 'She really is. Honestly.' It seemed vital she should make him believe it.

'D'you speak Russian then?'

'No, but I . . . understand a litle, and she understands quite a lot of English, so we each talk our own language.' Lucy paused a moment and added, 'She's a bit shy, you see.' She saw Geraldine's mouth quiver.

'You're pulling my leg,' said the first youth, but his friend turned to Geraldine and said very slowly, moving his lips with great care, 'Will you dance with me?'

Geraldine stared at him blankly and the organist played louder than ever.

'Why don't you translate?' said the first youth.

'She's a bit deaf as well,' said Lucy, feeling vicious.

'What's her name?' his friend asked, thumping his chest. 'Me Peter.'

'Me Tarzan, you Jane,' said the first youth to Geraldine with a coarse laugh.

'No, me Jane,' said Lucy. 'She Natasha.' Oh well, why not? she thought.

The hangers-on, bored, started to drift away, but the friend repeated carefully, pointing at himself, 'Me Peter,' and then pointing at Geraldine, 'You Natasha.' Lucy began to feel sorry for him.

'Tell her to say something in English,' said the first youth.

Just then the organist stopped playing; there was faint applause, and in the ensuing silence, loudly and clearly Geraldine said, 'Prick.'

Lucy saw incredulity on the faces of the two young men. Right, she thought, that does it. Time to go home before we get into real trouble. 'She's feeling sick,' she announced, seizing Geraldine's arm and jerking her to her feet. 'We must go.' Nobody moved and Lucy, beginning to panic, added, 'Come on, you'd better move, she might throw up all over you. You heard her say she feels sick.'

The young men drew back, still looking puzzled, not sure now what they had heard. Lucy frogmarched Geraldine to the door and into the car park.

'I hate men,' said Geraldine.

'They were harmless,' said Lucy.

Geraldine sat in the car with Lucy beside her and began to laugh. First the kitten chuckle, then the tiger roar. Then she started to cry.

'Please, Geraldine,' Lucy said. 'Let's go. Are you okay to drive? Please don't let's just sit here.'

Geraldine started the car. 'I don't know what I did wrong,' she said. 'I had children, I cooked dinners, I was good in bed. I entertained his friends. Why didn't Charlie want me?'

'Let's go home,' Lucy begged.

Geraldine drove slowly this time, so slowly and carefully that Lucy was sure that the police, should they meet any, would stop them. When they were nearly home Geraldine suddenly said, 'Well, he was a proper Charlie then,' but neither of them laughed. Lucy had heard of people being tired to the bone but she thought that her own exhaustion went beyond that: she was tired right through the marrow of her bones and could easily melt into a little exhausted pool on the floor of Geraldine's car.

Geraldine stopped outside Lucy's flat. 'Well,' she said, 'Keep in touch.'

'Yes,' said Lucy.

'I mean properly,' said Geraldine. 'Not just Christmas cards. And any time you fancy a weekend in Bristol, just give me a ring.'

Lucy kissed her on both cheeks. 'Take care,' she said. 'Drive carefully and good luck with everything.'

'It was lovely seeing you again,' said Geraldine.

Lucy waved until she was out of sight. Going upstairs and into her empty, silent flat, she felt curiously light and optimistic. Apart from the exhaustion, she seemed washed new, as on the day after a hangover. There were, it appeared, worse fates in the world than being alone. She had learnt that much; Geraldine had taught her something.

She opened the windows to get rid of the smoke. If someone new came along, so much the better, but if not, well . . . She stood on the balcony and looked at the sea and found herself smiling.

# A Long Way from Paradise

When the letter with the airline ticket arrived, Abigail didn't know what to do. She carried it around with her for several days and kept looking at it, on the bus or in her desk at school. At night she put it under her pillow. She knew she would have to tell her mother about it eventually but she needed time to think and she wanted to keep it a secret while she thought. She didn't want to talk to anyone about it until she had decided what to do.

At first there was a temptation to tear it up and send it back to him with no letter, nothing, just the pieces in an envelope. That would show him how she felt, and serve him right too. But she didn't. Then she was angry with herself for being so feeble. If she gave in as easily as that, he would only think he could buy her off with a holiday. It was like a bribe to make her forgive him, to pretend everything was all right.

She took out his letter, a bit crumpled now, and read it again.

Darling Abby,

I do wish you'd write to me. I know you're very cross with me for going away and you've every right to be, although I did try to explain why I had to go. But I'd still rather have a cross letter than no letter at all. I miss you very much. Can't you write and tell me how you feel and I'll answer you the best I can. It's awful writing all these letters and never getting a reply. It's as if my letters have got stuck at the post office and never reached you at all.

I'm enclosing a ticket for you to come out here in the Xmas holidays. All you have to do is ring up the airline for dates and flights. Please come – we've got a lot of catching up to do. Apart from that, I think you'd like it here. Now that the rainy season's over, it's lovely, warm and sunny. There are brightly coloured birds everywhere that come and steal the sugar at breakfast, and the flowers are amazing – you almost need sunglasses to look at them. Just think – you could be lying on the beach getting a fantastic suntan while all your friends are getting chilblains in the snow.

There was more, but she didn't read it all again. His letters were always like that, telling her how nice the place was and how much she'd like it, and often enclosing a few snapshots of himself against some scenic bit of landscape. He was always alone, which reminded her of the person who must have taken the photograph. The only difference with this letter was the ticket.

The temptation was enormous: she ached to see him again. Already his image was becoming faint and when she looked at the pictures he seemed somehow unfamiliar. Perhaps it was the unaccustomed suntan, making him appear younger; she tried to tell herself that. But she was afraid he was beginning to look like a stranger enjoying himself on a beach, a stranger who wrote her letters she did not answer. They had never been apart before, so these were the first letters she had ever received from him.

She finally decided to tell her mother when they were washing up. It was easier for them to talk about important things when their hands were busy and they didn't have to look at each other. Even so, it was hard to get the words out and when she did, they came in a rush.

'Dad's sent me a ticket.'

For just a second Mum's hands stopped moving in the soapy water; then they darted about faster than ever. It was still odd to see them without a wedding ring: as if she and Dad had never been married at all. When she first took

it off, Abigail had hoped it meant she was ready to start
going out with people again, like the man at work who
was always asking her. But it hadn't turned out that way.
It meant she was giving up. She had stopped wearing
make-up at the same time, stopped wearing rubber gloves
for washing up, like now, as if she didn't care what she
looked like any more.

It was so unlike her: she had always been so smart and
modern, keen to look nice, proud of her job. She and Dad
had even argued about her dressing up for work. He'd
hardly recognise her now, Abigail thought.

'He wants me to go out there in the holidays,' she went
on, bolder now it was out. She hated having to feel sorry
for Mum: it hurt and made her angry. She didn't want to
be grown up and responsible. She wanted Mum to look
after her and make Dad come back. 'But I shan't go,' she
added sharply.

'Why not?' Mum asked, sounding oddly casual.

'I don't want to.'

'Course you do.' She stopped washing up, wiped her
hands and put an arm round Abigail. 'It's only natural. Of
course you want to see him again.'

Abigail squirmed away. She hated it when Mum hugged
her. It didn't happen very often but it always made her
want to cry. She was afraid that if she cried Mum would
cry too and somehow that seemed very dangerous, as if it
would make everything fall apart. She had never seen
Mum cry, though she had heard her often enough through
the bedroom wall. She did her own crying at night too, but
silently, and sometimes, if she really couldn't avoid it, in
the loo at school. She resented it bitterly: she was sure Dad
wasn't crying. He was too busy enjoying himself in the
sunshine with that girl. If he could manage so well without
them both, then she and Mum should be able to manage
without him.

'I don't,' she said. 'And anyway, I'd have to see her too
and I'm not going to do that. He must be joking if he

thinks I'd go out there for a holiday while she's hanging about.'

Mum went back to the sink. 'You'll have to meet her eventually,' she said, sounding very calm and reasonable.

'I don't see why.'

'Because he's probably going to marry her.'

'But you're not divorced.' It was a shock, a blow to the stomach, to hear her worst fears put into words.

'No, but we will be next year.' Mum emptied the washing-up water and it gurgled away. 'He's got a new life out there, lovey, and he's not coming back. You need to see him. He still loves you, you know. It was me he wanted to leave, not you.'

'Yes, you told me all that,' Abigail snapped. Before Dad left, he and Mum had got together and explained it all to her, about how they had got married too young and how they had changed over the years and that was why they had been having a lot of rows until they got very polite and hardly talked at all. Now they were going to separate, but it was all for the best and she would have two homes instead of one and of course they both loved her as much as ever. It was quite a speech, quite a double act: in fact the most united thing she had seen them do in years. But it reminded her of American films and she didn't believe any of it. They were saying what they thought they ought to say.

She was right. After they'd finished their big speech and while she was still dumb with shock that the thing she'd always feared had actually happened, Mum added sharply, 'Well, aren't you going to tell her the rest of it?'

For just a second Dad looked like a cringing dog that knows it's going to be beaten, then he became very angry. 'I see. You want to play it that way, do you?'

'She might as well know the truth,' said Mum, looking at her nail varnish. 'She'll have to know sooner or later.'

'Your version, you mean,' Dad said.

'Just the facts,' said Mum.

Abigail wanted to scream and run away, but she didn't move.

'He's got this girl at work.' said Mum. 'She's one of the waitresses and she's twenty-six and he's going away with her.'

'God, you're a bitch,' said Dad.

'I mean really away,' said Mum. 'Far away. They're going to run away to an island in the sun and live happily ever after.'

'Shut up,' Dad yelled. Abigail put her hands over her ears. She pictured the waitress as someone with wild hair and a slightly tarty, cross-eyed look, rather like Karen Black in *Five Easy Pieces*. She was desperately embarrassed to think of Dad with a girl.

'I know it's a shock,' Dad said to her gently, 'and I'm sorry, but I'm sure once you meet her −'

'I'm never going to meet her,' she said. 'I hate her.' Dad had become disgusting and ridiculous, like vicars and schoolteachers you read about in the papers when they ran off with teenagers.

'I'm sorry,' Mum said. 'I shouldn't have told her like that.'

Abigail rocked herself to and fro, the way she did when she had a painful period, to make the backache go away. Her parents became united again. They tried to hug her but she wouldn't let them. They apologised to her as if she were grown up. They made tea and tried to persuade her to drink it.

'I'm going to bed,' Abigail said. In some perverse way she almost enjoyed seeing how guilty and miserable they looked. When she got to her room she put on a record very loud, knowing that for once they wouldn't dare ask her to turn it down. She lay on the bed and tried to think about what had happened but none of it seemed real. The music drowned it out.

Dad moved into a bedsit and she was supposed to visit him at weekends but then she found out that the girl was sharing the bedsit with him. Julie, her name was. After that Abigail wouldn't visit him any more and they had to meet in parks and coffee bars.

He tried to explain about the island, how it was a great opportunity. He tried to make it sound like work, not a glorious holiday.

'Julie has friends there and they're opening a small hotel. I'd be in charge of the restaurant. It'd be almost like having my own place.'

The name still hurt, making her sour. It seemed to intrude into every conversation they had. 'I don't see why. You'd still be working for someone else, just like now.'

'I know it's a long way,' he said, picking up what she hadn't said, 'but you could come out there in the holidays. And if you go to college next year I'd only see you in the holidays anyway.'

All that was true, but surely he didn't imagine that made it all right. She punished him by saying she had to go home early to do extra homework, since he was so keen she should go to college, and she wouldn't have time to see him on Sunday. She thought he sounded almost like someone of her own age when he talked about the restaurant, and it made her angry.

'He always wanted his own place,' Mum said when she mentioned it. 'When we got married, that was what we were going to do.'

'Why didn't you?'

'It cost too much. And I thought – oh, it sounds silly now, but I thought working together would be a mistake.'

Abigail wondered why she didn't say it was simply more fun to work in publishing, to start as a secretary and become a press officer. It was liberated; it was glamorous. It fitted in with all Mum's ideas about women being entitled to exciting jobs. Abigail agreed with her. But how had Dad felt about it? By the time he got home from the restaurant at night, Mum was asleep, and by the time he woke up in the morning, she had gone to work. It had only left Sundays for them to be together, and after they had read the papers and argued about who was going to cook, there was hardly time to do anything except watch television. Cooking seemed such a silly thing to argue about, but they always did. Either Dad complained that the last thing he wanted to do on his day off was cook, and Mum replied that she'd done it for six days already and why should she keep a dog and bark herself; or Dad went out of his way to stop Mum cooking by finding fault with what she cooked and saying he might as well do it, at least he'd get it right. Sometimes Abigail cooked, just to shut them up, but it didn't seem to make the atmosphere any better, so more often she went out.

'They're probably arguing about something else,' said her friend Lorna, who listened to lots of phone-in problems on the radio and considered herself quite an expert. 'I expect it's sex or money. It usually is. Do they shout a lot?'

'They used to,' Abigail said. 'But they stopped. They haven't had a proper row for ages.' At first she had been relieved: it had been awful to lie in bed and listen to their raised voices. But now that Lorna made her think about it, the silence she had welcomed as peaceful did in fact have an ominous aspect. She didn't count the Sunday arguments as rows: they were only bickering.

The night before he left, he took her out to dinner as if she were grown up, but she couldn't eat much because her throat was so tight with trying not to cry. He kept saying they'd soon be together again and she mustn't feel he was deserting her because he loved her more than anything in the world.

Not more than anyone, though, she wanted to say. Not more than Julie, or you wouldn't be going away with her. But she couldn't say it. She couldn't hurt him the way he'd hurt her, and besides, she didn't want him to agree with her.

'It wasn't something I did, was it?' she said instead.

She'd been longing to ask that because the idea hung about in her mind, although Lorna said it was childish, the sort of thing kids got in their heads. It was always coming up on her phone-in programmes and Abigail was too old to think like that, she said. People got divorced all the time and it was sex and money and boredom, nothing to do with their children. Abigail wished she thought Lorna was right.

'No,' he said, 'no, you mustn't think that. Promise me you won't, not ever.' And she saw tears come into his eyes. She was horribly embarrassed but relieved as well, as if he was crying for her and she could believe him now. He gave her a big, tight, almost suffocating bear-hug (the sort she had liked as a child, squealing with fright) when he took her home, and she couldn't cry at all. She kept thinking of Mum inside the house with the radio turned up loud, and Julie back at the flat waiting for him to come home and help her with the packing. Perhaps he would say, 'God, that was awful,' and she would put her arms round him and say, 'I know, darling, I know, but it's over now, don't think about it.'

They couldn't say goodbye. When she disentangled herself from the hug, she ran up the path to the door as fast as she could and let herself in without looking back. Mum called out, 'Abby?' and she called back, 'Mm,' which was all she could manage without breaking down. Mum's voice sounded strange too and she didn't say any more, but let Abigail run upstairs to her room without asking if she wanted a hot drink or anything, the way she usually did.

Abigail thought she would lie awake for hours but she didn't. Exhausted by the evening, she fell asleep almost at once, only to wake early, at peace for a moment, before she remembered that there was something bad to remember. It was a sensation she had previously only associated with exams.

She lay in bed, staring at the clock and picturing Dad at the airport, with Julie a self-satisfied blur beside him. She

imagined them so hard that they became like people in a
film. She concentrated on wishing Julie dead and when
that didn't work, when the Julie-figure simply wouldn't
collapse, no matter how much she willed it, she pictured
instead Dad changing his mind, and that seemed to work
better. She could see him shaking his head and saying, 'It's
no good, I can't do it, I just can't leave them.' Then he was
running away from the departure lounge, leaving Julie
alone. She didn't follow, in Abigail's film; she just looked
sad and resigned, admitting defeat. In her heart she knew it
served her right.

Dad sprinted through the airline terminal, not bothering
to ask about getting his luggage back. All he wanted was
to get to a phone. Abigail lay very still, almost holding her
breath, waiting for the phone to ring. The silence went on
and on.

Presently Mum came in with a cup of tea, not something
she usually did, and sat on the edge of Abigail's bed, as if
Abigail were ill. Together they watched the clock racing on
to departure time.

'I thought I'd make pancakes for breakfast,' said Mum,
who usually didn't have time to make anything. 'Would
you like that?'

Abigail felt empty rather than hungry but she couldn't
let Mum down. They both had to get through the next
hour somehow.

'Thanks,' she said. 'That'd be great.'

As the weeks passed, it was odd getting used to Dad not
being there, getting used to being just the two of them,
although he had never been there very much really, which
ought to have made it easier. She didn't notice so much on
Sundays because *she* usually went out and in any case it
was a relief not to have him and Mum going on about who
cooked lunch. But weekdays were awful, the time between
four thirty when Abigail got back from school and six
thirty when Mum came in from work. That had always
been their special time, before Dad left for the restaurant,

when they could watch silly programmes on television and talk about the day, cuddling up together on the sofa. The house became unbearably empty then.

Abigail took to hanging about after school with Lorna, mooching around the shops. They couldn't go to Lorna's house because her Mum would find them something useful to do. She didn't believe in idle hands. Wandering around Woolworths with Lorna, Abigail was shocked to find herself suddenly longing to steal something, for the first time in her life. A lipstick or some nail varnish. She was puzzled as well as shocked because she didn't wear lipstick, she didn't like the feel of it on her mouth, and she couldn't wear nail varnish because she still bit her nails. In fact she only wore eye make-up, but it was not eye make-up she wanted to steal. She didn't tell Lorna in case she produced some theory about it from one of her phone-in programmes.

Mum said they had to tell Mr Williams the headmaster that Dad had gone away. Abigail argued, but Mum said he had to know. She wouldn't say why. In case I do something weird, Abigail thought resentfully, like stealing from Woolworths. So he can Make Allowances. Perhaps Mum was right, but she hated it all the same. It seemed to make everything more final. There were lots of people at her school whose parents had split up, but she had never imagined herself as one of them, had even enjoyed feeling comfortably superior. Now she had suddenly joined their ranks and she felt unclean and embarrassed, as if she had been found with nits in her hair.

Mum had promised her no one else would know but overnight the whole school seemed to find out. At least, that's how it felt. Lorna swore she hadn't said a word and Abigail couldn't very well ask Mr Williams, but someone must have talked because people started coming up to her to sympathise or make jokes. Michael was one of them. 'Sorry about your Dad, Abs,' he said. 'Maybe your Mum can get it together with my Dad and then we'll be brother and sister.' He winked at her, and she wasn't sure if he was trying to be nice or nasty. She had gone out with him for a while after his mother ran off with the man next door, leaving Michael and his father alone, and she had liked the kissing and cuddling and the sense of importance that came from going out with someone other people fancied, someone who looked like Sting. But Michael had wanted her to go to bed with him when his father was out at work and she was frightened. She knew she wasn't in love with him and she wanted the first time to be with someone special; she also wanted to look forward to going to college, not worry about getting pregnant.

'You're old-fashioned,' Michael had teased her, and she lost her temper.

'I think it's old-fashioned to do something just because everyone else is doing it,' she said. She wasn't sure she meant it but it sounded good. 'I think you should make up your own mind, and anyway, if you really liked me, you wouldn't mind waiting.'

But he hadn't waited, he had shrugged his shoulders and gone off, saying he'd phone her, and now he was going out with Tracey, who was on the Pill.

She'd been meaning to ask Dad about it, whether she'd done the right thing and whether boys always behaved like that. It was easier to talk to Dad than Mum, and in any case he ought to know more about how boys thought. But she'd put it off, waiting for the right moment, and now it was too late. She almost wished she had got pregnant, or fallen off Michael's motorbike, so Dad would have been really worried about her. He might even have come rushing back.

When she didn't answer his letters, he started ringing up. She had not expected that: it was as if she imagined the island as a place too primitive to have telephones. Or perhaps it was that once he got on the plane she pictured him in limbo, falling into a dark hole somewhere, like the Bermuda Triangle, dropping off the edge of the world. Or even, more simply, that he and Mum had argued so much over the phone bill in London that she never dreamed he could ring up from the Caribbean. But of course Julie wouldn't nag, would she? Phone bills would mean nothing to Julie. She would be smiling all the time and encouraging him in whatever he wanted to do.

Abigail knew who it was on the phone before Mum said anything, just from the look on her face. A look of hope, turning swiftly into disappointment and resignation. Her face crumpled up, making her look at once like a child and an old woman, the way people always said babies looked like Winston Churchill. Abigail was scared: if Dad still had the power to do that to Mum's face, what might he do to Abigail? She backed away from the phone as Mum said, 'Yes, she's here' and held it out to her. She shook her head.

'Come on,' Mum said, 'he wants to talk to you. Don't be silly.'

Abigail put her hands behind her back. The temptation was so strong, the longing to speak to him, to hear his voice saying he missed her, maybe even saying he was coming home, he'd made a mistake. She couldn't do it. She was terrified of breaking down and making a fool of herself. And she didn't want to hear how happy he was on his beautiful island with Julie. She wanted to punish him for going away and leaving her. She wanted to make him as miserable as he'd made her.

'I'm sorry, David,' Mum said into the phone, and to Abigail's surprise she really did sound sorry. 'She won't. It's no good.' There was a pause. 'Yes, I'll tell her.' She hung up and turned to Abigail. 'He sends his love,' she said. 'And he misses you. Why wouldn't you speak to him? You're hurting yourself as much as him, you know.'

Abigail was shaking. She could see Mum moving towards her to give her a hug and she wanted the hug desperately but she also didn't want it. It would only make both of them cry.

She turned and ran out of the room, but she noticed as

she ran that she felt something else besides shaken and tearful, a new sensation. She felt powerful.

After that she made a plan. She decided never to answer the phone in case it was Dad. Refusing to speak when Mum took the call was one thing; hanging up on him would be quite another. She didn't think she could manage that. So she arranged with Lorna to ring once and hang up, then ring back, so she'd know who it was. Lorna was the only person who rang her often. She felt safe then; she thought the system was foolproof.

The call when it came caught her off-guard. She was home early from school, not roaming round Woolworths trying not to steal, because Lorna had gone to the dentist. Abigail rang her at five to see how she was. Lorna always made a big fuss at the dentist and she liked Abigail to take her suffering seriously.

'He's a butcher,' said Lorna, sounding as if she still had a mouthful of wadding. 'Let me ring you back. I want to make a cup of tea and take some aspirin first.'

Abigail hung up, amused. She didn't really believe Lorna was in agony. When the phone went, five minutes later, she was so relaxed, so sure it was Lorna, that she picked it up at once without waiting for the signal.

'Abby?'

She froze. He sounded so close he could have been phoning from the restaurant.

'Abby, I know it's you, don't hang up, please.'

She couldn't. She wasn't even tempted. She hung on to the phone as if it might escape, and shut her eyes, imagining Dad with his arms round her. He had the sort of caressing voice that always made you feel he was hugging you. It was something to do with being Welsh.

'Did you get the ticket?'

'Yes.'

'Are you coming?'

'I don't know.' And the next moment: 'Yes, of course I am.'

She heard him give a great sigh as if until that moment he had been holding his breath.

'When?'

'I don't know. As soon as I can.' She felt as if her brain had a life of its own, not safely confined in her head but darting about all over the place, out of control. 'But I can't leave Mum for Christmas.'

'Yes, you can, she won't mind.'

'No, I can't.' But already she was beginning to feel she could.

'No, of course you can't,' he said then, sounding resigned, as if she were another adult making adult decisions.

'How about the twenty-seventh?' she said. It began to be real, once she named a date. 'If I can get a flight.' How she regretted all the time she had wasted. What if they were all booked up?

'Fine. Terrific,' he said. 'Whatever you say.'

An idea came to her then, hearing those words. 'The only thing is,' she said, 'can it be just us? I don't want to meet her, I can't. And it's not fair on Mum.'

There was an agonising pause. 'Well,' he said, 'that's a bit difficult, it's such a small place and we're both working here . . .'

'Please,' she said.

'All right, caryad. I'll do my best.'

Triumph surged through her. She felt as if she had rubbed Julie's unknown face in the dust, trodden on her, banished her. They talked for some time after that about how much they missed each other and when she hung up she felt warm and comforted. Mum knew as soon as she came in.

'You've spoken to him,' she said. 'I'm glad.'

'I said I'd go out there after Christmas,' Abigail said. 'Is that all right? You don't mind, do you?'

'Of course I don't mind,' Mum said, smiling. 'But I think you should go sooner. It's crazy to go all that way for ten days. Go as soon as term ends and you can have three weeks out there.'

'But what about Christmas?' Abigail said.

'To tell you the truth,' Mum said, not looking at her, 'I've always wanted to spend Christmas in an hotel. To be waited on, and not have to cook. To meet new people. To catch up on sleep. This could be my big chance. Go on, you book your flight. Get the first one you can.'

After that it all became real very soon. She felt like *Alice Through the Looking Glass*: everything went into reverse. From refusing to go, from being static and miserable, she was flung into a world of action and excitement, racing about trying to sort out her ticket and buy clothes, arousing envy among her friends. At first there were no seats to be had, but before she had time to slump into gloom and despair, the travel agent came up with a cancellation. Someone had gone down with appendicitis.

'I can come on the nineteenth,' she said, shaking with joy, when Dad rang again. 'Someone got sick.'

'Hurrah,' Dad said, and they both laughed.

'Aren't we callous?' she said, feeling guilty but elated.

'Who cares?' said Dad, sounding suddenly very young.

Mum bought her a new bikini and a sundress, and she got herself some sandals. Lorna gave her a pair of sunglasses, very smart, that got darker or lighter according to the weather. She was touched because Lorna was generally both poor and mean, and the sunglasses must have been expensive. She let news of her trip leak round the school and soon she was floating on a warm tide of envy.

'Huh,' said Michael, 'it's all right for some.'

Abigail smiled. You should have stuck with me, she thought. I shall come back brown and beautiful, and you'll be sorry. Tracey had sandy hair and freckles.

She was so excited it was like being drunk, which she had been only once in her life, but nicer because there was no hangover to follow. Everything had to be done in a hurry because she had left it so late to decide. At the airport she felt a great wave of pity for Mum, who looked suddenly small and alone, still insisting that she was really looking forward to spending Christmas in an hotel.

'You could go to Aunt Isabel,' Abigail said, worried about her.

'I know. But this is what I want. I'll be fine. You have a good time, that's all. Really enjoy yourself. Don't punish him any more. Talk to him. Relax.'

Abigail nodded. They hugged, both smiling and tearful. She wanted to say she would bring him back with her, that she was going on a rescue mission, but she was afraid to raise Mum's hopes, in case it could not be done.

'Give him my love,' Mum said, as she turned to go.

The fantasy persisted on the long flight, haunting her through the noisy film and recurring meal and drinks, piercing through the music on her head set. She got tired and she dozed but wasn't sure if she was ever completely asleep, if the image of Dad saying yes, he wanted to come home, was her imagination or a dream. The only reality she was sure of was that he would be there at the airport to meet her, bronzed and smiling and alone; he would put his arms round her and she would hug him and that would make it all right. They would have time to talk about everything.

But when she landed she couldn't see him anywhere. The crowd thinned out, the pale tourists and the black residents, and still he wasn't there. How could he be late? How could he spoil it all?

A girl came up to her, smaller than herself, a sun-tanned girl with dark hair, wearing jeans and a T-shirt and no make-up. She smiled but she looked sad.

'Hullo,' she said gently. 'You must be Abigail. I'm Julie.'


The empty beaches below them were glaringly white in the sun, and the sea water was the colour of peacock feathers, a blue-green so dazzling that it hurt Abigail's eyes and she had to put on the new glasses, Lorna's extravagant present. It was a good excuse, but she needed them anyway, to shield her from Julie. She didn't think she was going to cry because she was still too stunned to believe what Julie had said. Luckily they did not have to talk any more now: the growling of the tiny aircraft, like an airborne terrier, made speech impossible. It was taking them from the big island to the small one, where in a sense she still believed Dad would be waiting with his arms outstretched.

Faced with Julie, and groggy from the seven-hour flight and all the anticipation, she had at first been furious and uncomprehending. How *could* he send Julie to meet her? He had promised. It wasn't like Dad to break a promise.

'I know,' Julie had said, as if hearing the thought, or perhaps Abigail's face had said it all. 'I'm sorry it's me. I know he said we wouldn't have to meet, only – there's been an accident.' Then Julie's own face crumpled up, reminding Abigail oddly of Mum, although they weren't alike. It was the same look, of someone whose world had just ended, of someone with nowhere to go to be safe. Abigail stared at her, silent. She knew the word accident meant something worse, something more final, although she couldn't believe it.

'We were diving off the boat,' Julie said, 'and he didn't come up and then, when he did, he . . . wasn't all right.' She started to shake; she clasped her hands together and looked at the floor. All around them people moved about the small airport: there were unfamiliar smells of heat and dust, fruit and flowers. Abigail felt very strange, as if she might wake up at any minute.

'They think it was a heart attack,' Julie said. 'We did everything we could. We did the kiss of life and everything. But they think he had a heart attack under water.'

Never to see Dad again. Not to be hugged, not to be told it was all right, he was coming home. It was too much to

bear. She sat on a bench, speechless. It couldn't be true.
Julie must be telling her lies. It was a spiteful trick, just to
upset her, because Julie was jealous at being left out.

'I'm so sorry,' Julie said. 'I couldn't ring you, you'd
already left. And I didn't dare ring your mother. I didn't
know what to do. You were on the plane when it
happened. There was nothing I *could* do.'

Abigail kept shaking her head, to brush Julie's words
away, as if they were bees trying to settle on her.

'I didn't know how to tell you,' Julie said. 'I had to come
and meet you and I didn't know what to say. I still don't.'
She looked at Abigail pleadingly; she seemed almost to
expect sympathy.

'It's all your fault,' Abigail heard herself say. She hadn't
known the words were in her mouth, waiting to leap out. 'I
hate you, I hate you, you made it happen.'

'I know,' Julie said in a desolate tone. 'That's how I feel
too. It's all my fault.'

After that there was nothing to say. They sat on the
bench side by side and the silence spread out.

'He wouldn't have been here but for me,' Julie said.
'That's what you mean, isn't it?'

Abigail didn't answer.

'But don't you see?' Julie went on angrily. 'I've lost him
too. I loved him as much as you did. It's the same for both
of us.' She started to cry.

It occurred to Abigail that Julie wasn't grown up at all,
that she was like Lorna with her phone-in programmes,
someone who enjoyed listening to real life but never
expected to have to take part in it. She was suddenly
furious with her father for lumbering her with someone of
her own age who was going to be no help to her. If you had
to do this, she thought, enraged, you should have left me
with Mum, who could help me bear it. But Julie was
twenty-six. She was supposed to be grown up. She had
stolen Dad and let him have an accident, but she was
behaving like Lorna with toothache. Abigail felt confused.

She was so angry with Julie that she wanted to kill her and at the same time she felt Dad might arrive at any moment and make it all right. Julie's tears seemed theatrical: they embarrassed her. Dad couldn't really have had an accident, not now, not when she'd finally come to see him and bring him home. She couldn't be never going to see him again; that simply wasn't possible.

'I don't know what you want to do now you're here,' Julie said, blowing her nose. 'Do you want to ring your mother? Or go straight home? Or come to the island? I don't know what to say for the best. You must be so tired and it's such a shock – I just don't know.' She put her head in her hands and left the decision to Abigail.

So now they were in the little plane whirring and buzzing above the blue-green water, sitting side by side and not speaking. When they landed, they drove in Julie's ancient car along a dirt track across the island. Somewhere Dad waited, Abigail felt, to tell her this was all a bad joke, a mistake, a false alarm. The car shuddered over pot-holes in the road and Julie's hands shook on the wheel. Abigail thought she could drive better than that and she hadn't even taken her test yet.

Crossing the island, they lost sight of the sea; there was only the lush vegetation that Julie said was a banana plantation, as if it mattered, and the dazzling flowers. The sun hammered on the roof of the car, and Abigail's head throbbed with exhaustion and grief. Then they rounded a bend and (it seemed very sudden after the long journey) they had arrived at their destination. A beach of soft white sand littered with pink shells. Half a dozen thatched cabins a few yards from the water, and everywhere an abundance of red and purple flowers like the ones Dad had told her about, exploding like fireworks. Out at sea, several boats drifted at anchor and on the beach half a dozen couples lay browning in the sun. Abigail wondered if they knew yet that there was no one to cook their dinner. She felt suddenly hysterical and yet she still half expected to see

Dad come running to meet her. If she started to laugh, would Julie think she was heartless and peculiar? But why did she even care what Julie thought?

Julie's friends emerged from a large white building behind the huts on the beach. The man had grey hair and a beard and was wearing frayed denim shorts, like somebody trying to look young; the woman had bleached frizzy hair and wore a kaftan. They both looked sympathetic but distracted, as if they had got more than they bargained for when they asked Dad and Julie to join them. They looked heavy with responsibility, and glanced anxiously from Julie to Abigail and back again. Wondering how we're getting on, Abigail thought bitterly. Whether I'm going to be a nuisance. Whether I've taken it well. She felt it was rather like Mr Williams the headmaster being asked to keep an eye on her.

'Cathy and Morris,' said Julie. She sounded exhausted. 'And this is Abigail.'

'Oh, my dear,' Cathy said, advancing. 'I'm so sorry.'

Abigail stepped back, afraid Cathy might be going to touch her. After a moment Cathy held out her hand and Morris did the same, so Abigail shook hands with both of them. So long as they don't put their arms round me, she thought. So long as nobody does that, I might just be all right. I might just be able to get through this on my own.

'It's terrible, terrible,' Morris said, getting her luggage out of Julie's car. She had the impression that they were both extremely embarrassed and didn't know what to say to her.

'But don't you look alike,' said Cathy in a sudden surprised voice. 'You could be sisters.'

'Please, Cathy, don't.' Julie sounded quite sharp. 'That's the last thing she wants to hear.'

They offered her food and drink but she had consumed so many different things on the plane, although it already seemed a lifetime ago, that all she could manage was some fruit juice. Morris carried her luggage to one of the huts on the beach and left her alone with Julie. Inside it was surprisingly cool, with a fan over the bed; there was a bathroom, and she even had a fridge of her own. But there was fine mesh on all the windows, which made her feel like the Sunday joint in her grandmother's larder on long-ago trips to Wales when she was a tiny child.

She was suddenly very tired, tired to the bone, the sort of tiredness she felt she might die of, and perhaps that would be the best thing.

'Shall I leave you alone now?' Julie asked.

Abigail nodded. She lay on the bed for a bit but she couldn't sleep so she unpacked her things instead. She kept thinking what a paradise the place would have been with Dad: the sea right outside her door and the thick white sand, the pink shells and the palm trees, the flowers and the little boats. It was easy to see why someone would run away to such a place.

She sat and watched the sun setting over the sea, turning the sky all shades of pink and orange, purple and red, until it finally disappeared so abruptly that she almost expected to hear a plop. Then the tropic night came down with darkness as sudden as a drawn blind, heavy with stars.

She hurt all over, like the time she had had flu. Mum had given her pills and drinks, let her sleep, changed the sheets, tempted her appetite with ice cream. But she had felt sore everywhere. She had been hot or cold but never just right, whatever Mum did, whether she brought a cold flannel or a hot-water bottle. She had dreamed strange dreams and wanted Dad to be there. When she woke, he was bending over the bed.

'How's my lovely, then?' he said, and suddenly she felt better, her fever gone, her skin no longer aching. Dad was magic. Mum had done all the work but Dad was magic.

Not any more though.

She slept at last beneath the whirling fan and dreamed of Dad coming out of the sea, holding out his arms. She woke screaming, soaked in sweat, and Julie came running in.

'It's all right, it's all right,' she kept saying, and tried to hug Abigail.

'No, it isn't,' said Abigail, and lashed out at Julie, catching her quite a heavy blow on the arm. 'It'll never be all right again.'

Julie subsided on to the bed. 'No,' she agreed, sounding unperturbed by the blow, even calm and fatalistic. 'That's true.'

Abigail sobbed and punched the pillows. 'I had a nightmare,' she said. 'He was coming out of the sea.'

'It's not going to happen,' said Julie. 'I only wish it could.'

'Go away,' said Abigail. 'Just go away and leave me alone.'

'I'm only in the next hut,' said Julie, going. 'Call if you need me. I don't sleep much.'

After she had gone, Abigail wished she hadn't sent her away. The night outside seemed very black and the sea didn't sound as friendly as it had before. Her throat was dry and her eyes felt gritty, so she got up and bathed them and had a drink of water from the fridge. There was a bowl of fruit on the table and she felt suddenly hungry, so she ate a banana and a mango. They tasted different from the ones she had had in England: richer, more creamy, spiced with sunshine. Odd disconnected thoughts came into her mind: fruit laid out in the greengrocer's at home; Dad teaching her to swim when they went on holiday to Wales, and telling her never to be afraid of the sea but always to treat it with respect.

Then she noticed the spider. It was big by English standards, hugely black against the white wall over her head. She watched it with horrified fascination as it crawled for a bit, then scuttled suddenly, then settled down and spread out as if it had all the time in the world. She got as far away from it as she could and waited till her heart had stopped thumping, while she considered what to do. At home Dad had always removed them for her in a bunch of tissues while Mum told her not to be so silly. She knew they were harmless and possibly more frightened of her, but what use was that knowledge when she was terrified? She couldn't sleep in the room with it; she daren't put out the light. She would have to sit all night and stare at it, when it was the last thing she wanted to see. But if she took her eyes off it for a moment and it moved, she would never be sure where it had gone.

Suddenly she was very tired as well as trapped. Only in the next hut, Julie had said. Call if you need me. So how had Dad intended to keep them apart, so they never met?

It was awful to need Julie, but there was no one else. And if she waited too long, the creature might get between her and the door so she couldn't get out. Already it was moving lazily in that direction. Making up her mind in a hurry, before she had time to hesitate, she ran to the door and flung it open, her feet plunging into the surprisingly cold soft sand. 'Julie,' she called. 'Julie.' She was ashamed of herself but she yelled quite loud.

Julie came out of her hut at once. It was almost as if she had been expecting the call. 'What is it?' she said. 'Are you all right?'

They stood on the beach looking at each other. Still Abigail half expected Dad to come out of the sea or the hut and join them. 'There's a spider in my room,' she said. She felt brave just using the word: at home she would have called it a creepy, which seemed to make it less menacing, but Julie wasn't to know that, unless of course Dad had told her.

'I'm sorry,' said Julie, as if it were her fault. 'They don't often come in, so near the sea. Shall I get rid of it for you?'

They went back to the hut together and several moths followed them in, but Abigail didn't mind that. 'It's over there,' she said.

'Oh yes, I see,' said Julie, unperturbed. She scooped it up gently in her hand and tossed it out of the doorway, closing the door after it like a weary hostess. 'I used to hate them too but I've got used to them now.'

'I know it's silly,' Abigail said, grateful and resentful. She couldn't get the words 'thank you' to come out of her mouth.

'It's not silly at all,' said Julie. 'It's just one of those things. I'm still frightened of worms but at least they don't turn up in your bedroom.'

Abigail found herself looking at Julie for the first time. She hadn't really seen her before; she had been too busy hating her. She saw a face that was calm and friendly, tired and sad. She didn't look at all like the film-star waitress, tarty and cross-eyed. In fact she looked rather like some of the younger teachers at school, like someone Abigail might have trusted, if she hadn't taken Dad away and killed him.

'I can't believe it either,' Julie said. 'I can't believe I'll never see him again. I know you hate me and I don't blame you, but you must believe I loved him. And you had him for seventeen years. I only had him for a year.'

'What about my mother?' Abigail said. She felt it was somehow unfair, invoking Mum when it should be just between the two of them, but she wanted to hit back with everything she had.

'I'm sorry about her, of course. But he told me it was over. They were really separate, even though they still lived in the same house.'

'And you believed him?' Abigail was shocked. Was Julie lying to her, or had Dad been lying to Julie? How could Mum and Dad have been separate? They never used the spare room, even when they had a row. And why had Mum cried so much when he went away?

'Why shouldn't I?' Julie said. 'He wouldn't lie to me.' She swayed slightly on her feet. 'D'you mind if I sit down?' she asked almost humbly. 'Only I feel a bit faint. You see, I'm going to have a baby.'

In the late morning Abigail sat on the verandah savouring

the unfamiliar taste of paw-paw for breakfast and wondering how she could even eat when Dad was dead. Julie had talked far into the night about the baby and how thrilled Dad had been about it and how she had only ever wanted a husband and a family, not a career. Eventually they had both fallen asleep, Abigail in the bed and Julie across the end of it, like a guard dog, Abigail thought when she woke in what was left of the night and saw her there. In the morning Julie was gone.

Now she came across the sand barefooted with a letter in her hand. 'Look what I've found,' she said, pleased like a child. 'I was looking at his things to cheer myself up and I found this. It's for you. I haven't read it.'

Abigail took it from her. She felt very strange, almost numb. A letter from Dad. Now. When he wasn't there any more. When she couldn't answer him. Julie went away. Tiny green lizards flickered up and down the wall. Abigail began to read.

Darling Abby,
    If you won't answer my letters and you won't speak to me on the phone, what can I do to reach you? Are you even *reading* my letters?
    You're my only hope. How can I approach your mother direct after all I've done to her? But *you* must know how she feels. D'you think there's any chance, any remote hope she might even consider letting me come home?

The familiar handwriting was a shock, almost a bigger shock than the words. It made Dad seem alive.

    I'm not going to pretend I don't love Julie any more because I do, but I've never stopped loving your mother. It's quite possible, indeed fatally easy in my case, to love two people at once, only in different ways, as you'll probably find out when you get older. I don't expect you to believe me now and I don't suppose your mother will believe me either, as I've hurt her so much. But she hurt me too when she made me feel her job was more important than our marriage, when she was too tired to make love, when she didn't care that the hours we both worked meant we hardly spent any time together.

There were sailboats and windsurfers out at sea, and beyond them a big boat from which people dived. Abigail wondered if that was the boat that Dad had been on when it happened.

I probably shouldn't be writing to you like this but who else can I turn to? You're in the middle of this mess and you do love us both – at least I hope you do.

The thing is, Julie is pregnant. We didn't plan it but she's so thrilled I had to pretend I'm thrilled too. In a sense I am – new life can't fail to be exciting and it's always a compliment when a woman wants to have your child – but in my heart I feel terror. Suddenly it's not a love affair any more. I had such a precious fantasy of Julie and me running away to the sunshine with no responsibilities, just each other and the restaurant, and now it all begins again, trying to be a husband and father.

This must sound terrible but I'm trying to be as honest as I can. If I have to be married, I only want to be married to your mother, and if I have to be a parent, I only want to be a parent to you.

The thought of Julie's child reminds me of your childhood. I can't do better for another child – I only want to make up to you for all the times I let you down. It's asking too much to make me live through all that again with another child instead of you.

I must be such a disappointment to you as a father and I don't know how to explain. There aren't any excuses but sometimes middle-aged people go a little crazy and want to be young again and they find someone they think can make that miracle happen for them. It can't be done of course but by the time they find that out they've caused a lot of pain and perhaps it's too late to repair the damage.

I don't know what I'm saying really – I can't leave Julie if she's pregnant and yet I'd rather stay with her if she wasn't.

I'm not making sense. You must be thinking very badly of me by now if you're reading this at all. I suppose what I really mean is, I want the best of both worlds, to be back with you and your mother, but still to see Julie at the restaurant. I'm terrified at how fast my life has changed and I don't know how to cope with it. I just go from one unbearable situation to another.

The letter ended there. He must have stopped writing it when he knew she was going to visit him. She sat for a while just holding the pages. When she had stopped crying she read it again, but it still made no sense to her. She felt frightened, that adults didn't know what they were doing any more than teenagers did, so there was no hope for her; she was only going to grow up into a greater muddle, like Dad.

One thing was clear, though. He didn't want Julie to be pregnant. She had only to show Julie the letter and all her happy memories would be ruined. She'd see what Dad was really like, how he wanted Mum back, and maybe Julie as well, but not her baby.

It would be so easy. She had it in her hands, the power to hurt Julie, to punish her for all the trouble she had caused. She could just say, 'Read this,' and Julie would be destroyed. The letter had been lying in Dad's room like a landmine and she had only to set it off with a touch.

Eventually Julie came back. Her face looked soft and hopeful; she said gently, 'Was it a nice letter? Did it help?'

Abigail hesitated. She could see plainly in Julie's face how much she had loved Dad. The letter burned in her hand.

'Yes,' she said. 'It's a lovely letter. Thank you.'

Julie smiled. 'I'm so glad,' she said. 'D'you want to ring your mother now?'

Abigail shook her head. 'Not yet,' she said.

'I'm going out in the motor boat,' Julie said. 'Come with me. You can't just sit here. He'd have wanted you to do something.'

They took the boat to another beach. Their feet made fresh marks in the white sand where no one had been before them. There were huge greyish lizards among the trees; they looked very old. Julie said they were iguanas. They seemed friendly but shy. The water was very clear and Abigail wanted to swim.

'You don't think I'm heartless, do you, coming here?' Julie asked. 'Only we used to come here a lot. I'm sure he'd want me to bring you here.'

'No, I don't think you're heartless at all,' Abigail said. 'I'd like to swim.'

They swam side by side, a little way apart, and she felt her tears flowing easily into the salt water, as if they belonged. The sea was warm and clear and buoyant.

'There's a coral reef out there,' Julie called to her. 'You can see all kinds of fish. Amazing colours.'

Back on the beach they lay on their towels in the sun.

'What happens next?' she asked Julie, when she felt brave enough.

'I'm not sure. They may want to have an inquest before the funeral.'

'Will I . . . I mean should I see . . .?' But she couldn't say the words.

'You can,' Julie said. 'But I shouldn't if I were you. Remember him the way he was.'

When they got back to the hotel Abigail rang her mother. She held the letter because it seemed to give her courage. She told Mum what had happened, but they had a bad line and she had to say it twice, which was painful but in an odd way calming.

'Oh no,' Mum said. 'Oh no.' And there was a long silence.

'He was writing a letter,' Abigail said. 'You can read it when I get back. It's addressed to me but it's meant for you really.' She felt herself starting to cry again but they were healing tears this time. 'It'll make you feel lots better.'

There was more silence from Mum, then she said in a

sort of blurred voice, 'Should I come out for the funeral?'

'I don't think so,' Abigail said. 'You'd only get tired and upset and spend a lot of money. And what would be the point?'

Mum sighed, sounding relieved, as if she were the child and Abigail the adult, telling her what to do.

'I thought about coming home early,' Abigail said, 'but I think I'll stay on. I might as well just be here for a bit, the way we planned it. I feel closer.'

'Yes, of course,' Mum said. 'You must do whatever you think best.'

Abigail didn't mention the baby. Time enough for that when she got home. She needed to be in the room with her for that: Mum might need a hug. Meanwhile she would sit in the sun with Julie and talk about Dad the way they both remembered him, and get brown the way he had promised her she would. She could do that for him at least. She would collect shells and walk through the icing-sugar sand and photograph the iguanas with their ancient faces and stare at the coloured fish and the coral reef through Julie's snorkeling mask. She felt oddly at peace. Nothing worse could happen to her now. And there would be the child. In a way Dad was still there: he would go on in her, and in her brother or sister, whichever it turned out to be. Julie had destroyed something but she was creating something too.

Abigail sat in the sun and looked at her nails. She had forgotten to bite them for two whole days and they were beginning to grow.

'I shall stop biting my nails,' she decided. 'I'm really too old to do that any more.'

# Jessica in Love

The first time Jessica came to London she fell in love: it was the blind instantaneous passion you were supposed, in popular folklore, to feel for a man, although she had fallen in love with Colin very slowly. It was everything that pop songs promised: some enchanted evening, and strangers in the night and fly me to the moon. She felt frightened and elated, yet at the same time entirely comfortable because of the intense familiarity of this town where she had never been before. This was her place: she recognised it. In fact she wanted to hug the whole city, to fling her arms round it and embrace it like a person. It gave her a strange mixture of security and excitement. Anything was possible here.

'You haven't been here ten minutes and already you're being unfaithful to me,' Colin teased her when she tried to explain. 'But it's all right. I forgive you. I'd rather have London as a rival than another bloke.'

Lying on her narrow college bed after making love, they would listen to the city breathing and purring outside the window ('You can even make traffic sound romantic,' Colin said) then get up and dress and wander through leafy Hampstead, up and down hilly streets, their arms round each other, to catch a Japanese or Swedish film at the Everyman. The dusk turned London gently purple, but when they came out in search of a pizza, it was evening with that curious rusty light, the amber glow of the dark city's lamps suggesting it was distantly on fire. Rationally she was aware of the noise and the dirt all around her, but

emotionally it seemed remote, dwarfed by the magic, like
tiny endearing faults in a lover. Sometimes they would go
on to listen to jazz on the South Bank and she would stand
entranced, hugging Colin, her back to the Festival Hall,
her face to the river, dazzled by the lights on the water,
weaving a fantasy in which they both became so rich they
could have a permanent suite at the Savoy. Then they
would walk slowly across Hungerford Bridge towards
Embankment tube station, pausing to pick out landmarks,
and Jessica would feel the city belonged to her.

Leaving Euston for a visit to her parents, she always felt
homesick before the train left the station, wrenched away
from her city, and apprehensive, as if something terrible
might happen to it in her absence. If she was travelling
with Colin she would try to distract herself by studying his
face. His hair was so thick and heavy that it always
flopped forward, making him look untidy, and his
eyelashes came down straight like a cow's, veiling his eyes.
It was odd that she found this so attractive in him, whereas
cows didn't move her at all. His nose was broad and
squashed, tending to spread across his face, and his mouth
turned slightly up a the corners, making him look good-
tempered even when he was angry. Jessica herself was dark
and dramatic, like a gypsy, with glossy hair and sallow
skin. People who didn't know them often took them for
brother and sister, which amused her.

Feeling her scrutiny, he looked up and smiled at her. The
smile warmed her, as if she had held out her hands to a
fire. 'It's all right,' he said, knowing she'd been thinking
about London. 'It'll still be there when we get back.'

Her parents always made a fuss of her when she arrived
and pressed her to eat more than she wanted. She told
herself it was their way of expressing love. 'You're just
skin and bone,' her mother said. 'You need feeding up.'
But by Saturday afternoon the visit was wearing itself out
and the talk shifted to her sister Jennifer and her husband
and baby, who would all presently arrive for tea. Jessica

felt that praise of Jennifer implied criticism of herself, that there was not enough love and approval in the family to spread over both of them. Yet she loved Jennifer and was fiercely protective of her if anyone outside the family attempted to criticise her. It was confusing to feel jealous of someone she loved. The baby confused her, too, sometimes making her long to be pregnant and sometimes making her long to run away. 'I'm glad I don't have to read all those books,' said Jennifer, eyeing the pile Jessica had brought with her as a defence.

If her parents stayed in on Saturday evening, she and Colin would go to a film or a disco, but if the house was empty they would stay in and watch television like an old married couple. Making love here felt illicit, which could be thrilling or uncomfortable according to their mood. Sometimes they didn't bother. But when the news came on Jessica always felt a pang of loss at the sight of the London skyline. 'Relax,' said Colin, kissing her. 'We'll soon be back.'

On Sundays she went to lunch at the farm with Colin and his father and Dave, his brother. It felt odd to be the only woman there. Colin could not even remember his mother. The three men talked about what needed doing on the farm and what had to be done, and Jessica smiled and stared out of the window, wondering how anyone could live without the reassuring sight of buildings. The fields stretched away into the distance, seemingly endless; even the animals looked lonely, she thought. It always surprised her to see how effortlessly Colin melted back into the language of the farm, instantly talking technicalities with Dave and his Dad like somebody born bilingual, as if he had never been away, as if London were a foreign country and this was home. It frightened her; she didn't feel he belonged to her then. He wasn't her Colin any more. She couldn't wait to get him away and back to civilisation.

'Come on, Jess, get some fresh air in your lungs,' said Dave, who liked to tease her. And she would tramp obediently over the fields for hours in gumboots and anorak, knowing that somehow she would get her revenge: by the end of the afternoon she had always managed to catch cold.

Then it was back home with Colin for an early supper with her parents before getting the train back to London. Sneezing merrily by now, Jessica would be faint with triumph at proving she was allergic to the countryside, dizzy with excitement at the prospect of the escapist train journey. She was all hugs and kisses, Dave forgiven, Jennifer forgotten, her parents beloved and so soon to be left behind.

'Back to the smoke then,' her father always said. 'You take care of yourself now. You look after her, Colin.'

Jessica felt that they saw London as an alien place, that there was an unspoken criticism of her for choosing to go there when she could have picked a local college. She felt like a naughty child who had run away from home. She couldn't have explained what it was about London that gave her such a charge; she didn't do any of the usual tourist things, although she had at first, and she couldn't afford any treats on a student grant. She just knew that as the train raced towards London she was flooded with relief, as if she had come through some danger and survived. There was something essential mixed in with the noise and the dirt, addictive as a drug, and as vital to her well-being as oxygen.

They had their lives all planned. Colin was going to teach and Jessica was going to be an estate agent. But jobs were harder to find than they'd thought, when the time came; it was a shock not to be students any more with subsidised accommodation, travel and food.

'If you got work up here, you could live at home,' her mother said. 'Think of all the money you'd save.'

'We can always use an extra pair of hands,' said Colin's Dad.

It had never occurred to Jessica that both families

cherished a dream of them going home after college. How could they think that London was not for ever? 'They really expect us to go back,' she said to Colin. 'Isn't that amazing?'

'Well, maybe they've got a point,' he said. 'It would be cheaper. We could save much faster up there and get a place in London later.'

Jessica was terrified. If they once went back, they might get stuck there and never get away again. 'You don't want to go back, do you?' she said. 'You can't. You're winding me up.'

He smiled. 'I want to be with you,' he said. 'And you want to be in London.'

So Colin took the job at the comprehensive in Battersea and Jessica enrolled for a secretarial course. 'All those exams and you end up as a secretary,' said Jennifer, watching her pack. 'It doesn't make sense.'

'I'm not ending up as anything,' said Jessica, trying to stay cool. 'I'm just beginning.'

'Oh well, I suppose you can always do a bit of temping when you have kids,' said Jennifer, who had to have the last word. In childhood Jessica remembered occasionally banging her head on the ground in an effort to shut her up.

They told their families they were going to share a flat with other people. Everyone knew that meant living together but it was easier than saying it. They rented a room in a mansion block near the river at the wrong end of the King's Road where lorries thundered past on their way to the M4, making the whole building shudder and keeping them awake until sheer exhaustion got them suddenly adjusted. It was Chelsea, but only just. On Sunday mornings they would stroll down the road to buy the papers and have a drink at the pub or take their glasses across the road to lean on the wall and admire the houseboats floating gently on the brown water.

'Maybe we can live on a houseboat one day,' Jessica said. Jennifer's remark about kids haunted her and she thought no one could expect her to have kids if she lived on a houseboat.

'Maybe,' Colin said. 'But it might smell a bit. People chuck refuse in the river.'

'Hey,' she said lightly, 'that sounds like criticism. This is our town, remember?'

'It's yours,' he said. 'I'm only here by invitation. You belong.'

She was shocked into silence. She had always wanted to believe that he loved London as much as she did, though on some level she had known that nobody could. 'What is it?' she said eventually. 'What's the matter? You sound so sad.'

'Oh, I don't know, Jess,' he said, not looking at her. 'I'm just a bit disenchanted.'

'Is it the kids?' she said, frightened, hoping that was all he meant. 'Are they getting you down?'

'Well, they never stop thumping each other, if that's what you mean. I suppose I'm bloody lucky they don't thump me. Barry got duffed up the other day; he was off sick for a week. They put razor blades in our teacups if they get half a chance, and one of them told me his father found a baby in a dustbin on their council estate. What did he do? Call an ambulance? Not on your life. He called the *News of the World*.'

'Why didn't you tell me?' Jessica said, feeling inadequate.

'I told you they were rough. I didn't know you wanted a daily bulletin.'

'You could teach at another school.'

'They're all like that.'

'Well, a private school then. They can't be like that.'

'Oh, Jess,' he said hopelessly, 'if I do that, then I've really sold out.'

'I don't see why.' But she knew what he meant.

'Anyway,' he said, 'it's not just the kids. We're not saving anything. It'll be years before we can get our own place.'

She hated to see him so defeated. 'It'll be all right, you see. Once I get a proper job. Once I start pulling my weight. You're carrying me at the moment, that's why it's tough.'

She took him home, cooked a wonderful lunch, got him rather drunk and made love to him. He slept heavily afterwards and she watched him with protective tenderness, wondering if that was how Jennifer felt about her child. In the morning he went back to work as if nothing had happened, but Jessica felt the conversation marked a turning point in their lives.

She got a job as secretary to an estate agent and started learning as much as she could about the business. It excited her so much that sometimes she felt quite breathless. Sooner or later she would be a negotiator, selling properties as if the whole of London was hers to sell.

At the end of the year Colin left the school in Battersea and went to another one in Wandsworth. Jessica hardly dared ask him what it was like, but eventually she had to. 'It's just the same,' he said. 'I'm not a teacher, I'm a policeman. But don't worry. I can cope.'

At weekends they went to art galleries and museums; during the week to theatres and films. Colin was far more hungry for culture than Jessica. 'Otherwise we might as well not be here,' he said.

They rented a flat of their own in Fulham. It had tiny rooms but a large roof terrace. Jessica sunbathed to the hum of traffic. When she went home to visit her family, the silence kept her awake.

'It's highway robbery,' said Jennifer, leafing through one of Jessica's property magazines. 'You could buy a whole house up here for the price of one of your tarted-up studios in London. Are you going to be selling rubbish like that?'

Next year Jessica got the job as a trainee negotiator and at last it was all happening, the dream coming true. Colin said he was happy for her and they drank champagne and went to Covent Garden to celebrate. She spent all her spare time studying and she bought a second-hand car with her savings that had been meant for the deposit on a flat, so that she could get to know her area as well as a taxidriver and drive clients around from one property to another. She had exams to take, too; she was very busy. Colin kept telling her how well she was doing, but he didn't talk about school any more and he didn't make love to her as often as he used to. She was suddenly afraid. She felt a chill where before there had been warmth.

When the blow fell it was without warning: a phone call from Dave to say Colin's father had had a heart attack. By the time they reached the farm he was dead, and Jessica, who had surreptitiously packed black clothes just in case, felt guilty and responsible, as if she had made it happen. Colin and Dave formed an instant alliance of mutual support and she felt relieved but excluded. At the funeral she surprised herself by crying a lot while they didn't cry at all. Afterwards they went for long walks together to have whatever private conversations they could not have in the house while she was there, and she watched their broad backs disappearing over the horizon with a sense of dread.

Colin didn't tell her until they were back in London. Then he put it very plainly. 'I'm sorry, Jess,' he said. 'I'll have to go back. Dave can't manage without me.'

She stared at him with absolute horror, saying, 'Just for the holidays, that's what you mean, isn't it?' while knowing it was worse than that.

'No, to stay. Dave can't cope – well, he probably could but he's panicking, he's talking about selling the farm. If I'm there I can steady him down. Don't look like that, it's not yet. I'll have to give a term's notice, of course.'

Jessica didn't know how she got through the next few weeks. They both went very quiet as if keeping their heads down, keeping a low profile. They made love with particular intensity but didn't talk. Then Colin suddenly said, 'Would you like to get married? I've always assumed we would one day but maybe I should have asked you before.'

She didn't know what to say. She couldn't imagine life without him but she knew life on the farm would be a death sentence for her. So she just gave him a big hug. 'Let's talk about it another time.'

'I know it's a lot to ask,' he said, 'uprooting you like this.' And then she realised he was expecting her to agree.

'It's so soon after the funeral,' she said. 'We can't make decisions now. We're not thinking straight, either of us.'

'I know how much you love London,' he said. 'I just hope you love me more, that's all.'

'Of course I do,' she said, but she wasn't sure she meant it and he looked as if he didn't believe her.

'We could come down for weekends,' he said. 'We could even move back in a few years. It wouldn't have to be for ever.'

They were both crying when they said goodbye on Euston station. 'See you soon,' were his last words, and he waved till he was out of sight. Jessica went home in a taxi she couldn't afford and the phone was ringing as she walked in. 'What's the matter with you?' Jennifer said. 'You love him, don't you? You can't let him go.'

'Yes, I love him,' said Jessica, crying, 'but I can't leave London.'

'You're mad. How can a bloody city be more important than a man?'

Jessica went out and walked about. She came home and slept heavily; she went to work in a daze. Colin wrote letters and rang her up to ask when she'd be arriving. She said she didn't know yet; she had work to finish; people were relying on her. He sent her a cassette of Roberta Flack singing 'Jessie, come home, there's a hole in the bed,' and she started crying all over again. She thought it was the hardest and most important decision she'd ever make and she had to make it alone. She went to Kensington and sat on a bench in Edwardes Square to calm herself. The white stucco houses in all their tall thin perfection were full of enchantment still.

When she had written the letter she went out to post it at midnight, in case she lost her nerve. It was a bright cold night: the stars were watching her as she posted goodbye into the box, and the lights were plunging into the river. She felt sad but she didn't feel alone. Perhaps they could still be friends; perhaps he would come back because he missed her; perhaps there was someone else out there who loved London as much as she did. She didn't know yet. She was in pain but the pain made sense because she had not betrayed herself. She was staying at home. This was where she belonged.

# Christmas Magic

If only it could be optional, Laura thought, like holidays. Then you could say, without loss of face, 'No, I'm not having one this year, I can't afford it,' or 'I'm saving up to have a really good one in three years' time,' and no one would think any the less of you. Or, failing that, if it could come round at regular but infrequent intervals, like Leap Year, and then you might just be able to cope with it. Or if you could choose when to have it, perhaps when the weather was better and you were in a good mood and you felt like some spontaneous rejoicing. But no, it was a birthday and so of course it had to come round relentlessly on the same day every year. For the whole of your life, on 25 December you were obliged to be full of goodwill.

'Don't be such a misery,' Kate said when she moaned about Christmas. Kate had taken to calling her Scrooge, and although she managed to laugh, it hurt. They had read the story at school and Laura couldn't remember if Scrooge had always hated Christmas or if something had happened to trigger him off. In her own case she knew perfectly well what it was. Christmas had been wonderful, literally full of wonder, when she and Kate and James could hardly go to sleep for excitement about Santa Claus, and woke at dawn to slide down their beds and kick the rustling pillowcases packed with goodies. It had been even more wonderful when she grew up and fell in love and spent Christmas with John or Stephen or Tony, as well as with her family. And it was still wonderful for her parents, because they were religious, and wonderful for Kate, because she had children to get excited, and wonderful for James, because he had Caroline to make love with. In short, Christmas could be wonderful if you were religious, or a child, or a parent, or if you had a lover. But if you didn't fit into any of these categories, then it could be pretty bloody awful and turn you into Scrooge, although you knew that no one liked a misery and you were digging your own social grave.

What had happened to her was Michael. Three years of being in love with someone who could never spend Christmas with you because he had to spend it with his children. That proved he was a good father but didn't do much for your self-esteem. He couldn't spend your birthday with you, either, because he had to spend it with his wife, as it was her birthday too. That confirmed your belief in astrology but otherwise it was pretty bad news. And of course Bank Holidays and weekends were out; it would have been silly to ask about them. They were spent digging the garden or laying concrete paths or building shelves or, just occasionally, putting the car on the ferry to France to load up with cheap wine, a nice day out for the family, of course, but you didn't mention that. So you had to make do with long lunch hours (alibi the dentist, the hairdresser, or sudden illness) and the occasional evening, where the strain of the lies that had to be told seemed to crawl into bed with you and nearly, but not quite, wreck the whole thing.

Of course it was stupid to fall in love with a married man, she realised that, especially when you were only twenty-three and quite attractive, to anyone who liked blonde hair and green eyes; when you had a good job, your boss claimed you were the perfect secretary and he'd be lost without you, and your friends said you deserved the best of everything. But none of these people knew how delicious Michael's skin smelt or the way he looked when you made love or the jokes he told you while he was getting dressed. So they couldn't really understand what made you waste three years of your life and not regret it. Because of course you had come to your senses eventually and broken it off, knowing you were doing the right thing because the pain had finally made you numb to everything and you were like an animal in a trap that would bite off a limb to escape. There had to be more in the world for you than this, being on the fringe of someone's life and fitting into the tiny spaces he made for you. But she hadn't expected it would take so long to recover, to pick up the friends who had grown sick of her never making plans but always sitting by the phone just in case; to make new ones at evening classes, dramatic society, health club, new ones who knew nothing about what an idiot she had been. She hadn't known it would be another two years before the pain finally went, leaving merely a great emptiness. Was it so unreasonable to hate Christmas after all that?

She made a joke of it at the office, the Scrooge joke that Kate had begun. She started a Society for the Abolition of Christmas and found enthusiastic support through October and November when the pressure was on to buy presents you couldn't afford for your loved ones and cards for people you disliked, but around the second week of December she noticed that the momentum of the season took over and SAC members fell away. Somewhere inside them, behind all the token resistance, was a hard core of festivity. They started ordering turkeys and buying holly and tinsel and brightly coloured paper. They still complained about it all, but it was a ritual complaint, put on for her benefit, to conceal the fact that deep down they were really enjoying themselves and they wanted an excuse for celebration.

'It's only the back end of a horse,' said Kate crisply on the phone, 'so you won't need much rehearsal. Arriving on Christmas Eve will be quite all right. Of course Mum and Dad would like you to come sooner but if you can't, you can't, I suppose.'

Oh God, the fearful jollity of Kate's house loomed before her like a punishment, and then to be jammed up against Kate inside the suffocating skin of a pantomime horse, more intimate than they had been since childhood when they shared a room and terrified one another with ghost stories and thrashed each other with pillows.

'Can't you find someone else?' she said.

'No, I can't,' said Kate, with the confidence of two years' seniority, 'or I would. Are you driving down?'

'Yes, of course.' Lucia was her pride and joy, her very first car, the second-hand Mazda she had bought in the spring, as soon as she finally passed her test. She didn't go anywhere without Lucia. If possible she would have liked to take Lucia upstairs to bed with her.

'Well, be careful,' said Kate, who had passed first time at seventeen. And hung up.

So it was that she came to be driving to Hastings on Christmas Eve with a bootful of presents and a glum expression, like a reluctant Santa who had exchanged his reindeer for something a bit more modern, but was still wishing he could have stayed at home in Lapland with the duvet over his head. She had had Lucia serviced three weeks before, in preparation for the journey, so felt confident enough to do a bit of speeding on the motorway, hoping the police would be too full of goodwill to catch her. She was still enough of a new driver to feel an illicit thrill at breaking the law, however marginally, (seventy-five was normal, eighty was daring and eighty-five was positively wicked) plus a sense of smug self-righteousness at keeping Lucia in mint condition. Coming off the motorway, she noticed the windscreen was rather murky and the wipers didn't seem to be clearing it, so she stopped in the next village and got out of the car, armed with a roll of kitchen paper. Then she noticed she was at a bus stop and virtuously got back in and moved Lucia further up the street. The windscreen was surprisingly hard to clean and seemed covered with gunge, but she persevered.

When she started the engine again, the oil light came on. And stayed on.

Instant panic. This was definitely not supposed to happen. Especially not after a service when Lucia was full to bursting with expensive oil. She got the manual out of the glove compartment to check if she was doing something stupid, something only new drivers in their ignorance might do, but it told her to check the oil level and if it was low not to move the car but to seek help, or oil. She knew all that already.

'Come on, Lucia,' she said. 'You can't let me down now. Not on Christmas bloody Eve.'

Maybe it was just an electrical fault. Maybe if she turned off the engine and waited and started it again, all would be well. At some level, she still believed in magic. But she tried it and all was definitely not well, there was no miracle, only the oil lamp still glaring malevolently at her. Swearing under her breath she got out, opened the bonnet, pulled out the dip stick, wiped it on the kitchen paper. Then she realised that she wasn't near enough to a street lamp to see where to plunge it back in, never mind read it when it came out again. She felt very silly. And right at that moment it started to rain.

She looked around for a phonebox but couldn't see one anywhere. They were like policemen, she thought, never around when you needed one but always lurking when you didn't. Besides, she would look like a really stupid woman driver if she phoned the AA when what she really needed was a torch. There was nothing else for it. She rang the doorbell of the nearest lighted house.

A man opened the door. He was a few inches taller than she was, slim and muscular. She couldn't see his face clearly against the light, but he was wearing a rather nice striped jersey and corduroy trousers, and he had the busy, abstracted air of one who has been interrupted in an important task.

'I'm sorry to disturb you,' she said, hating her image as

helpless woman, 'but could you possibly lend me a torch, just for a minute? I think I've run out of oil and I can't see to check it.'

'Of course,' he said, as if it was the most natural thing in the world. 'Come in for a minute while I find one.'

All her mother's childhood warnings about not talking to strange men, let alone going willingly into their homes, flooded back into her mind. On the other hand, she could hardly expect him to be crouching behind his own front door with a torch between his teeth, waiting for her to ring his bell, and she didn't want to stand on the step in the rain. So she went in and waited in his hall while he disappeared into the back of the house.

The hall was bright with decorations, festooned with tinsel and holly and hung with balloons. Another Christmas freak, she thought. Not a likely candidate for membership of SAC. She expected a wife and children to leap out at her, but the house was strangely silent.

'Here we are,' he said, reappearing with the torch. Now that she saw him clearly for the first time, she had the oddest feeling that she had met him before, although she knew he was a stranger. He was about her own age, with curly brown hair and blue eyes that looked at her keenly but reassuringly, rather like a family doctor. Not at all the mad rapist of her mother's fantasies. She told herself sternly not to be ridiculous, but the blend of novelty and familiarity made her start to shake inside.

He didn't give her the torch, but came out with her on to the pavement.

'Oh, very nice,' he said when he saw Lucia. 'They're good, aren't they?'

She warmed to his praise and let him hold the torch while she inserted the dipstick. It came out bone dry. There was no oil in Lucia at all.

'But I only just had her serviced,' she said, aghast.

'Maybe your sump plug has fallen out,' he said hopefully, and to her amazement spreadeagled himself on the wet pavement, heedless of his good jersey, to peer under Lucia's engine. 'That's it, I'm afraid,' he added, surfacing. 'There's a great pool of oil.' And he shone the torch for her to see.

'I'll kill my garage,' she said. 'May I use your phone?'

'Of course,' he said. 'Come and have a Christmas drink. After all, you won't be driving. Sorry about that.'

The living-room was a mass of decorations too. Was he doing all this for himself or was he expecting someone? She felt more embarrassed than ever when the AA told her it would be an hour or two before they could come. People were breaking down all over the place, it seemed.

'Stay as long as you like,' he said. 'My friends aren't arriving till late. It's nice to have company.'

'You've really got the Christmas spirit,' she said, looking round.

'Actually, I hate it,' he said, 'but they've got children so I thought I should make an effort. It seems pretty pointless on your own, don't you think?'

Magic words, she thought. She could hardly believe it. If she'd met him at a party she'd be trying to chat him up by now, appear glamorous and interesting instead of silly and helpless with a broken-down car. They were saying such trivial things to each other and yet she had the oddest feeling they were really talking about something else.

'Absolutely,' she said. 'I've promised to be the back end of a pantomine horse on Boxing Day, just to please my sister. So it's really important I get to Hastings tonight. I've got to rehearse.'

'That sounds like a traditional English Christmas.' He smiled. 'I've forgotten what it's like. I've been working abroad and I only came home six months ago.' He was staring at her all the time.

'What do you do?' she asked politely, conscious now of feeling absurdly comfortable with him, more comfortable than she had felt with any man since Michael, and yet at the same time extremely tense. It was an odd, invigorating ambivalence. Must be my hormones, she thought. I'm out of practice. Perhaps I'm going mad.

'I'm a physicist,' he said. 'I've been helping people find oil.'

In her mind she could hear Kate, ever the matchmaker, saying, 'My God, he sounds perfect, wherever did you find him?' and herself answering flippantly, 'Oh, it's easy if you know how. I just rang his bell.'

'How ironic,' she said, too frozen with excitement to flirt.

'How far did you drive after the light came on?' he asked, as if he was really interested.

'I don't know,' she said. 'I think I noticed it right away but maybe it was on before. Not on the motorway but further back down the street when I stopped at the bus stop.'

'Hey,' he said, 'we may be on to something. Hang on, Watson. Maybe it fell out right there. Got shaken loose on the motorway because your garage didn't tighten it properly and fell out when you stopped. Change of temperature and all that. Why don't I go and look for it?'

What a terrible idea, she thought, when all I want to do is sit here for as long as it takes the AA to arrive, sit here and get to know you and show you I can be wonderful too when you get to know me. 'That would be very kind,' she said faintly.

'Not at all.' He got up. 'A two-legged horse might ruin the pantomime. Besides, I rather fancy myself as a mechanic. Won't be long. Make yourself at home.'

While he was gone, she studied the room. It had a good, warm atmosphere. Lots of books and records. Honey-coloured walls and rust carpet. Deep comfortable sofas. It was a real home, as if he didn't mind being alone, no matter what he said. And everywhere the wretched decorations. She didn't believe he really hated it. Deep down he was a Christmas freak like everyone else and she envied him.

Presently he returned with a smug expression and oil all over his hands. 'Got it,' he said. 'Right there by the bus stop. I've put it back really tight and I've put some oil in. Simple. You'll be okay now.'

He wants to get rid of me, she thought suddenly, with an ache of disappointment. I'm a nuisance. He really wants me out, that's why he's doing all this. 'I can't thank you enough,' she said, chilled, and rang the AA to cancel her call, abandoning all fantasies of exchanging names and phone numbers with him, meeting for drinks, meeting for dinner, living happily ever after.

'It was really nice meeting you,' he said when she was standing on the step.

'Happy Christmas,' she said bitterly. And drove off.

For the rest of the journey she berated herself, first for having the idea that they already knew each other, then for not trusting her instincts and doing something about it. By the time she arrived she had a violent headache and was wondering if she had imagined the whole thing.

'God, you're a wimp,' said Kate when she told her the story. 'You'll have to call in on your way back, that's all. Take him a present. Say you want to thank him properly.' She laughed the suggestive laugh that had made her the heroine of the fourth form.

'I couldn't possibly,' Laura said, wondering if perhaps she could. 'He couldn't wait to get rid of me.'

'He was trying to impress you, twitbag,' said Kate. 'God, that Michael has a lot to answer for. Where's all your self-esteem?'

Her parents fussed over her, declaring she needed more food, more sea air, more early nights. They still resented her running away to the big city, the bright lights, the unsuitable men. Kate's children climbed all over her and Kate's husband carved the turkey and James and Caroline canoodled on the sofa until she felt quite sick with envy. By four o'clock they were all sleepy and full and knee-deep in wrapping paper.

She went for a solitary walk along the sea front to clear her head. The tide was in and wild spray crashed on to the promenade. She loved it here in winter when there were no tourists and the sea could belong to her alone. But in her mind she kept seeing a stranger's familiar face and a warmly decorated room.

It was hot inside the cloth skin as she and Kate lolloped around the stage next day, falling in and out of step. But she was cheered by the howls of laughter from the audience and even more by the thought that Christmas was over for another year. She began to nurse a fantasy that she really could drop in on her way back, that he'd be pleased to see her, that he too felt as if they'd met before, maybe in a previous incarnation. She liked the idea of that. But she knew she wouldn't do it when it came to the crunch and the knowledge made her sad.

Kate put her head round the door of what passed for a dressing-room at the church hall. 'Someone to see you,' she said, and went away.

'I thought the back legs were absolutely brilliant,' he said. 'Best back legs I've ever seen. But I've had a hell of a job finding you. Why didn't you give me your name and address?'

Laura felt a huge delighted smile fill up the whole of her face. 'Why didn't you ask me?'

'Don't laugh,' he said, 'but I didn't think of it till after you'd gone. I felt as if I knew you already.'

'That's amazing,' she said, shaken. 'That's exactly how I felt too.'

Kate peered round the door, saw them grinning idiotically at each other, shook her head and disappeared.

'Tell you what,' he said. 'Let's start again. I'm Tom Mallison and I really like your hooves. Could we take it from there?'

'I'm Laura Nichols,' said Laura, 'and I really love Christmas. Did I mention that before?'

# The Consolation Prize

In the summer, she went to live by the sea.

'Do come,' Penny urged her. 'Jean wants to go to Vancouver and she needs someone to water the cat and feed the plants. I could do it but I'd have to drive there every day. It won't cost you anything and you can let your flat and make a fortune.'

Annie felt she was being manipulated. The idea of a summer spent away from London, away from Daniel, threw her into a panic, and yet at the same time it was perversely attractive. It would serve him right. He was always away for most of August anyway, down in Cornwall with his family, and they only met three or four times a month for a few hours each time, so if she did go away for the summer she was probably only missing about twenty-four hours of Daniel.

It was sad arithmetic. It evoked a day and a night of unbroken time, which of course they had never spent together, and it made her angry that she was managing on so little.

'Besides,' Penny added unfairly, 'now I'm pregnant I need you more than ever. Just imagine, a whole summer only five minutes apart. It'd be almost as good as sharing a flat again.'

Annie still wasn't used to the idea of Penny being pregnant. The bump wasn't very obvious yet but she found herself staring at Penny's stomach every time they met and thinking with a certain amount of apprehension about the miracle that was taking place. Would it come between them mentally as it already did physically when they hugged? Would Penny be too tired, too preoccupied, too *maternal* to sit up late and hear about Daniel and care about people who didn't have children? Pregnancy was something they had discussed so often, inevitable but remote, like the end of the world, and here was Penny already doing it. Was summer by the sea a last chance to make the most of Penny in case she was submerged when the baby came?

They went to look at the flat together. It was small, like Annie's place in London, two rooms, kitchen and bathroom, but it had a balcony overlooking the sea. Annie stood there for a long time watching the windsurfers with their gaudy butterfly sails. Sometimes they capsized ignominiously; sometimes they were swept along fast in a straight line. The sun on the water dazzled her and the sea and the sky merged, making the horizon a distant blur. She was conscious of Jean waiting for a decision, the tiny diamond glinting on her left hand. She was younger than Annie but she had the confident air of one who knows she has got her life in order. She would be much too sensible to get involved with a married man. 'I just need someone to look after the flat,' she said, 'while I visit my fiancé.' She had an open honest face with no make-up, and she was decidedly overweight, but Annie still couldn't like her. The word 'fiancé' took her straight back to her teens when your parents paid for the reception and your father gave you away and your first marriage was also your last.

'It's a lovely view,' she said, as the cat twined itself round her legs. She thought of Daniel and how surprised he would be if she went away.

'So we're going to be neighbours,' Steve said that evening when she joined them for supper.

'Well, I haven't really decided yet. I said I'd ring her next week.'

'She wants to talk it over with Daniel first,' said Penny.

Annie was grateful for the way she always made it sound as though Daniel were part of her life, instead of belonging to someone else. Penny understood even though she couldn't approve. Annie didn't blame her for not approving; after all, she didn't really approve herself.

'How is Danny boy?' Steve enquired.

'Fine,' said Annie, 'but d'you have to call him that?'

'Sorry, sorry.' Then he whistled a few bars of the 'Londonderry Air'.

'Lay off, Steve,' said Penny. 'Not everyone appreciates your warped sense of humour.'

Annie couldn't understand why Penny had married Steve. Apart from the fact that he looked rather like Warren Beatty, he didn't seem to have much to recommend him. But perhaps that was enough. Perhaps he was wonderful in bed. Perhaps he was also very kind and had a lovely nature hidden away under his silly jokes. Perhaps they had proper conversations when they were alone. Sometimes when she visited them she felt like Blanche in *Streetcar* staying with Stella and Stanley Kowalski, and very much hoped it wouldn't end the same way, with her getting raped and going off her head and being carted away by men in white coats, dependent on the kindness of strangers. The whole situation with Daniel made her feel a little crazy at times, as if she was living two half lives, or as if she were a puppet kept in a toy cupboard, not an adult woman in charge of her own fate. Perhaps that was why Penny had married Steve, so as not to feel like that.

'Just think,' said Steve, perhaps trying to make amends, 'if you were only down the road, how much work you and Pen could do on Lydia Snake.'

This was their pet project. In a rare idle moment in the staffroom long ago they had come up with the idea of a series of children's books, written by Annie and illustrated by Penny, about Lydia Snake, a charming reticulated python who lived in an airing cupboard and had various adventures when she was off duty from busking with her owner. She was in love with Peregrine Python, but he was a bit of a snob and preferred Anna Adder, so Lydia Snake spent a lot of time pouring out her troubles to her best friend Cindy Cat. They had great fun planning the series and how to spend the vast royalties, but so far Penny had done one rather tentative charcoal drawing of their heroine coiled up on a striped bath towel, and Annie had written half a paragraph beginning, 'Lydia Snake really wished people weren't so prejudiced against pythons.'

'After all,' Steve added, spoiling it all, 'you'll have to find something to do with those endless holidays you teachers get.'

'Absolutely right,' said Annie, refusing to rise to the bait. 'And now I'm teaching adults, my holidays are even longer.' She knew from experience that the best way to deal with Steve was to smile and agree with him, but she didn't always remember in time. 'I shall think of you, Steve, when you're out driving your minicab and I'm sitting on my balcony looking at the sea and writing a bestseller.'

Steve grinned, acknowledging defeat, Penny giggled and poured some more wine, and the evening ended more amiably than it had begun.

When she got home Annie rang Jeremy for advice. He seemed delighted to be asked and insisted on taking her out to dinner next day to discuss it. She protested feebly; she always felt guilty about letting him spend money on her, but he would never let her pay her share, no matter how often she suggested it. 'There are other reasons than sex,' he would say solemnly, 'for a man to buy a woman dinner. Her nut-brown hair. Her cheekbones. Her sense of humour.'

'I don't think I have much sense of humour,' said Annie, who couldn't deny the hair and the cheekbones but felt bad about the number of times she had cried on Jeremy's shoulder.

'You laugh at my jokes, don't you?' said Jeremy. 'What more proof do you need?' And she hadn't the heart to tell him that he didn't make very many jokes.

Proposals, now, that was a different matter. She had lost count of how many times Jeremy had proposed to her. She had learnt to take him seriously, although she had to keep saying no. Now he had stopped asking her, and contented himself with telling her to let him know if she ever changed her mind. 'I'm going to leave the offer on the table,' he said. 'Okay?' She was ashamed to admit that she actually missed being asked. Now when they met he would simply say, 'Still Daniel?' and, when she nodded: 'Lucky chap.'

Jeremy was thirty-eight and lived with his mother who said plaintively at intervals, 'Annie, my dear, I do wish you'd marry Jay and take him off my hands. He's such a responsibility and I want to grow old disgracefully.' Jeremy said his mother needed protection from unsuitable men who were after her money rather than her body, but since knowing them both for five years Annie had reached the conclusion that they needed each other.

She had tried hard to fall in love with Jeremy. If anyone could have fallen in love by sheer willpower, she would have managed it. He was tall and thin, with sandy hair and anxious brown eyes behind thick glasses, but he had nice hands and a lovely voice and he was kind and intelligent and he cared about her. They had met when he sold her a flat after her divorce and for a couple of years the relationship stayed platonic while she described herself as the walking wounded.

Then one fatal New Year's Eve they had tried to make love, perhaps feeling it was expected of them after such a long friendship, or that it was silly not to, with so much goodwill around. It was a dismal failure and left them both feeling embarrassed. Even their arms and legs didn't seem to fit, quite apart from the more important bits. Jeremy was not well-endowed and she didn't feel filled up

at all; he didn't seem to have heard of foreplay, or
afterplay, come to that; and the whole performance, if she
could call it that, was over almost as soon as it had begun.
'Was that it?' she felt like saying but didn't because she had
a kind heart and besides, like every other woman, she
knew that the male ego was a delicate thing: since puberty
she had been conditioned not to damage it.

'It'll be better next time,' he promised her, breathing
hard, and she longed to say, 'If there is a next time.'

Even their mouths were ill-matched: their teeth clashed
and their tongues were tentative. Jeremy didn't smell of
anything either: sweat or soap or skin. He was totally
bland. If you shut your eyes, you could pretend he wasn't
there, which she did. They were obviously meant to be
friends and that was that. They shouldn't have pushed
their luck. The best part had been when he put his arm
round her and stroked her hair.

'I'm afraid I'm not very good at this,' he added
disarmingly, 'because I don't get enough practice.'

'I'm rather out of practice myself,' she said, to comfort
him. It was true but irrelevant. Making love was not something you forgot how to do, if you had ever known. She
felt bitterly disappointed that the two miserable celibate
years since her divorce should end in this undignified
fumbling. Then she began to wonder if she was at fault,
not sufficiently erotic or skilful to get the best out of
Jeremy. Like most women, she had been trained to blame
herself for men's shortcomings.

'I shouldn't have drunk so much, trying to get up my
courage,' he said.

'Neither should I,' she said dutifully, although they had
only had two gin and tonics, and a bottle of champagne
with their dinner. She wondered how long it would be
before they could both pretend the whole thing had never
happened.

Then he had really surprised her. 'Of course,' he said, in
the same casual, excuse-making tone, 'if you were just

anyone I'd be much better. I've really made a hash of it because I'm in love with you.'

She was so overwhelmed by this statement that she couldn't think of anything to say.

'Story of my life,' he added.

'Jeremy, you're a lovely person and I'm very fond of you, but I'm sure we're just meant to be friends. It feels a bit incestuous. The chemistry isn't right. It's nobody's fault. Or maybe I haven't got over Peter yet.' Words poured out of her now, anything that came to mind that would make him feel better and make sure it never happened again.

'I do wish you'd marry me,' he said. 'I'm sure I could improve a lot over the next fifty years.'

On the whole he seemed to get over the incident, as she thought of it, rather faster than she did. She went on feeling embarrassed on his behalf for quite some time, whereas once she'd made it clear to him that they were going to be platonic or nothing, and no hard feelings, he relaxed and seemed to recover all his old zest for taking her out for dinners and concerts and drives in the country. He held her hand in the street and kissed her goodnight in the hall, but he never again tried to get her into bed, and she thought she detected relief rather than disappointment. If he wasn't allowed to try, then he could not fail. For herself, she enjoyed his company; she was also grateful to have someone to talk about when her ex-husband Peter rang up with news of his new wife and child.

And then she met Daniel. It still made her go cold when she thought how easily she might not have met him. Liz had invited her to the latest private view at the gallery as usual, but she was late home from school after rehearsing *Saint Joan* and due to meet Jeremy for dinner at eight. She was thoroughly exhausted and really wanted nothing more than a bath and an early night. Besides, the gallery seemed to be moving away from the splashy dramatic abstract paintings that she enjoyed towards huge heavy badly drawn nudes. Perhaps that was the new trend. It was probably just like skirt lengths and she was out of date as usual. Just as she was deciding that she liked modern art after all, they went and changed it.

But Liz had rung up at the last moment and said, 'Don't you dare cancel, I'm counting on you. Gian-Carlo's bringing his *wife*, for God's sake, you can't let me down now, I need some moral support.'

So Annie had gone, half out of sisterly loyalty to Liz, and half out of curiosity to see the legendary Gian-Carlo, Liz's Italian lover, at close range. She recognised him at once, although she had never seen him before, because he was supremely beautiful, like a film star, a god; she found herself wondering how Liz could possibly go to bed with him. It would be like sleeping with a work of art: too awe-inspiring to be fun.The wife was predictable too: plump and plain and confident, her status reinforced by many children. Annie felt comfortably above it all, divorced and celibate, and ready to be soothed by yet another peaceful dinner with Jeremy. Then she saw Daniel.

He was shorter than Jeremy and wider, so that he formed a rather delectable rectangle like some of the paintings, which were not all the ugly figures she had feared. He had dark hair turning grey and an air of weariness, as if he had seen it all before and found it wanting. There were exhausted shadows beneath his eyes, which were a murky green. But he had a smile that made you feel you were the only person in the room, and dark hair escaping from his collar and cuffs, suggesting it must be all over his body. She fell instantly in love, or was it lust? She didn't care. Her knees sagged and she could feel herself salivating, as if, starving, she had pressed her nose against the window of a top-class restaurant serving rare steak.

'Who is that?' she said faintly to Liz.

'Where?' Then she followed Annie's eyeline. 'Oh, him.

That's Daniel Hurst, Gian-Carlo's accountant. We call him the gorilla.'

Annie gulped. 'I nearly poured my drink over him and he said, "Excuse me".'

'Oh, terrific,' said Liz. 'Sounds like an old Doris Day movie. That's really sparkling dialogue.'

'Introduce me, Liz, please. I'll do anything you like. I'll hem your curtains. I'll walk the dog. I'll even unblock your sink.'

'Follow me,' said Liz instantly. 'He's heavily married, of course. But you expected that, didn't you? All the good ones are.'

They crossed the room together and she heard Liz say, 'Oh Daniel, have you met Annie? She needs some advice about her income tax and I told her you were just the chap.'

'We nearly collided just now,' he said, smiling the irresistible smile. 'Hullo again.'

Then Liz was suddenly gone and they were alone in the crowded room. Annie heard herself telling him about the Lydia Snake project as if it were a reality and he said something about Schedule D and spreading her (as yet non-existent) self-employed income over three years, but she didn't really take it in because she was too busy looking at his mouth.

'It sounds like great fun,' he said. 'I'm sure my children would love it.'

The word children gave her a pain in the heart, the sort she had not had since Peter announced he was leaving her for pregnant Linda Jones in the upper sixth. She wondered if they looked like him. That large squashed crooked nose of his would look odd on a child. She thought he looked rather Roman, like someone out of *I Claudius* or possibly *The Godfather*. Maybe he was in the Mafia. She remembered Liz saying that the gallery was meant to be a tax loss for Gian-Carlo, while the ceramics shop next door made all the real money. Perhaps Daniel was a crook.

She wondered if she were going mad. She had never been so instantly devastated by anyone. She heard herself talking as if she were perfectly in control of herself, and she must have said something amusing because he laughed.

'Perhaps we could discuss it over dinner,' he said. 'My wife's up in Scotland with her parents and I do hate eating alone.'

That of course was her cue to say no, thanks all the same, she didn't go out with married men.

'I'd love to,' she said instantly. 'I'll just have to make one phone call.'

Off she went to the cloakroom, feeling above the ground, although she had only had one glass of wine, pitying all the other poor ordinary mortals who were not going to have dinner with Daniel. She rang Jeremy and said she had the curse and needed an early night. The lies poured out effortlessly, without hesitation or guilt; she could hear him being embarrassed and sympathetic and she was so convincing she almost convinced herself and started to look around for Tampax. Then she set about repairing her make-up. The face that looked back at her seemed utterly changed: young and hopeful and eager, not at all the face of a deserted wife or a celibate divorcee. She hardly recognised herself. Spraying herself with scent, she felt a sudden surge of confidence, as if anything were possible.

He took her to a very smart Indian restaurant where the waiters all seemed to know him and were very attentive. She caught herself wondering if he took his wife there too. Or was it just a safe place for other people? Over dinner he told her that he had been married twice and had two children from each marriage. It was worse than she thought. His first wife Deborah had gone back to Newcastle to be near her parents. Once a month he went up there to see the children and spend the weekend in an hotel. It was not an amicable arrangement. And once a month the children came to London to spend the weekend with him and his second wife Judy. This was not an amicable arrangement either. The two sets of children did not get on and Judy found being a stepmother more difficult than she had expected. 'I think she's beginning to realise she's made a terrible mistake,' he said with a wry smile. He did not tell any of this in a tone of self-pity, rather with a mixture of factual reporting and mild surprise, like a man who had been innocently walking down the garden path when a ton of cement fell on his head.

I should get up and run away now, she thought. I am a fool to be sitting here listening to this.

The dark hairs that escaped from his cuffs went all the way down his fingers and she found herself looking at them tenderly and wanting to kiss them.

'Not a good track record, I'm afraid,' he said. 'As a husband I'm a bit of a walking disaster. Let's say as a husband I make a very good accountant.'

In return she told him about marrying Peter at nineteen, when they were both at college, against their parents' better judgment, and agreeing not to have children until they had qualified and got jobs and saved up enough for a place of their own.

'I know,' he said. 'The right time. It just never comes.'

'Oh, but it did,' she said. 'Only when we tried nothing happened. So we went on trying, getting more and more worried and bad-tempered and pretending it didn't matter, and then Peter started having affairs and then he got this student pregnant and that was the end.'

He looked at her steadily for a long moment, the muddy green of his eyes reminding her of the colour of avocados, somewhere between ripe and rotten. Again she thought that she ought to flee for her life.

'Did you have affairs?' he asked.

She hesitated. 'Yes. But that gives the wrong impression. I didn't really want to, it was just a way of getting my own back when I felt miserable.'

'It can be very comforting,' he said.

She tried to be honest. 'Yes, I know. What I meant was, it didn't happen easily. I'm not a casual sort of person.'

'You're very beautiful,' he said. 'And very young.'

'I'm thirty,' she said, thrilled and embarrassed by the simplicity of the compliment, trying to hide behind a joke. 'The big one.'

'I'm forty-five,' he said. 'That's half way, even to an optimist. You're a child, a mere beginner. I envy you. You've still got time to get it right.' He smiled the smile that had been her undoing in the gallery and she felt a curious kind of knot in her stomach, as if he had locked into a private space that no one else had touched.

They had ice cream for pudding, needing the coolness after the delicious spicy food, and it came in a curious phallic shape that made them both laugh as if they were conspirators. They looked each other very straight in the eyes and didn't say anything. It was hard for her to attack the ice cream with her spoon.

He paid for the meal with a gold American Express card. In the street on the way back to the car he touched her hair very lightly with his hand. It felt as intimate as sex and she was truly frightened, but nothing would have made her run away.

He drove her back to her flat and parked outside. They sat in silence for what seemed like a long time, the tension between them feeling almost palpable, a dark presence filling the space, like another person in the car.

Eventually she said, 'Are you going to come in?'

'If I'm invited.' Still he didn't touch her and her skin began to crawl and ache with longing, as if she had flu.

'Then I'm inviting you.' She resented his making her do all the work and yet she appreciated it too. At least it left her with a free choice; there was no pressure, except in the silence.

Inside the flat she made coffee while he prowled and looked at the pictures, making the odd appreciative comment that they were much better than the stuff in Gian-Carlo's gallery. When the coffee was ready they sat on the sofa to drink it, still behaving like polite strangers. Her old cat of the marriage, the original Cindy Cat, was still alive then and came to sit on the back of the sofa between them; she always flirted outrageously with male visitors. Daniel began to stroke her and she responded as usual.

'What a loud purr,' he said. 'Do you have a loud purr?' And his hand came to rest on Annie's shoulder.

'Sometimes,' she said, turning her head to look at him, dizzy with relief that he had finally touched her.

They kissed then, and she sensed a tremendous hunger in him, as if he were starving and needed to devour her. The mug of hot coffee was still clutched in her hands and he paused to take it away and place it carefully on the table. Then they began to explore each other, undoing buttons and zips, kissing and stroking the skin they uncovered. Their clothes left a trail from living-room to bedroom until they finally fell on the bed and began to make love in real earnest. She found herself back in a world of sensation she had almost forgotten existed, or had never fully explored. She was in bed with a large warm furry animal and they were giving each other every sort of pleasure. Their bodies shifted easily from one position to another, like experienced dancers anticipating one another's movements, and their faces acknowledged each other's delight. It was so long since she had made love properly that at first she got stuck on the edge of a climax and feared it would never happen, that it was tantalisingly close yet beyond her reach, but he somehow made her understand that there was no hurry, no urgency, so suddenly it didn't matter, she could relax and she was able to come, over and over again until she was exhausted and replete, and when he finally came she was triumphant that she could at last make him lose control.

They had a long cuddle and didn't speak at all. She felt she had returned from a long journey, very tired and yet

full of energy, as if she could have jumped up and gone to a
party, but might have fallen asleep in the taxi. Out of the
long silence he suddenly said, 'Would you like to do this
again with me?'

No one had ever asked her that before in bed; they had
all gone off and rung or failed to ring. It was odd to be
asked, odd and touching and sweet, and she felt quite
overwhelmed by such unexpected courtesy. It was as if he
didn't take her for granted although he had seen the full
extent of her need. Could it be that he too felt insecure?
Then he would not exploit her, perhaps.

'Yes,' she said, and just managed to stop herself adding
the word please. To her surprise he then started making
love to her again. 'I thought you meant another time,' she
said, delighted at this indulgent luxury.

'I did,' he said, 'but why not now as well?'

'What a good idea,' she said.

This time it was very relaxed because they had nothing
to prove: it was friendly, light-hearted and fun, and they
laughed a lot. When it was over she lay there smiling, still
revelling in all her warm wet sensations and the smell of
his furry skin, so it was quite a shock to hear him say
presently in an everyday-sounding voice, 'Well, I suppose
I'd better get dressed.'

She felt like Cinderella at the ball, the glass slipper
falling off, the coach turning into a pumpkin. 'Can't you
stay?'

'Babysitter,' he said simply and started pulling on his
scattered clothes.

A great chill of disappointment settled on her and she
curled up in resentful silence for a few minutes, watching
him dress, the glow of the street lamp illuminating his fur
before it disappeared back into his shirt and trousers and
jacket. Then she got up and put on a dressing gown. They
stood facing each other in the hall and she felt like an
abandoned child. No more treats. Back to school. She
could see herself in the mirror looking crumpled and

dishevelled, make-up smudged or worn away, lips swollen, hair all over the place, whereas he looked almost the business man again, back in his suit.

'I'll ring you,' he said, combing his hair.

She had heard that before.

'That is,' he added patiently, 'if you give me your number.'

She was startled, as if he should have known it by telepathy. She wrote it down for him on a scrap of paper from the telephone pad and he handed her his business card, an obvious way, she thought, of telling her she wasn't of course allowed to phone him at home. Then he kissed her goodbye and it felt all right again, while they were touching.

As soon as he had gone, it didn't feel right at all.

'The trick is not to fall in love with them,' Liz said. After two years with Gian-Carlo she considered herself an expert on married men. 'Then you don't get hurt.'

It was two days later and Daniel still hadn't phoned. Annie had gone through several years of agony while she waited, punishing herself with expressions like making yourself cheap, throwing yourself at him, having no self-respect and behaving like an unpaid tart, but Liz insisted it was their mother's voice she was hearing.

'If you don't fall in love then what's the point?' Annie asked. 'You might as well hold out for somebody single who can stay the night and give you his home number and take you out at weekends.'

'But they don't stop you meeting this person, if he exists,' Liz pointed out. 'They just make sure you get plenty of good sex and hot dinners while you're waiting. It's only like taking a temporary job until a permanent one comes along. You've already got that wimp Jeremy. Now you've got Daniel to balance things up. It's ideal.'

'If he rings,' said Annie, trying not to stare at the phone.

'Two days is nothing for an Englishman,' said Liz

comfortingly. Then she spoilt it all by adding, 'Of course if he was foreign you'd have had flowers by now. Gian-Carlo sent me red roses every day for a week, the first time I went to bed with him.'

'Perhaps he fell in love with you,' Annie suggested.

Liz laughed. 'Don't be silly. He's in love with himself. And he loves his wife and all the little bambini. I'm just something exciting and decorative like a ceramic tile or a Lamborghini that he feels he deserves. When men get to forty and they're successful, they feel they've earned a mistress. I'm a status symbol, that's all.'

Annie wondered if she meant all the cynical things she said. It was difficult to tell with Liz.

'I should have played hard to get,' she said, watching the phone.

'Rubbish,' said Liz. 'He might have been run over by a bus and you'd have missed your night of bliss. Worse still, *you* might have been run over by a bus. At least this way you can die smiling.'

There was a long silence.

'I should never have gone to bed with him so quickly,' Annie said sadly.

'If he's shocked by that,' said Liz, 'then he's not worth having. In fact it's a good test of character. You didn't do it all by yourself, did you? It's like two people robbing a bank and then one says to the other, "I don't want to speak to you, you're a bank robber".'

'You see,' Annie said, 'you *do* think it's a crime.'

'God give me patience,' said Liz.

Annie picked up the phone to check it was still working and quickly replaced it.

'Of course,' Liz said, 'there is another solution to this. You can ring him.'

Annie shook her head.

'I see. You can go to bed with him on the first night but you can't ring him up. Terrific. Why do you think he gave you his number?'

Annie sighed. 'His hair smelt of incense,' she said, remembering.

'That's just a miracle shampoo for the over forties, to stop them going bald.'

'And his sweat is like scent.'

'Oh dear,' said Liz. 'Now that really sounds like love.'

And at that moment the phone rang. 'Hullo,' said Daniel sounding perfectly ordinary except that he had the most wonderful voice she had ever heard. 'I was wondering if you'd like to meet for lunch next week? Or a drink after work?'

Gradually a pattern established itself. During term time they met between five and seven. In the holidays they met from twelve till three, or one till four. Some weeks he was too busy to meet at all. Some weeks he didn't even phone. But if she rang him he always seemed to be delighted and usually made an arrangement to meet. Very rarely they managed to spend an evening together and go out to dinner. Never a weekend. Never overnight. Time was so short that they spent most of it in bed, though not always making love. Sometimes he fell asleep and she was torn between tenderness and rage. One day he fell asleep on the sofa with a coffee cup in his hand and she worried that he might fall asleep at the wheel of his car. He talked a lot but revealed very little and she had to work out for herself that supporting two families and travelling between them was an exhausting life. She suggested going with him on one of his trips to Newcastle but he said the children liked to visit his hotel room and he would be busy with them all the time. She lacked the courage to suggest going along just for the ride because she felt sure he would refuse; moreover she thought it would indicate that she was really mad.

Sometimes they quarrelled. It seemed to happen about every six months and became known as their bi-annual quarrel, so that in between they could joke about it. That was how long it took for all her resentments to build up, as if they had a fixed gestation period of their own. Too many phone calls missed, and meetings cancelled or postponed. Too many evenings alone in front of the television with a takeaway pizza. Too much sympathy from her friends on how neglected she was.

She would fantasise about giving him up and how shocked he would be, which was rather like fantasising about committing suicide to make your family feel guilty for not appreciating you: small comfort for you at your own funeral. She felt like a child muttering, 'Then he'll be sorry.' She could fill her evenings if she chose to, seeing Liz or Jeremy, Penny and Steve, other friends and colleagues; she could be busy and it was all very pleasant. But she was too honest not to feel a hollow ache at the centre of all this activity. I deserve more than this, she thought.

She envied couples who were entitled to be together, who did not have to make love with one eye on the clock, who had time to talk, to make plans, to go out, to see films, to take holidays, to do ordinary things, like meeting each other's friends, and even perhaps grow bored and take one another for granted, the ultimate luxury.

Quarrelling did not come naturally to her and she had to wind herself up to it, dwelling on her resentments like somebody biting on a sore tooth. She was afraid of anger, her own and other people's, remembering arguments with Peter that had been ugly and explosive and achieved nothing except to hasten the end, although they were supposed to clear the air. But eventually she would lose her temper with Daniel and unleash all her grievances, shaking inside, scarcely hearing what she said, terrified that he would reject her.

He always listened in silence. He did not shout or sulk, as Peter had done, or (worst fear of all) walk out. 'I'm sorry you feel like that,' he would say mildly, a soft answer, she thought, to turn away her wrath. 'I must try to do better in future.' Then he would describe all he had to do in an average day or an average week, both at work and at home, and she would end up amazed that he could fit her in at all. She would feel washed clean and new by being so outspoken, so assertive; they would make love, and he would go back to the office late.

And afterwards everything would go on exactly the same as before.

One evening she drove to Blackheath to find the road where he lived. She told herself she just wanted to see his house; in truth she was terrified that she might also see his wife and children. She went after dark to minimise this risk, but even so her heart beat very fast as she approached the street. She felt like a trespasser but she was also very angry that she could never visit him, that he came always to her flat and went away, leaving her alone again, and that she was weak enough to tolerate this arrangement. Driving past his house seemed a way of expanding this boundary, even in secret.

And then she saw him, wearing a tracksuit, out walking the dog. Her heart turned over with shock at seeing him out of context, doing something so ordinary and domestic, a routine chore, part of his other life that she so much wanted to share; and she had time to notice that he looked somehow deglamorised, tired and sad and old; then her guilt at spying on him, as it now seemed she was doing, made her accelerate away before he could notice she was there. At least she hoped he didn't notice. In all the panic and haste she didn't even see what his house looked like and she dared not return another time. She never mentioned the incident and neither did he.

'That's nothing,' Liz said, when Annie told her about the narrow escape. 'When I was in love with my psychiatrist I used to go round to his flat and kiss his car. Can you imagine? God, women are fools. One day the bonnet was hot, he must have just come home, and I nearly burnt my lip.'

Annie laughed and laughed, and realised she wanted to cry.

'Gian-Carlo would never behave like that,' Liz added. 'He'd be too busy at home slurping up the pasta or designing another memorable tile.'

'Liz,' Annie said seriously, 'does Gian-Carlo say he loves you?'

'All the time.'

'Daniel never says it.'

'Don't worry,' said Liz. 'They don't mean it, so it really doesn't matter if they say it or not. The result's the same. Here we are and here they aren't.'

'But I want to say it to Daniel.'

'God, you're a glutton for punishment,' said Liz fondly.

When they were touching, she always felt all right. Whether they were making love or holding hands, skin contact and body warmth reassured her that all was well. Sometimes in bed he held her so tight she felt she might suffocate or drown, engulfed in sweat and pleasure and fur. Then it was like a bear hug. She couldn't equate this person with the other in a grey pin-striped suit who kissed her goodbye on her forehead and made harsh jokes that kept her at arm's length. She felt she was allowed to get close to him only in bed.

Sometimes he let slip tantalising details of his past life, like the time Judy was about to have their first child and one of his other children was seriously ill in hospital up in Newcastle. He had spent most of his time zooming up and down the motorway.

'That must have been awful,' she said. 'You must have felt really torn in two.'

'Just as well I had a fast car,' he said.

She sensed that he dreaded pity more than anything and would always defend himself against it with flippancy.

'You don't like me to sympathise, do you?' she said, greatly daring.

He looked amazed. 'Why should you sympathise when all my troubles are of my own making?'

She wanted to discuss his two marriages, to find out why he had left Deborah for Judy, and what had gone wrong there too.

'I'm just not a monogamous person,' he said, 'as you must have noticed by now.' And he smiled to take the sting out of the words.

'But what were they like?' she persisted. 'What *are* they like? Are they very different?'

'I'm not sure I know the answer to that,' he said. 'They're probably quite alike, I think I tend to go on making the same mistakes.'

'So do I,' she said bitterly.

'Well, I can't discuss you with them,' he said, 'so it hardly seems fair to discuss them with you.'

When she finally told him about the seaside plan, he looked surprised for a moment, then said quickly, 'How nice, you'll enjoy that.'

She took a deep breath. 'Will you be able to come down?'

'I'll try.'

'That sounds like no.'

He smiled again. 'Don't be so pessimistic.'

She wondered if he had noticed that for the first time it would be her leaving him, instead of the other way round, no longer waiting by the phone to be slotted into his life. If he wanted to see her this summer he would have to make the effort, travel, tell lies.

'Come on,' he said, glancing at his watch. 'Let's go to bed.'

So now she sat with Penny on her new balcony, wearing dark glasses against the sparkling of the sun on the water, gazing at the shimmering sails of the boats and the windsurfers. Already London seemed remote. She felt she had stepped back into the past: the little seaside town was small and quiet, even when, as now, it was full of visitors. Life was conducted at a different pace here. People smiled at you in streets and cafés; shopkeepers let you exchange things without a receipt. You could sit outside eating fish and chips or a cream tea; you could watch children making sandcastles or playing with seaweed on the beach and dream of your own childhood. The shops were full of cheap sundresses and comfortable sandals; old ladies wandered about together window-shopping, or sat in deckchairs on the promenade wearing white cardigans and sensible shoes. It was the sort of place she might once have hated but now she found it restful and calm. She liked collecting seashells and coloured stones; she enjoyed the muddy sand between her toes and the crunch of the shingle underneath her feet; she revelled in pottering about the antique shops which contained not just furniture and mirrors but amazing collections of bric-à-brac. One day she found a snowstorm paperweight and it reminded her of the relationship with Daniel: no matter how much you shook it up, afterwards it was exactly the same.

Officially she and Penny were meant to be working on Lydia Snake, but so far instead of getting on with the story they had begun, they had amused themselves making a list of titles for other future stories. It was more fun. Lydia Snake at the Seaside. Lydia Snake joins the Circus. Lydia Snake at Boarding School. And – an X certificate version for parents only – Lydia Snake in Soho.

'There's a lot of mileage in this,' Annie said. 'It could go on for ever.'

'That is if it ever gets started.'

'Ah, you've just hit the hidden snag.'

Penny was more obviously pregnant now. It made Annie feel protective, just seeing her like that, with the un-accustomed curve that she herself had been unable to achieve. She had begun to warm to Steve, too, as she saw him more considerate of Penny in her touchingly vulnerable state. He would leap up now to fetch and carry for her in a way he had never done before. Perhaps she had been wrong about him and he was really a nice person after all.

She spent a lot of time with them both, having lunches and drinks and dinners. Sometimes they invited single men specially to meet her but she thought of Daniel and failed to find them attractive. Steve took a keen interest in Lydia Snake and enjoyed coming up with ever more suggestive titles: Lydia Snake's Skin Flick, or Lydia Snake Gets It Off.

One night he drove her home because her car was being serviced. She was feeling totally relaxed with him by now, so the shock was even greater when he put his hand on her knee as he parked outside her flat. 'Aren't you going to invite me in?' he said, like the worst caricature of a leering escort.

'No,' she said inadequately, feeling that to ask him to remove his hand from her knee would turn her too into a caricature, only of offended virtue. Perhaps she could freeze it off by sheer willpower, make him feel so embarrassed that he would remove it of his own accord.

To her horror he took this passivity for encouragement, leaned across and tried to kiss her. Instantly they were locked in a dreadful old-fashioned battle, Annie feeling like an indignant teenager again as she fought not to unclench her teeth. The hand was still on her knee and the other hand seemed to possess a life of its own, darting about into all sorts of places uninvited. Annie stopped pretending to be grown up and tactful: she simply hit him and he reeled backwards with surprise, banging his head on the windscreen. He swore and Annie laughed. She had been right all along about *A Streetcar Named Desire*.

'I'm sorry,' Steve muttered, holding his head in both hands as if to make sure it had not come loose. 'I must have had too much to drink.'

Annie found this a particularly insulting excuse. 'Don't be ridiculous,' she said sharply. 'I wouldn't have let you drive me home if you had.'

'No, that's true. Sorry,' he said again. 'I've always fancied you, okay?'

'That's better,' Annie said. Simple lust was preferable to

alcoholic frenzy any day, she thought. 'Just don't do it again, that's all, it's very embarrassing. And how can you be sure I won't tell Penny? It would serve you right if I did.'

'I assume you wouldn't want to hurt her,' he said simply. 'Any more than I would.'

'Then for God's sake think before you jump on someone again. Penny's friends may not all be as understanding as I am. I'm sorry if you're getting frustrated while she's pregnant, but it won't last for ever.'

She thought she was trying to make allowances for him, to smooth it over, since she would have to go on seeing them both, but he said, sounding surprised, 'Oh, it's not that, she's as randy as ever, bless her heart, it's me, it turns me right off her being like that, I can't think of her that way, know what I mean?'

Something Daniel had said came back to her then, something about children changing everything; and she had replied that not having them changed everything too.

'Yes, I think so,' she said, getting out of the car, 'and I'm going to pretend this never happened.'

'I thought you'd understand,' Steve said through the window. 'You knowing about married men and all that.'

When she got up to the flat she stood for a long time on the balcony, watching the moon making a sharp silver path on the water. She wanted Daniel desperately: to be here, to hug her, to listen, to make love. The worst part was, she did find Steve attractive, not as himself but as a Warren Beatty lookalike. If she had not been in love with Daniel . . . If Penny had not been her friend . . . Yes, she could imagine circumstances in which she might have gone to bed with Steve.

She tried to think about it honestly, without prejudice. Perhaps if you didn't take a sternly moralistic view, there *was* something inherently difficult about watching your girlfriend turn into a wife and then into a mother, when the mother you knew best was your own. In another culture there would have been other wives and concubines lined up to share the strain. Perhaps fifty years of monogamy was too much to expect of anyone.

This is ridiculous, she thought. Here I am actually making excuses for my best friend's nasty husband because he's greedy and self-indulgent and wants a bit on the side. He thinks I'm cheap, fair game, an easy lay because I have a married lover. It's as simple as that.

But it didn't feel simple at all and she was making excuses for herself and Daniel as well as Steve. I can't have it both ways, she told herself. I've been the deceived wife and now I'm the other woman. Who gets the better deal? Do you want quantity or quality? In another culture I might have been actually grateful to fertile Linda Jones for giving my husband a child when I couldn't. I might have seen it as a blessing, letting me off the hook. And if I'm honest I must admit I enjoyed those affairs I had, particularly as I could blame Peter for provoking them.

She remembered that Judy had been Daniel's mistress before she was his wife and wondered which role she preferred. She must know him well. There must be some level, even subconscious, on which she knew that someone else was playing her old part. It would probably always be so. Was that really such an enviable situation?

Oh well, I can't solve it all tonight, she thought, as her mother used to say, only about different subjects, as she poured the cocoa. It was amazing that a casual pass from Steve had conjured up so much introspection. Except that everything made her think of Daniel because he was usually in her mind. She spent so little time actually with him that she had to make up the difference by thinking and talking about him.

She took a quick swig of whisky instead of cocoa and went to bed, soothed by the sound of the waves. But it was a long time before she slept.

In the morning she was busy getting ready for Liz and Jeremy. Usually she saw them separately, so that Jeremy could flirt with her and Liz could talk about Gian-Carlo, but as she hated cooking and they both wanted to see the flat, it seemed sensible to invite them together for once. Besides, she owed Jeremy a good meal for letting her place in London to some rich Americans. Liz had immediately said she'd save petrol and ask for a lift.

While she was waiting for them to arrive, the phone rang and it was Daniel, calling from the golf club. A weekend call was a rare treat and she was overcome by joy.

'D'you want the bad news or the good news?' he asked.

'Both.'

'The bad news is I can't get down to see you this month. I just can't take that much time off. The good news is I could manage a stopover in August when I've taken the children back to Newcastle.'

August. The holiday month. The family month. The desert. Suddenly there was an oasis with palm trees, sparkling fountains, sherbet. She felt an absurdly wide smile spreading across her face.

'Stopover,' she said. 'That means when people actually stay the night. Get into bed and sleep. Have breakfast and conversation. That kind of thing.'

'That's right.' He was smiling too; she could hear it in his voice.

'Could you confirm that in writing?' she said.

The prospect of such delight suffused the day, giving it a warm pink glow, lending new meaning to the words rose-tinted glasses. She found it hard to concentrate on Jeremy and Liz, who finally arrived a bit later than expected, but when she did manage to notice them she thought they seemed a trifle edgy. Perhaps they had found the two-hour journey a strain. Alone with her, Liz had always said Jeremy was nice but dull, and Jeremy had implied that Liz was amusing but rather tarty, so maybe it proved how wise she had been to keep them more or less apart all this time. And yet they looked good together, both tall and thin. Liz was looking particularly well, wearing a cream dress Annie had not seen before, her skin lightly tanned, her hair newly streaked. How lucky Gian-Carlo was, Annie thought.

'Daniel's coming to stay the night in August,' she announced in triumph.

'Big deal,' Liz said. 'It's only taken him three years.'

'It's different for you,' Annie said. 'When Gian-Carlo comes to London he can always stay the night because his wife is back in Milan. You take it for granted. You're spoilt.'

'I don't know about spoilt,' Liz said. 'He's beginning to snore and get a paunch. I think Maria's cooking is finally catching up with him.'

'Isn't Daniel coming down this month as well?' Jeremy asked.

'He can't,' Annie said defensively. 'Two wives and four children take a lot of supporting, you know. Driving down here and back would mean taking a whole day off work. It's hard enough for him when I'm in London, just taking a few hours off.'

'He doesn't deserve you,' said Jeremy.

It was annoying having to defend Daniel when privately she agreed with what they said about him. But it was more annoying to have them criticise him. She was entitled to complain, but they were not supposed to attack, even though she knew they only did it out of concern for her. Nevertheless they had a nice lunch and a stroll on the beach until it came on to rain and they ended up back in the flat reading the Sunday papers and playing Scrabble. The cat seemed greatly taken with them both and kept sitting on them and purring and kneading them with her claws.

'You should get another cat, Annie,' Liz said.

'I know,' Annie said. 'Maybe I will But it's such a cliché, the spinster teacher with her cat.' In her heart she longed for a cat and did not know how she had lived without all that comforting warm fur since Cindy died. 'Anyway, I'm out a lot,' she added, wishing it were true.

When they had gone she rang up Penny to gloat about Daniel, her joyfulness having completely wiped out the memory of Steve's clumsy grope, until he answered the phone. Hearing his voice filled with sudden apprehension brought it all back, and she nearly laughed because he sounded so obviously terrified she was going to report him to Penny. Instead she told Penny about Daniel's impending visit and heard Penny doing her best to sound delighted and not succeeding very well.

'Well, I think it's wonderful,' Annie said sharply.

'Yes, of course it is. I'm really pleased for you, you know I am. It's just – oh, I just wish you could find someone who could really be with you. I'd like you to be as happy as I am.'

There was no answer to that. She didn't feel like ringing anyone else with her news: obviously no one could appreciate it as she did. So she spent the evening vaguely watching television, feeling almost dizzy at the prospect of a night with Daniel. She wondered if she would be able to sleep at all. At times like this, or when she was waiting for him to arrive, her happiness was so overpowering that it made all the deprivation in between seem like nothing. It was a privilege to be allowed to feel so intensely.

She fell asleep in front of the television and was woken at midnight by the phone. It was Liz.

'Annie, I've got to ask you something,' she said, sounding nervous. 'I can't sleep till I do but I don't think you're going to like it. Would you – well, would you mind very much if I married Jeremy?'

Annie, half awake, felt as though she had been kicked in the stomach. 'Jeremy?' she echoed feebly. 'You and Jeremy? But you've always said he's a wimp.'

There was a long sigh from Liz. 'I know,' she said, 'but he *is* awfully nice.'

'D'you think I hadn't noticed?' Annie was suddenly furious. 'Why d'you think I've been going out with him all this time? Has he asked you then? When did all this happen?' A whole plot seemed to be emerging from behind her back.

'Well, I've always liked him,' Liz said. 'You know I have. I mean, we've liked each other. And you don't want him, do you? You've had five years to make up your mind and you've always said no.'

Annie took deep breaths, trying to calm herself. 'Is that what he says?'

'No, but it's true, isn't it?'

'But you don't love him.' She was still making an effort to understand. 'Do you?'

Liz sighed again. 'We get on well. And we'd both like to have children before it's too late. I want to get married, Annie, I can't help it. It's all right for you, you're divorced, but I've never been married and I don't want to sit around here till Gian-Carlo trades me in for a newer model.'

'Well, you don't need my permission.' She was amazed at the anger she felt. No more candle-lit dinners, no more proposals, no more moral support, no more sad eyes gazing at her with hopeless longing. No more Jeremy.

'It needn't make any difference to you,' Liz said as if telepathic. 'You've always said he was like a brother. Well, now he really will be.'

'Why tonight?' Annie demanded. 'What happened tonight? He's known you for five years too. Why should he suddenly ask you to marry him?'

'Oh well,' Liz said reluctantly, 'we got chatting in the car and then I asked him in and, well, you know, one thing led to another.'

'You went to bed with him.'

'Well, yes.'

'And?'

'Well, he wasn't nearly as bad as you made out. Maybe it's because he's not in love with me. Maybe he's been practising on someone else. Anyway. It was all right.'

All right. This from someone who had always implied that Gian-Carlo was in the Olympic gold medal class.

'Anyway,' Liz added, 'sex isn't everything. I'm lonely, Annie. I want someone of my own, and he's kind, he won't treat me badly.'

'I hope you'll be very happy.'

'Don't be like that.'

'No, I mean it. I really do. I'm just . . . surprised.'

Silence. Expensive telephone minutes ticking away.

'What about Gian-Carlo?' Annie asked suddenly.

'Well, I said I'd give him up, of course.'

'Will you?'

'How do I know till I do it?'

Annie was still in shock, as if they had finally proved that the earth was flat and shown her the evidence.

'I'm being honest with you,' Liz said. 'You can wreck the whole thing if you want to.'

'No, I can't,' Annie said. 'And I don't want to.'

'Please forgive me,' Liz said. 'Jeremy's going to ring you tomorrow. He's gone home to tell his mother.'

Next day there was a large bunch of flowers from Jeremy with no message. But he didn't phone.

August was hot, with sudden bursts of rain. She sat on the balcony or lay on the beach, trying to get brown for Daniel. Once or twice she even swam in the icy water. One night there was an electric storm and she stood at her living-room window watching it, while the cat cowered under the sofa and she tried to persuade her that storms were fun. Great jagged forks of lightning crackled across the sky beyond the sea. It was an awesome sight, quite different from a storm in town. She felt she had dropped out of London life and was now a part of some elemental world. Would Daniel enjoy seeing her in this new environment? There was so much she didn't know about him.

She and Penny abandoned all pretence of working on Lydia Snake. Penny was knitting. Various tiny garments in white and yellow, blue and pink, sprang from her needles.

She was keeping her options open. Annie sat and watched her while she talked about how happy she was. It felt odd, seeing Penny so transformed. As the bump grew larger, the Penny she knew seemed to disappear behind it. When Steve joined them he was so polite and considerate that Annie hardly recognised him. She almost wanted to ask him to tease her, so as not to arouse suspicion. She found herself wondering if she would have been like Penny, had she ever got pregnant by Peter.

Jeremy wrote an embarrassed letter from which she gathered that he and Liz had been seeing each other ever since Annie left town. It made more sense, it made the decision less sudden, but she wondered why Liz had not told her, when she was bound to find out. He implied he was marrying Liz because she reminded him of Annie. It didn't sound very complimentary to Liz but perhaps he was trying to be tactful. Annie was shaken because she had never thought that she and Liz were alike at all, except in the most superficial way. She wondered what sort of a marriage it would be, if Jeremy saw Liz as a substitute, a sort of consolation prize, and Liz was still secretly involved with Gian-Carlo. She felt shocked: it was against all her romantic principles. But perhaps she was wrong and they would be all the happier for having low expectations. After all, she and Daniel had both pursued grand passions and ended up getting divorced. Perhaps if the flames never burnt very high, they would never burn out either. Liz and Jeremy might be able to simmer away together into contented old age. It didn't sound very exciting, but it might be cosy.

As the day of Daniel's visit approached, she caught herself wishing that it could be forever postponed, like jam tomorrow, so that she might have the pleasure of looking forward to it indefinitely. She hated to think that the time would actually come and therefore pass. And yet she was also impatient to the point of desperation. She smiled to herself, thinking that her students would hardly recognise this crazy, obsessive person. They only saw her as someone cool and confident, efficient in her work, friendly and distant.

Daniel arrived about seven. He looked very tired, having driven from Cornwall to Newcastle with two children, stayed the night, had a row with Deborah, and driven from Newcastle to Sussex. When he got home he would probably have a row with Judy, if they both had the energy. The two sets of children had all continued to loathe each other and had spent the entire holiday fighting. He had also paid brief visits to widowed parents and in-laws, and dug gardens, painted walls, laid carpets. He told her all this in a casual, throw-away style, as if it was a joke, and she hugged him, knowing better than to sympathise. He seldom hugged her first, but always responded when she hugged him. He seemed to need her to make the first move. Now when she put her arms round him he looked down at her, smiling fondly; he smelt the same as ever, and felt just as solid. It was like hugging a tree or a bear. Sometimes she thought that if he were not furry and heavily built with a special smell, none of this would have happened. She undid his shirt buttons and kissed his fur, breathing in the scent, which did not remind her of anything but him. In the dark or blindfolded, she would have recognised him.

'You feel good,' she told him inadequately. 'And you smell wonderful.'

'So do you.'

They kissed. It was extraordinary to see him in this new space, in the flat overlooking the sea, doing ordinary things he had never done before with her, like unpacking his overnight bag. She looked tenderly at the items as they appeared: toothbrush, electric razor, a clean shirt, a bottle of champagne. They had a drink and went to bed, making love quickly because it had been so long since they were together. She was so moved at having him inside her again that she cried. Our longest separation yet, she thought, but did not say so, in case it sounded like a reproach. Afterwards, the cat came to join them, purring and sniffing the sheets.

She had prepared a feast, but he said they could have it for lunch: he wanted to take her out for dinner. Crossing the road, he held her back from the traffic and she said lightly yet with an undercurrent of bitterness, thinking of all the time she had spent without him, 'Oh, you could always replace me.'

'I don't think I could,' he said. 'You're unique.'

He so seldom paid her compliments that she was silent with surprise and did not dare ask him to elaborate in case he took refuge in jokes and told her that surely everyone was unique.

Over dinner she told him about Jeremy and Liz, Penny and Steve, presenting each story as a joke. She felt he needed light relief. It occurred to her, not for the first time, that this was her role in his life: to provide amusement, warmth, acceptance, just as his role in her life was to be a focus for all her intense feelings. It was a strange bargain and it made her feel rather sad, but she did not want to spoil their time together with any negative emotion. And yet this was a unique opportunity: at last they had time to talk.

'Why don't we do this more often?' she ventured to say, as she ate the delicious food. 'Or is that a silly question?'

'Because it would make waves,' he said. 'I lost my children that way. I can't go through all that again. Two weekends a month and a summer holiday aren't the same thing at all. I spend all my time trying to mend fences.'

'So I've just got to put up with it,' she said.

'Only if you want to.'

'Obviously I do.'

'I don't take you for granted, if that's what you mean.'

Well, there it was, she thought. You could ask a man to leave his wife, perhaps, but you couldn't ask him to leave his children. She agreed with him really. Two sets of abandoned children would be unbearable. She would never survive the guilt, and neither would he.

'But we never make plans,' she said. 'And I find you very hard to talk to.'

'I just live from day to day,' he said, 'and I've never found talking helps. We're talking now, aren't we? But it doesn't change anything.'

'I only feel all right when we're touching,' she said.

'Then let's touch some more.'

'But you never say anything reassuring or encouraging or . . .' She gave up and simply held his hand under the table.

'What's the point when I've got nothing to offer you?' he said.

Outside the restaurant the sea sucked at the pebbles, drew itself back, then sprang at them again.

He paid the bill and they went back to the flat, looked at the moon, finished the champagne and went to bed. He warned her to kick him if he snored and she promised she would, but he didn't snore, just breathed heavily on his back, and then, turning with a sudden movement on to his side, slept so silently that he might have been dead. She curled round him, breathing in the smell of his skin, and feeling, much against her will, sorry for him as well as sorry for herself. It was hopeless. His burdens hung around him like the panniers on a donkey, preventing anyone from getting really close to him. There simply wasn't enough time or energy for all he had to do. She remembered how once she had watched him walking down the road to her flat and he had looked like a man with all the troubles of the world on his shoulders; yet the moment she opened the door he had been flippant and bright as usual. I've either got to accept this the way it is, she told herself, or get out: there are no other options.

She fought against sleep, wanting to extend the luxury of spending the night with him, just as she had wanted to postpone his arrival, but eventually sleep overcame her. She woke in the night several times, though, feeling him move restlessly beside her. She was so unused to sleeping with anyone that at first in her semi-conscious state she thought she was back in the days of her marriage and panic engulfed her until she remembered that it was Daniel.

In the morning it felt strange, seeing each other tousled and bleary for the first time. They made love differently; already it seemed more domestic. She found she was exhausted from all the excitement, the disturbed night, and slightly hungover from the champagne: it was almost as though she had jet lag. Her body was out of sync and her mind was buzzing.

They had breakfast on the balcony and the sea soothed her as it always did. They compared suntans in the harsh daylight. They watched the bright sails skimming across the water and occasionally plunging in.

'What time d'you have to leave?' she asked.

'After lunch.'

They went back to bed and made love as if they might never meet again. As usual it felt so right that while it lasted she did not care that they hardly talked and seldom met. They were in another world where they could communicate through their skin.

Around noon she got up and served the feast she had prepared the previous day. It was raining by now so they had to eat indoors. The lovely food stuck in her throat and he had to eat most of it. All she felt now was time passing like an express train, wrenching them apart. It was almost a relief when he said he had to go; she could not bear much more waiting.

When he kissed her goodbye he held her face in his hands as if he really cared about her.

'See you soon,' he said, as he always did, although it was seldom true.

'Take care,' she said as usual.

After he had gone she curled up in their scented sheets and slept and slept.

She lived on her memories far into September, replaying their time together like an old film. She felt curiously content. It occurred to her that Daniel was a consolation prize as much as Jeremy had been, that each represented half a relationship, that neither could change, that both were fixed like the scene in the snowstorm paperweight. She was safe. Involved and yet detached. She could not be hurt again as she had been with Peter. Perhaps in her heart she preferred it that way. Perhaps she wasn't ready yet to take such enormous risks again. The realisation calmed her. It was reassuring to decide that she wasn't the masochistic idiot her friends seemed to think, but a sensible grown-up woman in charge of her life, taking care of herself as best she could.

Time passed and Daniel didn't ring, but she was unworried. He had never been good at telephoning. She read books and prepared lectures and walked on the beach. The week before she was due to go home she rang the office and they said he was sick. That alarmed her. One of her worst fantasies had always been that he would die in an accident and no one would tell her because they did not know she existed.

The call came the same night and she knew at once something was wrong. He had never before rung her so late.

'Hullo,' he said, sounding remote and self-contained. 'Sorry I haven't been in touch.'

'Are you all right? I phoned the office and they told me you were ill.'

He managed to laugh. 'Well, I'm not at my best. Judy's left me.'

She was too shocked to speak. It was the one thing she had never expected.

'Just took the kids and left me a note.'

She said slowly, 'I can't believe it.'

'Why are you surprised? I'm not. I told you three years ago she knew she'd made a mistake. She's just been biding her time.' But he sounded shell-shocked all the same.

Daniel alone. It was unthinkable. It changed everything. 'I'm sorry,' she said. 'I don't know what to say.'

'When are you coming back?'

'Next week.'

'Well, don't be too surprised if you find me on your doorstep with a suitcase.'

She was silent, shocked to find that her strongest emotion was terror. Underneath the terror was a mixture of excitement and rage.

'Don't panic,' he said, hearing her silence. 'That was a joke.'

'Maybe she'll come back.' It didn't sound like a joke.

'I rather doubt it,' he said. 'She's got somebody else.'

'I can't believe it.'

'Why not? I told you I'm a walking disaster. She's only doing to me what I did to Deborah. It's almost funny, isn't it?'

'Not really,' she said gently.

'I've never lived alone,' he said. 'It'll be an education, won't it?'

Penny actually laughed when Annie broke the news. 'You know the old saying, "Be careful what you wish for, because you may get it." '

'But I'd just decided I like it the way it is,' Annie said, aghast. 'It's all I can handle.'

'The great editor in the sky must be working to rule,' Penny said. 'For three years you've been telling her you want more of Daniel. Obviously your new message hasn't reached her yet.'

'But we hardly know each other,' Annie said. 'Except in bed.'

'Well, now's your chance. I think it's wonderful.'

'But . . . two broken marriages . . . four children to visit . . . what's he going to be like? Where does that leave me?'

'It's make or break time,' said Penny. 'Real life has caught up with you.'

Annie drove back to the flat in a daze. In less than three months at the seaside, everything had changed: Liz and Jeremy, Penny and Steve, and now herself and Daniel. It could be the end of something or it could be the start of a whole new life. But it could never be the same again.

Jean was due back in the morning. Annie fed the cat and watered the plants for the last time, then stood on the balcony watching the sea.

It was time to go back to the city.

# Signs of the Times

Autumn always seems melancholy to Jo, its falling leaves and dark afternoons and relentless slide towards Christmas, with Bonfire Night thrown in as a rather desperate attempt to cheer everyone up. It's even worse near the end of a decade, she thinks, forcing her to review more than the past year. She says to Madelyn, 'I've decided I don't like the eighties.'

'Never mind,' says Madelyn, 'they're nearly over.'

The sisters are sitting over the remnants of lunch, finishing the last of the wine, having a forbidden cigarette.

'That's like saying a hurricane's nearly over,' says Jo. 'What about the damage?'

She treasures these Saturdays alone with Madelyn, just the two of them. Because she has known Madelyn all her life, they could be any age when they are together. And because their lives are so different, together they make up a whole extra person, a phantom third, who just might be able to solve problems too much for either of them separately. She doesn't even resent the fact, as she did in her teens, that Madelyn has cornered the market in beauty. They both have the family face, but on Madelyn it looks better. She has a certain bony elegance, while Jo has somehow managed to get both wrinkled and flabby. The same red hair on Jo looks gingery; on Madelyn it has the sheen of copper. Having children must be ageing, Jo decides.

'Are you thinking of Martin?' Madelyn asks.

'I suppose.'

Madelyn puts her hand over Jo's hand and squeezes it. 'He'll be all right.'

But it isn't easy to have a brother who lives with someone who is HIV positive. They've always known he's gay, well, almost as long as he's known himself. Since their teens, anyway. Because it was Martin, it was easy to accept, like different tastes in music or clothes; it didn't seem like something you read about in the newspapers, homosexuality, that big word, that could be a problem or a natural choice – however you preferred to see it. It was just Martin being himself. Until AIDS.

He told Madelyn first, about Simon having the virus. That still rankles a bit, but Jo tells herself it's only to be expected, he and Madelyn have always been specially close, probably something to do with being near in age. Their little brother. Mum's afterthought. Squeezed in and out just as the gates were closing.

'He wants to have the test,' Madelyn says.

Jo shivers. Until he has it, they can all pretend this isn't really happening. 'Did he ask you to tell me that?'

Madelyn ignores this. 'If it's positive then at least he and Simon are in the same boat. And if it's negative we can all stop worrying. And they'd know if they have to have safe sex or not.'

Jo still doesn't really want to think about what gay men do in bed. If that's old-fashioned of her, she thinks, well, she can't help it. She just knows she loves Martin and she doesn't want him to die. 'I thought they were supposed to anyway,' she says.

'Well, obviously if one's okay and the other isn't. But if they've both got it . . .' Madelyn shrugs.

'I thought it could still make it worse . . . there are different viruses or something.' She's read all she can on the subject but still it gets jumbled up in her mind so that she can't retain the information, as if anxiety has frozen her memory.

'I don't really know,' Madelyn says. 'I don't think they do either.'

She doesn't just mean Martin and Simon. She means the doctors too, the whole medical world, baffled by this new plague, constantly changing their minds and issuing different advice as fresh facts come to light. They are really saying they can't help and they're just as terrified as we are. We're on our own out here, Jo thinks.

'No, they don't,' she says bitterly.

'They'll find a cure eventually,' Madelyn says, perhaps to convince herself as well as Jo. 'They're bound to.'

The sisters both wonder silently whether this is true and even if it is, whether it will be in time. Jo is shocked to find herself wanting Martin, if healthy, to leave Simon, to run away, to save himself while he can. But she knows he won't. She likes Simon; she doesn't want him to die either. But he isn't family.

'The last time I saw them,' she says to Madelyn, 'Simon was in bed with a cold. I hadn't seen him for a while and he was so thin, I thought he was dying.'

'I know,' Madelyn says. 'I saw him like that too. He looked terrible, didn't he? But he's okay again now. You must go round and see him looking better.'

'Yes, I must.' Jo can't get the gaunt, shrunken vision out of her head. And that was just with a bad cold. God forbid Martin should ever look like that.

'Jo, I've got something to tell you,' Madelyn says suddenly. Her voice is odd, tense, highly charged.

'What?' says Jo. 'I can't stand any more shocks.'

'Not even a nice one?' Madelyn looks at her pleadingly. 'I've been trying to tell you all day.' And she rushes on, as if Jo might prevent her: 'I think I may be pregnant.'

'Oh, God, Maddy.' Jo doesn't know what to say.

'It's good news, if I am,' Madelyn says. 'Really it is. We've got it all worked out. There's no way Robert can leave Sarah and I wouldn't respect him much if he did, but

there's a crèche at the office and we can be together
Monday to Friday. It'll be just like now, only better.'

Madelyn has been in love with her boss for a long time
or, as she prefers to put it, a hundred years. Jo has hoped
and prayed she'd meet someone single and get married
instead of wasting her life on somebody who goes home
every weekend to his children and his wife, who has
multiple sclerosis. The situation is a mess and Madelyn
deserves better. But she loves Robert, who seems to Jo
amazingly ordinary, and she is thirty-nine. Her biological
clock is ticking away; Jo understands that. She just can't
bear the thought of Madelyn having only half a life and
Robert having two.

It seems only last week that she and Madelyn were
young and free, wearing long dresses in the daytime and
taking the Pill, burning joss sticks and smoking pot,
listening to the Beatles and the Rolling Stones. Now the
sixties are old hat and being pilloried in the media for
causing the moral decline of the nation. Her own children,
of course, can't imagine that she and Madelyn were ever
young.

Madelyn is watching her with a hopeful face. 'Go on,'
she says. 'Give me your good housekeeping seal of
approval.'

'Oh . . .' Jo says, blinking rapidly. 'Of course I do. You
know I do.'

'Mad by name and mad by nature,' says Madelyn
cheerfully. 'Don't tell the others till I'm sure.'

Jo thinks about the others on her way home. She won't
be tempted to tell them: she is used to keeping Madelyn's
secrets since childhood. She feels ashamed to be missing
her parents, though, as if she ought to be too grown up to
mind them running off to Portugal. That's how she thinks
of them, like naughty children playing truant or, worse,
like rats deserting a sinking ship, although the economy is
supposed to be much improved, she reads. Her parents
have taken against the government in a very personal way

and decided to leave the country as if on a matter of principle, though Jo thinks it also has something to do with the need for sunshine to warm their old bones and cheap wine to cheer them up. She feels older than her parents now, fighting a lonely rearguard action; she needs them to give her moral support. Before they left they switched channels every time there was a TV commercial about AIDS, sometimes with Martin in the room, going with one swift click from tombstones to 'Come Dancing', and Jo wanted to scream at them, He's your son, don't you care, can't you see what's happening?

'You must come and stay with us,' they said to the room at large, and then to Martin, 'Bring your friend.' Perhaps that was enough; Martin thought it was. But Jo was angry. She felt they were leaving her to face the problem for them. 'If they don't know already I can't tell them now,' Martin said. 'They don't even know I'm gay, for God's sake. It'd be like you saying you're getting divorced if they didn't even know you were married.' And he laughed, the way he always did about important things.

Jo is still surprised that her private life could be invaded by politics, something she has always thought of as being rather dull and belonging to the newspapers. After years of the whole family being vaguely Liberal, she has found herself with Socialist parents going to live abroad and feeling self-righteous about it, while her daughter has turned into a passionate Conservative since her boyfriend managed to become a yuppie. Jo still can't understand exactly what it is Dave does, though Debbie, flushed with pride, has often tried to explain it to her. All Jo can take in is that Dave, who used to run a market stall, now has something to do with futures trading that involves vast sums of money and a lot of shouting and telephoning and computer screens, and allows him to run a BMW, although he is only twenty-five years old. It seems incomprehensible to Jo; the job is so far removed from her experience that he might as well have become an astronaut.

But she is pleased for Dave, who is a nice boy, and happy for Debbie, who loved him long before he was rich.

She is less pleased at the way her peaceful home has become a battleground. Suddenly she and Matt are ridiculed by children and parents alike for voting for a party that cannot decide what to call itself. Debbie blames her brother for being on the dole; where once she thought him unlucky, she now calls him lazy. If Dave can get rich, then so could Ian, Debbie says. Ian disputes this hotly. Political arguments break out at meals, till Jo can't enjoy the food she's cooked, though her children seem able to eat and argue at the same time.

Matt bans politics at the table. Debbie talks about Dave's new flat in Dockland, the feeling of space, the view of the river from the terrace. She talks about motor racing at weekends, at Brands Hatch or Silverstone, about dinners at restaurants costing £100 for two with wine. Ian kicks her under the table and she lets out a shriek. Matt tells them both to behave themselves. 'I wasn't talking politics, Dad,' says Debbie, looking innocent. The corners of Matt's mouth twitch: Debbie has always been able to get round him. She is a real Daddy's girl. Ian has tears of rage in his eyes as he rushes from the table; Jo feels his pain as if it were her own.

Her parents suggest he should go and stay with them in Portugal for a while. He is sure to find a job more easily there, they say. As a waiter, for instance, in a restaurant run by some English friends of theirs. Ian brightens; Jo thinks it is a terrible idea. 'He could come and work for me in the garage,' Matt says. 'I've told him often enough.' Ian scowls and says that would be charity. Jo doesn't like to ask why help from his grandparents is more acceptable than help from his father: she is afraid of the answer.

Over the next few months, the scene is repeated with variations until it feels to Jo as if her happy home life has gone for ever. 'It's just a phase,' Matt tells her. 'They'll get over it.' Jo loves her children dearly but she thinks they have been having phases and inflicting them on her ever since they were born. Yet she can't bear the idea that one day they won't live with her any more.

Today when she gets home from lunch with Madelyn it is late afternoon and growing dark. Ian lies on the floor watching television with the sound down and a record on the stereo very loud. Jo has to shout over it. 'Dad not home yet?' Ian shakes his head, eyes fixed on the screen, feet waving in the air in time to the beat. 'Where's Debbie?' Jo asks. 'She said she'd start supper.' Ian shrugs. The record stops abruptly and the silence is quite a shock; Ian says, 'Mum, Gran rang up. They've found me a job. Will you tell Dad?'

'Oh, Ian.' She's quite overcome. And why didn't her mother tell her first? How can she steal her son without even asking permission?

'It's all right, Mum. It's a good thing.' His eyes fix on hers, daring her to object. 'You ought to be pleased for me.'

And of course she is. In a way.

Jo puts the stew in the oven and walks down the road to the garage. The air smells of bonfires and mist. She wants to be alone with Matt to tell him the news. All she can see of him is two feet sticking out from under a car he is repairing. Everyone else has gone home and the place is empty and echoing. Matt works harder than ever now he is in business for himself but he loves it; he says being made redundant is the best thing that ever happened to him.

She tells Matt about Ian and he comes out from beneath the car and gives her a big hug. 'It'll be good for him,' he says, 'but it's tough on you, love.' She sinks into the hug, smelling the warm familiar smell of Matt mixed with the garage smells, and lets herself cry a little. Matt kisses her. She says as she said to Madelyn, 'I don't like the eighties.'

'It's change you don't like,' says Matt, holding her.

She feels bereaved, as if Ian has died, and heavy with Madelyn's secret. They walk home together, arms round each other, and she thinks how lucky she is to have Matt when other women are lonely or married to horrible men. She shouldn't complain about anything, she thinks.

'It's all right,' Matt says. 'I'm not changing.'

'But you are,' she says. 'You're getting better all the time.' This reminds them of one of their favourite records twenty years ago and they both smile.

When they get home Ian has gone out to celebrate, leaving a note: 'Mum, I borrowed a fiver, hope that's OK.' Jo screws up the note and throws it away before Matt sees it. She pours them both drinks and checks the progress of the stew while Matt goes upstairs to have a bath. Debbie comes in and says, 'Oh, sorry, Mum, did I forget to turn on the oven? Look, I won't be in to supper, I'm just going to change and then go right out again, okay?'

'Everyone's changing,' Jo says, 'and it's not okay at all.' She tells Debbie about Ian and the job in Portugal and Debbie's face slumps. 'Oh, shit,' she says. 'I hate you using that word,' Jo says, 'and I thought you'd be pleased. You and Ian do nothing but fight these days.'

'I thought he'd be around when I'm not,' Debbie says. Suddenly she looks like Madelyn telling her secret, nervous and proud. 'Look, Mum, I've been waiting for a good moment but there isn't going to be one. Dave wants me to go and live with him. Will you break it to Dad?'

Jo slams the stew back in the oven. 'No, I bloody won't.'

'I do hate you using that word,' Debbie says, hugging her. 'And these aren't really changes, these are things you've known were on the cards for ages, you just don't like getting them both in one day.'

'You're only nineteen,' Jo says, feeling stupid, knowing they can't stop her, thinking how upset Matt will be.

'You were only nineteen when you married Dad,' Debbie says, as Jo knew she would.

'But you're not getting married.'

'We might. Eventually. When we're ready to have kids.'

The confidence of youth, Jo thinks, remembering. But she doesn't envy Debbie, she worries about her. Does she realise she is facing a lifetime choosing between condoms and monogamy? That she might end up a single parent? That she is growing up too fast?

'Anyway,' Debbie says, 'you ought to be pleased. You and Dad are like a couple of old love birds most of the time, you should be glad to have the place to yourselves again.' Suddenly she sounds almost jealous.

'I'm not telling him for you, Deb,' Jo says. 'You'll have to tell him yourself.'

'I'll get Dave to tell him,' says Debbie. 'Man to man and all that.'

'Try getting Dave to ask him,' Jo says. 'That might go down better.'

'Oh, Mum,' says Debbie, kissing her. 'You're so tactful.'

The week passes slowly at her dull office, but she needs the money and the people are nice. Next Saturday when she goes for lunch with Madelyn, wanting to be soothed, Martin is there and sudden panic ices over her spine.

'It's all right,' Martin says, and she knows he means just the opposite. He smiles reassuringly at her while his eyes look serious. Madelyn puts her arm round him as if to protect him. Jo feels they are all like children trying to face up to a new school, trying not to look scared.

'He's had the test,' Madelyn says, 'and it was positive.'

What a family we are, Jo thinks. We all have to be postmen for each other. She feels herself starting to cry as she looks at Martin, but she isn't surprised or shocked: it's as if she's always known this is how it would be.

'I'm not dying, Jo,' Martin says. 'I'm living with it. There's a big difference. I may never get it and even if I do, it doesn't mean I'll die.'

They have lunch and she tries to believe him.

'And you mustn't blame Simon,' he says, reading her thoughts. 'It may have been me who gave it to him.'

Jo knows this is true but she blames Simon anyway.

They eat in silence and she gazes at her little brother and thinks how cruel it is that she can't save him. She runs through his childhood and adolescence in her head as if she were using fast forward on the video.

'My test was positive too,' Madelyn says softly.

They both look at her and smile. Madelyn hugs her stomach and smiles back. Jo feels a sense of affirmation, a pledge of hope. Something to hang on to, a bit of the future. Madelyn's child, to be born in the next decade. Life going on, no matter what, against all odds. They hold hands, the three of them, thinking of the fourth.

'Oh, Madelyn,' she says, 'I'm so glad.'

'Isn't she clever?' Martin says lovingly.

'Martin for a boy and Joanna for a girl, I thought,' says Madelyn, looking pleased with herself.

Jo finishes her wine. Suddenly she can't wait to get home and tell Matt, face to face. And to hold him very close.

# *Casualties*

Neil rings her up to invite her to his wedding. Janis hears jubilation in his voice, clearly telling her that someone else wants him even though she doesn't. He and Sandra will be very pleased if she can be there. Janis congratulates him in what she hopes are warm, neutral tones, more like an old friend with whom he had lost touch than an ex-wife. She says it is nice of him to ask her and she will let him know. She needs time to think.

After she puts the phone down she checks herself, as if she had been involved in a road accident, and finds to her relief only surprise, even a bruise of envy, but no actual damage. She monitors herself precisely and she notices another emotion creeping in: a sense of relief that perhaps Neil will in future be less likely to ring her up to see how she is getting on without him.

She was never sure how to handle those phone calls. Did Neil want to hear that she was lonely and miserable or that she was happy with a lover? Either way, she always felt he was checking up on her, trying to control her behaviour, the way he had done when they were married, seeing if she was still available. She always feared there was the dreadful possibility that since neither of them had remarried he might ask her to try again and refusal would offend, like asking for credit in the corner shop. She has never found it easy to say no to Neil. Does that mean she has to go to his wedding?

She pours herself a large drink and remembers the party.

She finds she has not forgiven Neil for that: her resentment is still fresh. In those days it was called wife-swapping; later it became known as swinging or, as now, recreational sex. She thinks the original title the most honest because it suggests that wives are commodities to be bartered and exchanged, rather like cigarette cards or marbles in the hands of small boys.

She remembers urging Neil to have an affair, if that was what he wanted. She might want to have one herself one day. If you are both teenage virgins when you get married, it is galling to wake up ten years later and find that the whole sexual revolution has passed you by. But Neil says no, he doesn't want to have an affair, that is the whole point. 'I want to watch you with someone else,' he says.

Janis is chilled by this remark. (Jan knows it is a common male fantasy, good for reviving flagging interest. Jan knows a lot of things that Janis never knew.) She feels as if she has been riding along in a sledge, wrapped warmly in a nice fur rug, and he has suddenly taken her out and thrown her to the wolves howling behind them. She has never even kissed another man with her mouth open. She remembers a time when Neil used to stop her reading sexy books. She remembers being so in love she could hardly bear to turn over and go to sleep. She remembers saying, 'Oh King, live for ever,' to Neil when they made love on their honeymoon. Obviously things have changed while she was not paying attention.

She tells Neil she doesn't want to go to the party but he can go without her, with her blessing. He is not pleased. Apparently that won't do at all. It is for couples only.

Neil sulks. He sulks powerfully, having had plenty of practice and being temperamentally gifted at it. His sulking pervades the house like dark swirling fog. Janis is frightened of it. What if the Neil she knows and loves never reappears? She tries to think of the party as a trip to Australia. Perhaps if Neil goes there once he won't actually want to emigrate, whereas if she won't let him go there at all, he will blame her for ever. If only she didn't have to go with him.

(Jan wonders why Janis didn't just say no and the hell with the consequences. Simple. Jan thinks Janis was a wimp. Her psychiatrist thinks she secretly wanted to go and put all the responsibility on to Neil. Maybe he's right. He calls her Jan because that is what she calls herself these days: she thinks Janis has a childish, petulant sound.)

Neil tells Janis the party will make her less inhibited, improve their sex life. He says it's not fair that she can have more orgasms than he can. Janis says it's not her fault that she has a clitoris and he doesn't. But she knows it's her fault that she earns more than he does (they both work in advertising but she has been promoted) and her fault that she doesn't want to have a baby yet. She doesn't actually think she is inhibited. But admittedly she doesn't like it when he ties her up and pushes objects inside her, saying he wants to observe her reactions without being involved. And admittedly she doesn't like it when he makes her tie him up and toss him off for half an hour or so. If that means she is inhibited, then she definitely is. But she supposes there has to be give and take in every marriage. As she sits there, stopping and starting, looking at her watch to be sure she makes it last long enough, or he'll be angry, she is strongly tempted to leave him there, blindfolded and spread-eagled, and go to the pictures. She feels powerful and invisible, like God. She feels bad-tempered and silly. If she were doing all this for a stranger, she thinks, she would get paid. If they loved each other enough, perhaps she'd be happy to do it. Or he wouldn't ask her to. Whichever. She isn't sure if it's the activity he likes or the fact that she doesn't like it. She thinks they need psychiatric help.

They go the party. Janis can't hold out against all the sulking or maybe she really wants to go. She doesn't know her own motives but she knows it is easier to agree. She buys a new pink dress and puts fake tan on her legs. After

all, she will be taking her clothes off in a room full of
strangers. In the shop she suddenly wants to tell the sales
girl why she is buying the dress but of course she doesn't.
She is frightened that the party will be full of fat ugly
people who will laugh at her and be nasty to her, maybe
even spit on her, but when she says this to Neil he tells her
not to be silly.

The party is held in a Kensington basement. They are
both very nervous when they arrive. There are four other
couples, all in their twenties and thirties: the host Michel
and his wife Francoise, a woman called Sheena with long
dark hair and her husband Rob, who looks like Rupert
Brooke, a Welsh dentist called Evan and his blonde
mistress Margie, and another couple whose names Janis
can't remember because they are so plain and she is
already getting drunk. Everyone sits around drinking and
chatting and there is dancing; later they play strip poker. It
is all very civilised: everyone is clean and well spoken.
Janis fancies Evan: he is short, dark, and has a wicked
smile. She has never fancied anyone but Neil before and it
shakes her. She is also terribly worried about the plain
couple, that no one will fancy them and they will be
wallflowers, as if at an ordinary dance.

Eventually everyone is naked, dancing, touching, drunk.
It is odd seeing people's clothes come off and shedding her
own: the nakedness goes through various stages of
seeming exciting, absurd, embarrassing, and finally natural.
Janis is past caring what happens. She can't tell any more
whether it is daring and erotic or silly and sad. They have a
choice of staying in the living-room for group sex or going
into the bedroom to be private. She goes into the bedroom
with Rob because he has a kind face, and he kisses her and
strokes her but he has no erection and she feels terribly
sorry for him and both relieved and disappointed for
herself. How awful to be a man, a victim of such an unreli-
able mechanism. She hasn't given it much thought before: it
has never happened to Neil in all their years together.

Janis and Rob stay in the bedroom for quite a while, just kissing and cuddling in the dark. They don't talk much. Janis thinks they are both nervous and glad to be with each other, almost hiding from the rest of the party. It's a bit like the first day at school, the same sense of relief when you find someone to sit next to in class, or make a little friend in the playground. She likes him, and he is very attractive; she is sorry he can't make love to her.

Eventually she goes back into the big room with Rob and finds Michel having sex with Sheena. She has never watched people having sex before and she has to admit it excites her, the movements, the sounds. It looks comic, aggressive, beautiful, all at once. There is the curious thrill of seeing a private act done in public.

Neil goes into the bedroom with Francoise, who has very big tits. Oh well. Janis holds hands with Rob and watches Evan having sex with Sheena now that Michel is having sex with Margie. Janis wonders how Rob feels, watching Sheena with another man. Is that why he came to the party, to see his wife with someone else? Or is he, like Janis, here against his will? Do men get bullied into these things too? Sheena seems to be very popular and she comes very noisily, like someone in a film. The plain couple are in a corner glumly having sex with each other; Janis was right to fear that no one else would fancy them. But she feels someone should have made the effort, to be polite. Or maybe they are happy exhibitionists and she has no need to worry. Or maybe she has missed a lot of group activity while she was in the bedroom with Rob.

No one else offers to have sex with her or Rob, just as well really, she thinks, so they roll around together for a while in a friendly way near the others and Evan kisses Janis while she is underneath Rob and he is still on top of Sheena. 'Isn't she lovely?' he says, which sounds encouraging, although she doesn't suppose he has the energy to fit her in now and she keeps wondering how Neil and Francoise are getting on in the other room. But she

feels warmed by his approval nevertheless. She is so drunk
that her thoughts are coming through very slowly and it
only now occurs to her that it is odd of Neil to go off into
the other room when he had said he wanted to watch her
with someone else. She is beginning to get a headache too.
But she feels very friendly towards everyone.

(Jan is cross with Janis that she can't remember more
details; her psychiatrist tells her she has suppressed them,
but Jan puts it down to all the alcohol. Looking back, she
can't understand why they weren't all smoking joints
instead. And she envies them their Pill freedom. If it was
happening now they would all have to use condoms, not
the same thing at all.)

Eventually Neil and Francoise come back, but she can't
tell from their faces how it went. People start getting
dressed and Michel makes coffee, like an ordinary host. It
is two o'clock in the morning; the party is breaking up like
any normal party. Sheena says she and Rob must get home
to relieve the babysitter. Janis admires Sheena's long dark
hair and Sheena says her five-year-old daughter holds it up
for her when she goes to the loo. Michel invites Janis and
Neil for lunch with him and Francoise later in the week
and Janis hears herself saying yes.

She and Neil go home, too drunk to drive but driving
nevertheless. They don't talk much; they are very tired. She
wants to ask him how he got on with Francoise but
something stops her. She keeps thinking that now they are
on opposite sides of the fence. When they get home they go
straight to bed and they are so tired and drunk that they
fall asleep instantly.

In the morning she wakes with a colossal headache and
goes out to get the papers while Neil is still asleep. A lorry
driver whistles at her and for the first time in her life she
feels only flattery and exhilaration, instead of em-
barrassment or annoyance. The world looks different to
her. There are other men out there who fancy her, well, she
has always known that, but now she knows she can fancy

them back, and that is a big surprise. More than that: a revelation. It changes everything. She had always thought she would never fancy anyone but Neil, because she loves him. And last night she fancied three other men. Three. Now that he has given her permission, who knows how many other men she may fancy? She understands the split between sex and love at last: so this is what they mean. It's really very simple.

She goes home with the papers, feeling light-hearted despite her cracking, crashing headache. She wakes Neil with coffee. Only then does she discover he feels deeply depressed, humiliated. He failed to make love to Francoise last night. Or to put it another way, he failed to have sex with her. Or to put it yet another way, he was impotent.

Janis can see from his face that this is a big disaster. She tries to cheer him up by telling him that Rob failed too, so they are still equal, as it were. He looks marginally cheered up but stays in bed all day reading the papers while Janis runs up and down stairs with trays of food. To her surprise, all the men from the party ring up wanting to arrange to see her and Neil again. She relays this information to Neil, still in bed, but he tells her to say no to them. He is writing poetry now, in free verse, all about the party; Janis sits on the edge of the bed and reads it. Some of it is rather good, although he has never written poetry before. She is aware of feeling resentment at having to say no to all the men.

'I'm sorry,' Neil says, in one of his scary mind-reading moments. 'I know how much you'd like to see Evan again.'

Janis is struck by his calm tone, accepting that their wishes are different but there is no room for debate. She has gone along with his desire to attend the party, now she will surely go along with his desire to retreat. Has she ever gone against him? She runs through her memory for an occasion: probably not, unless you count the time she bought a cheap skirt from a street trader in the market, just after they had agreed to economise, in the early days when they were poor. She remembers they had a big row about that. She has obeyed Neil more than she obeyed her father, who didn't want her to get married so young, or to Neil, or perhaps at all.

She wonders if Neil realises they are at a crossroads, that the ground is shifting beneath their feet as in an earthquake, that their whole marriage is changing shape. She stares at him, eating the sandwiches she has made and writing another poem. He looks tired and she feels sorry for him but there is another feeling too, alarming and unfamiliar, like a stranger standing in a corner of the room, someone veiled or cloaked, with head turned away like the figure of Death in *The Seventh Seal*: anger.

'And you'd better tell Michel and Francoise we can't go to lunch,' Neil says.

After a pause Janis shakes her head. She is conscious of defying him and she waits for the sky to fall in. Nothing happens.

'I want to go,' she says.

During the week they argue about it and she surprises herself by pointing out that he made her go to the party so it is not fair to cancel the lunch. She is even more surprised to hear him agree with her and she feels a terrifying sense of power. Now there is no safety anywhere, no boundaries at all, if they can both get their own way by force. Anything can happen. At night they lie tensely back to back without speaking, each waiting for the other to fall asleep.

They go to the lunch. They eat homemade curry, which is very hot, as if by accident, somehow tasting hotter than intended, and Janis wonders if it is meant to be an aphrodisiac. If so, it doesn't work. They talk of this and that, rather awkwardly. Although she is on the Pill, Janis is also wearing her old diaphragm in honour of the occasion. She is very nervous and feels the need for belt and braces: she doesn't think Michel will be impotent like Rob. During lunch she watches Neil's face and wonders if he is frightened of Francoise, who seems extraordinarily relaxed. Perhaps she has done this sort of thing many times. They both compliment her on her curry and she smiles.

After lunch they adjourn to separate rooms, which is a relief but still makes Janis wonder why they could not have just gone off and had separate secret affairs in the first place. She has the same feeling of apprehension that she had before her driving test. Michel makes love to her carefully, as if she were a virgin, and as if he had read the same handbook as Neil, doing all the same things with his hands, his tongue, his cock. There must be a standard way to make love, Janis thinks. But he looks and feels and smells different; he is not the same size and shape. She doesn't do anything clever herself, she feels shy, but she responds, she welcomes his sallow muscular energetic body, and she keeps remembering he is foreign. She is crossing a frontier without a passport or visa. She is amazed how easy it all is and wonders why she ever felt frightened. She forgets about Neil in the other room with Francoise, but her last thoughts of him are benevolent, she actually hopes he is having a good time; she relaxes into sex with Michel and she comes before he does, feeling triumphant, as if she has passed an important exam.

Michel is pleased. He smiles down at her and says, 'Oh, you are very good, for an English girl.'

(Jan is disgusted with Janis that she did not hit him for this piece of male chauvinist piggery, but Janis only remembers being amused that he is so French he can't even pay her a compliment without insulting her at the same time. She is too grateful to be angry. He has set her free. Or helped her to free herself. She cannot help seeing him as a benefactor. She strokes his hair.)

The four of them reassemble in the living-room to drink tea. There is polite conversation, but Janis, watching covertly, thinks Francoise looks tense and Neil depressed. She interprets disaster and suddenly she is very fearful.

They leave with insincere promises of future meetings

and on the way home Neil tells her he had another failure and passed the time trying to fix a broken heel on one of Francoise's stilettos. He sounds angry and bitter and humiliated, full of self-disgust, but Janis feels all these emotions are directed at her. Now they are really in different countries and it is meant to be all her fault. Well, she rejects that, amazed at her own strength. It is her fault they went to the lunch but his fault they went to the party. They are quits. She identifies a strong spirit of revenge in herself that is new.

Neil takes to his bed again but this time he doesn't write poetry and Janis doesn't run up and down with trays. To her horror, he gives up his job instead and concentrates full time on being depressed. Janis feels herself to be without compassion; she telephones Evan and meets him for sex in someone else's flat. He is different from Michel, heavier, violent. Janis begins to discover things about herself through his body: perhaps, she thinks, that is what bodies are for. Was that what Neil was trying to tell her? Does he even know? Well, it is too late now. She contemplates all the bodies in the world waiting to reveal her self to her, all the bodies that Neil kept her from until he threw her to them. She is a changed woman now; she has great expectations.

Some time after this she realises she doesn't love him any more. It is a profound shock, like losing a parent or a religion. The divorce when it comes is a mere formality, like burying a corpse that has been frozen for a long time, pending the inquest.

(Jan decides not to go to the wedding. If she cries, they will think she regrets the divorce, and she is inclined to cry at weddings: all that optimism touches her cynical heart. And her current lover points out that she might drink too much and say something tactless. Besides, she doesn't actually want to see Neil again. Instead she sends a telegram saying: 'All the best', and signs it 'Janis'. He wouldn't recognise Jan.)

# *Luke's Women*

When Luke left me for Millie, I wanted to kill her. I
fantasised about putting a petrol bomb through her
letterbox, only I didn't know how to make one and I was
afraid of getting caught. That's always one of the big
problems of revenge. There was also the chance it might
kill Luke and I hadn't come around to that idea yet. He
was too beautiful to hurt, I thought then, and he'd had a
terrible childhood, and I'd always known he was easily
tempted. (Besides, oh, shameful secret thought, he might
yet come back to me, if I played my cards right.) But I'd
expected better things of Millie because she was a woman
and a neighbour and (I'd thought) a friend. The idea of
injuring Millie was terribly attractive.

Instead, I wrote their phone number in all the public
lavatories I could find. I had a lot of fun composing
variations on Miss Stern/French Lessons/Big Stud. Nothing
sexist about me: I believe in equal opportunities. It seemed
a while since I had had fun. Sometimes I got quite obscene
and surprised myself. It gave me a sense of purpose while
the children were at school. As a revenge it's pretty near
perfect: easy, harmless, anonymous, but very annoying.
The beauty of it was, Millie had just moved house, so at
first it looked as if they'd inherited a dubious phone number,
and however much they thought it might be me, they couldn't
prove it. Better yet, even when they changed their phone
number they still had to give it to me because of the children.

Don't let anyone tell you revenge doesn't help. It's very

soothing, like calomine lotion on sunburn, and it stops you feeling small and helpless. You grow to your proper adult size again, like Alice if she'd found the correct 'Drink Me' bottle. Many a night when I still had a pain like an open wound at the thought of Luke and Millie together, I managed to go to sleep with a smile on my face because I knew they were getting calls day and night from a whole bunch of lustful strangers. Better for me than lying awake crying, I thought, which clogs up your nose till you can't breathe and you just know that no one will ever love you again because you're a snuffling, snivelling wreck with puffy eyes, like some old punch-drunk boxer. It was better than being a brave little soldier, too, all frightfully civilised, pretending it was just one of those things and nobody's fault.

Eventually I gave up, of course, but not until I was ready. After two or three changes of number it became too much effort and besides, I was beginning to feel better, going back to nursing, having the occasional lover. But I felt proud of myself. At least I hadn't meekly put up with being kicked in the teeth.

When Luke left Millie for Barbara, she scratched his car. She just went out one night and dragged a rusty nail the whole length of his beautiful new convertible parked outside Barbara's flat. I heard about it all from Luke. We were quite friendly by then. At first we'd had to keep in touch because of the children (plus my absurd fantasy that he might come back to me) and by the time they'd grown up and gone off to college he'd got in the habit of ringing me or dropping in to talk about himself, the way men like to do. When he left Millie, the last splinter of pain came out of my heart and I felt washed clean, vindicated. She was suffering as I had suffered and Luke had proved himself no good to either of us. I laughed when he told me about her revenge. And I thought how much I had missed her over the years. A woman after my own heart, you might say.

Luke sprawled on my sofa and stared at me with that attentive soft-focused look that so many women find beguiling but which really means he hasn't got his contact lenses in.

'Barbara's thrown me out,' he said. 'She's afraid it might be her car next. She thinks I'm a liability.'

'Barbara sounds like a sensible woman,' I said.

Luke wasn't ageing well. He'd put on weight and he was going grey and bald at the same time. Looking at him dispassionately, I thought I'd had the best of him. But there was still the charm and the smile and the look. And he was the girls' father; there'd always be that bond.

'I don't like living on my own,' he said, stroking the back of my neck. 'It's not good for me.'

'Now's your chance to practise what you preach,' I said, removing the hand. 'Aren't you always urging your patients to find inner tranquillity without a partner?'

'That's why I need one,' said Luke. 'To replenish me. I give out so much of myself each day. You know, I really miss family life.'

I thought of all the times he had failed to visit the girls and I had tried to make up excuses for him so they wouldn't be too disappointed.

'You may miss it,' I said, 'but are you really suited to it?'

'I made a mess of it last time,' he said calmly. 'I'd like a chance to get it right.'

The next time I saw Millie in Sainsbury's I smiled at her and we ended up going for a long boozy lunch. Her five years with Luke had aged her, I thought, more than my fifteen had aged me, but perhaps having the girls had kept me young. Millie couldn't have children and Luke had got to her at a time when she was feeling particularly vulnerable because her husband had just died after a long illness. The more we talked and drank, the more forgiving I felt. It was a new sensation, warm and benevolent. I liked it.

'Scratching the car was a masterstroke,' I said. It would be nice to be friends again with a woman who displayed such initiative.

'I wanted to break into the flat and turn all the taps on,' she said miserably, 'but I hadn't the guts.'

'That would have been magnificent. I wanted to burn down your house.'

'Those phone calls were amazing.'

We smiled at each other. It all seemed a long time ago. What a lot of fuss about Luke, I thought, ordering another bottle of wine. How flattering for him.

One thing led to another, the way it does, Time the Great Healer did his usual stuff, and after a while I went to work with Millie in her executive catering business. I'd had enough of the NHS and this was much easier work and far better paid.

We had a lovely secretary called Sophie, who charmed all the clients. Our food was pretty good, as it happens, but I think they'd have eaten lukewarm cardboard if Sophie had delivered it. She was twenty-three, with long legs in short skirts, and tousled dark hair, as if she had just got out of bed; she had big dark eyes, and a large mouth with well-developed lips, as if she had been practising French all her life, though her accent was pure Sloane. She was punctual, her typing was good, she put a smile in her voice on the phone, and she never parked the van on a yellow line. In short, she was a paragon and we adored her. Millie even gave her one of Samantha's kittens. We enjoyed hearing about her various boyfriends in our coffee breaks, too, until one day she came in all starry-eyed and started talking about someone called Luke.

'Surely not *our* Luke?' I said to Millie after Sophie had gone home.

'I'm afraid so. He's got an accountant since he went into private practice and we've been catering for the accountant. It's rotten luck.'

This was serious news. This was incest. If Sophie found

out, horror of horrors, she might be so embarrassed she'd leave. And if she didn't find out, Luke might live happily ever after. A dilemma for all of us.

'I haven't told her yet,' Luke admitted. 'I don't want to put her off me.'

'Thanks a lot, Luke,' I said. 'Are you ashamed of us?'

'I think I'm in love,' said Luke, sounding dreamy and smug.

So for a little while we all colluded to keep Sophie ignorant. But of course it had to come out eventually and when it did her reaction surprised us all. We had reckoned without the habits of Sophie's class. She thought it was funny. Or, to use her exact words, 'a hoot'. It reminded her of a sitcom on television. Apparently Sophie's parents and step-parents had divorced and remarried so many times she thought having an extended family was the natural way to live. To Sophie the fact that we had both loved Luke and remained friends was additional proof that he was the wonderful person she knew him to be. The fact that he had left us belonged to the past. When she met him he was alone and that was all that mattered. She hadn't had to steal him from anyone.

Luke starts talking about marriage and children. I wonder how long it will last this time. Will it be five years, ten years, fifteen years before he does another runner, or is Sophie the true love he seems to think she is? He talks about her tenderly, in poetic phrases, but I have heard it all before, about me, about Millie, about Barbara. I should stop listening. I should tell him to go away. Instead I watch his mouth. Is it possible I am something as ordinary and humiliating as jealous? I don't want him back so why don't I want him to be happy? Am I really thinking of Sophie's welfare and her future as a single parent? Maybe I'm wrong and Luke has actually changed. But I believe a philandering man only comes to rest when he runs out of steam, whichever woman he happens to be with at the time. My father, for instance, stayed with his third wife mainly because he was eighty-two. Luke is only forty-three. He looks to me as if he has a lot of mileage left.

Luke's mouth goes on moving in praise of Sophie. I wonder if I would feel more charitable if I had remarried, if Millie had remarried. I wonder why balding greying middle-aged overweight rich charming selfish men are so much in demand while thin glamorous middle-aged solvent embittered women are not. I think I know but that doesn't mean I have to like it or that nothing can be done about it. Sophie is scarcely older than my daughters. Luke's daughters. They like Sophie but they are startled at the idea of her as their step-mother.

Luke books one of those ritzy package holidays to Barbados. A sort of pre-wedding honeymoon. Sophie looks up catteries in the yellow pages.

'This is a crisis,' I say to Millie. 'Desperate measures are called for.'

So Millie and I park outside Sophie's flat, waiting for the kitten to emerge. Millie has her doubts about the plan and keeps making feeble objections. But I am adamant. A little healthy shared anxiety will be good for Luke and Sophie. It will test their love. Why wait till they reach the labour ward? Why wait till they reach the Caribbean?

The kitten eventually comes out of the cat flap. It's quite big by now, nearly an adult cat, with wonderful black and orange markings. It roams in the garden, teasing us, climbs trees, stalks birds, strolls along the top of the fence, jumps down on to the pavement beside us. Millie tries to grab it but it skitters away from her.

'We shouldn't be doing this,' Millie says.

'Go away, Millie,' I say. 'Go and mind the store. Make sure Sophie doesn't come home early. You're too soft-hearted for this kind of work.'

It takes me several days and a parking ticket to capture the cat, but eventually it gets used to me and makes the mistake of rolling around in the sun and letting me tickle its tummy. I have it in the cat basket so fast it hardly has time to scratch me it's so surprised, and I zoom off home to imprison it in the spare room two floors up where there's no chance of Luke hearing it mewing if he drops in unexpectedly, where it leads an indolent pampered life like a concubine in a harem with me a devoted handmaid bringing it food and milk and litter trays. It miaows a bit but on the whole it accepts the privileges of imprisonment graciously. It sleeps a lot. It plays with ping-pong balls. It rips up the carpet. I get quite fond of it. At night, secure from interruptions, I even let it curl up on my bed.

Tension is mounting, as the newspapers say. Sophie talks about her loss to Millie, who nearly weakens at the sight of her tear-stained face, and Luke talks to me, quite immune to tears. He can't believe that Sophie would cancel a holiday because of a missing cat: it either comes back or it doesn't, regardless of Sophie's whereabouts. Let's be logical about this, he says: if it never returns, God forbid, is Sophie never to go on holiday? How can waiting around for a cat be more important than going away with him? Sophie on the other hand can't believe he would expect her to go away not knowing what has happened to the cat: how could she enjoy herself unsure if Tabitha is alive or dead? What if she came back during the holiday and found nobody there? She might go away for ever. Each is beginning to question the depth of the other's love. They are seeing each other with new eyes.

The holiday is cancelled. The money would not be refundable: the ritzy travel agents don't consider a missing cat sufficient reason for an insurance claim, but Luke of course is well placed for a fake medical certificate so all is well financially. They can always book another holiday. But they don't. Something has changed. Something has been spoilt.

Millie is stricken with guilt. 'We shouldn't have done it,' she says.

'Nonsense,' I say. 'One day she'll be grateful. Did you want Sophie to end up with Luke?'

Millie says no, but we should have let her find out for herself. I say nothing. I release the cat into Sophie's garden and it bolts through the cat flap. Next day Sophie comes to the office with a radiant face.

Time passes. There is a curious atmosphere, too amorphous to dissect, a message in the ether, that somehow Luke and Sophie suspect we had something to do with the cat's disappearance and yet they can't or won't accuse us. It is too improbable, too unseemly. Or perhaps they are embarrassed by their own behaviour. Sophie's manner in the office is reserved; Luke's voice on the telephone is cool.

After a while Luke and Sophie separate. Sophie gives in her notice: she says she is going to live in the country near her assorted relatives. Millie and I feel sad. We know we have come to the end of something important and the office will not be the same without her. Presently we decide perhaps we should not go on in business together. I think I shall take up agency nursing for a change.

More time passes. Difficult time. The girls go to visit Luke. They like his new wife. Apparently she is very pretty and great fun. They go to her twenty-first birthday party and they say the baby is gorgeous. They keep in touch with Sophie, too. They tell me she is very happy; she has married a vet.

Luke doesn't visit me any more. It's probably all for the best.

# *Memento Vitae*

Lionel reminds Naomi of her father: silent, warm, elusive. That is partly why she loves him; she knows that. He is tall and grey and heavy, good to hug, solid as a tree. He smiles down at her when she hugs him and kisses the top of her head. He looks as if he cares about her then, but she wouldn't presume he does. She has never heard him use the word love and she has been careful not to use it herself. But their bodies seem to understand each other.

When they have arranged to meet for lunch she watches from the balcony to see him arrive. The waiting is part of the pleasure. Earlier in the day she has been out to buy smoked salmon and chicken tikka, raspberries and cream. She has never found shopping so erotic before. She is drunk with the knowledge that she is doing all this for him and presently he will be climbing the stairs to her flat and she will be able to touch him. She smiles at strangers as she walks round the shop, gathering up all his favourite things and feeling her body making itself ready for his arrival. It is only just possible to contain such happiness: a few drops more, she feels, and it might spill over into madness.

She hopes he will be late and he often is, giving her more time to look forward to her treat. If he is going to be very late, he telephones. This is an extra pleasure, to hear his voice again, casual and apologetic, as if he were an ordinary person and they had a relationship with a future. Sometimes, rarely, he has to cancel, and even that has its merits, as he then has to rebook, prolonging her time of anticipation. Some friends tell her this is unhealthy and masochistic, but she thinks it's sensible, making the most of everything she is given. Other friends envy her for having a high which must, she thinks, be very similar to one induced by drugs. A hit or a fix. She isn't sure of her terminology; she is a bit out of date. But she knows about love. That doesn't seem to change. Only now there are books written about how to cure it, groups formed to support you while you learn to love moderately, without risk, making sure you get loved back in equal measure before you hazard yourself.

He arrives frowning, with some remark about the traffic or the weather. He is an angry person. She can feel the enormity of her smile splitting her face: she is smiling hugely, like an idiot. She is smiling for both of them. She is so joyful, her smile is out of control. What does he make of such a smile?

He walks in, past her. He doesn't kiss her or touch her. If she waits long enough he will, but often she can't wait and she goes to him and puts her arms round him, needing to touch him; she puts her head against his chest, opens his shirt, kisses his fur and breathes in that special scent of him. Pheromones. She has read about them. Sheer animal attraction, primitive, atavistic, the chemistry that makes for instant mating.

He returns the hug. He looks down at her and smiles at last and they say hullo. The back of his shirt is wet with sweat. Occasionally, he has an erection then and there, and they go straight to bed. But usually he doesn't: he is tired and irritable and wants a drink, lunch, time to unwind and dump his hospital morning. She has to let go of him by sheer willpower before he pulls away from her. She never gets enough of him but he, she fears, gets far too much of her. An unequal bargain. She feels like a puppy wagging its tail at an indifferent master, jumping up, licking his hand. She hates feeling like that but she doesn't know how to stop.

He talks about patients and administration while she pours him wine and prepares the food. He tells her he has fucked up his life: he has had too many children and he pays too much maintenance. It is always a shock when he says something important: usually he uses words to conceal rather than reveal. Over two years he has only told her a few things that really matter. She longs to talk to him, to listen to him, but feels an enormous pressure against it, blocking her best endeavours. He has a prickly self-protective casing around him. She is embracing a hedgehog. He is a crab, an armadillo: he won't let her touch his soft centre but keeps her outside, banging helplessly on his hard shell with her small useless fists.

He fills her eyes. The pleasure of having him in her space, of being able to look at him and touch him sometimes makes her deaf so that she has difficulty hearing what he says, although she longs to hear it. She tells him this, but he doesn't respond. Sometimes he seems so joyless she wonders why he is with her at all. 'I wouldn't be here if I didn't like it,' he says. Whatever that means. His idea of a compliment perhaps. In bed she presses her hands very flat against his furry body so that she can touch as much of him as possible while he sleeps. She knows she is obsessed but that knowledge doesn't make the obsession go away.

In restaurants, on the rare occasions when they go out and are therefore unable to make love, she can't stop herself touching him, stroking him, yet she worries that all this physical adulation may be cloying and oppressive. 'D'you like me touching you or do you think, Oh God, not again?' she asks him, genuinely wanting to know.

'I like it,' he says without emotion.

Once he comes round to see her and they sit for an hour talking of hotels in America while he holds her hand actively, fingers moving, clasping and reclasping, their hands making love while their words say nothing at all. Then he leaves for his next appointment. On another occasion she asks him if he would have liked to make love that day. 'I wouldn't have minded,' he says, 'but I was conscious of the time.'

When they met he told her his wife was going to leave him but she hasn't and this is never mentioned now. He has had three wives and seven children. He earns a lot of money but he is always in debt. He doesn't like her to sympathise with him: he prefers to blame himself for everything.

At the beginning he made love to her totally, with hands and tongue and cock, making her come over and over again, seeming to care about her coming. Now he gets into bed and pulls the duvet over his head; she gets in beside him and he puts his arm round her and sleeps. She lies there listening to his heavy breathing and watching their time together tick away. Talking time, if they could ever talk. Lovemaking time. He is so tired. He is exhausted. He needs sleep more than he needs her. He needs oblivion.

No matter how much she loves him, she can't make him love her. It doesn't work that way. She understands that: there have been people in the past who loved her, whom she could not love. She knows too that the person who loves gains more than the person who is loved. So she feels more sorry for him than for herself. She is richer; she can afford to be generous.

When he wakes he denies being asleep. He says, 'Make me hard,' and she takes his cock in her mouth. She loves it so much, this part of him, hard or soft. Usually her tongue and his hand and a little fantasy talk work the magic and it rises from the ashes. But sometimes it won't obey. She feels his shame and anger acutely: it is far worse than her own disappointment. And there is the extra burden of having to pretend it does not matter. He apologises; she is embarrassed. They both want him to be powerful. 'I'm sorry. My cock's not behaving itself,' he says.

She thinks it a miracle it ever does when they have so little time, trying to eat, drink, sleep, talk and make love in less than three hours once a fortnight. At his best he is the greatest lover she has ever had and she has told him so in the past, but this does not help them now.

'Well,' she says, 'you're not a machine.'

His reply amazes her so much she forgets to ask him what he means. 'Yes I am,' he says, 'and so are you.'

Sometimes he comes in her mouth and she swallows it. The warm spray flowering on her tongue like sparklers on the hand, soft and piercing, gentle and sharp. Before, with other people, lesser loves, she has always spat it out. But usually he comes inside her, needing to enter her as she needs to have him inside. 'I'm past my prime,' he says.

'What a good thing I didn't meet you any sooner,' she says, half meaning it, although in her heart she wants all his life. He would have been too much for her. If she finds him intoxicating now, what must he have been like when his cock always obeyed him, when the dark hair that covers his body also covered his head, before it started greying, thinning, before he put on weight, before he had responsibilities? Did he like himself any better when he was young, she wonders?

Sometimes he won't even kiss her. 'Don't I taste nice?' she asks fearfully.

'I'm not feeling very kissy at the moment,' he says. 'Nothing to do with you.'

She wonders if anything is to do with her. Sometimes she feels she is just servicing him. Often they make love without him even stroking her. She can do it for herself, which he likes, or do without. Then she feels lonely, angry, that he is destroying the only thing they have. He says he is lazy, she thinks he is nearly dead. Her compassion is greater than her anger. He has very little left to give, but she wants it, whatever it is. Everything could be resolved if they had more time, she thinks. She sucks him, strokes him; they work together on the magic mushroom, and then they fuck for a long time. Often she comes gloriously but sometimes she is too tense and anxious, too worried for him. Advice from sex manuals whirls through her head: relax, squeeze, fantasise, enjoy. Above all, don't let this powerful, fragile creature feel inadequate. Hearing his cries at the end and feeling the waves of his semen inside her, she feels privileged, set apart from ordinary mortals, joined to a god. She holds him while he sleeps and imagines a life where they could live together, knowing it will never happen. Each time he leaves she feels exhausted and bereaved.

She takes out insurance: she finds herself another lover, Paul. She doesn't believe in fidelity to a married man any more, no matter how much she loves him. It makes no sense; she had learned the hard way. In her experience they eventually give her up for a new woman or for their old wife. They get bored by familiarity or scared of intensity and they run away: it is only a matter of time. Paul is married too, but more happily than Lionel: it shows in his face. 'I don't want to be unfaithful to my wife emotionally or financially,' he says at the beginning, very clear, 'just sexually.' She understands: he means he will bring cheap bottles of wine and discourage her from phoning him at the office. His wife's name is Christine and he often mentions her casually as if to remind Naomi of her existence, or as if she were someone they both knew, as if it reassured him to bring her into the conversation.

'That's all right,' she says. 'I'm in love,' and she tells him about her beloved. He listens sympathetically, a rare gift, they have good sex together, and she thinks of him as a friend. She likes the perfect balance of it, the fearful symmetry: him with his wife and her with her lover. She hopes he will make her feel more relaxed, less desperate for Lionel, better able to survive the intervals between meetings. He is short and wiry, smooth-skinned, cheerful and energetic, and he makes love generously, doing everything she wants. He is content with his life and therefore he has more to give. 'Tell me what you want,' he says, as if offering her a menu. The luxury of it. She feels safe with him: there is no danger of her loving him. Each time she is pleased to see him arrive, smiling, kissing and hugging her as soon as they meet; each time she watches him leave with a light heart, feeling replenished.

Lionel would like her to find another man to join them, so she doesn't tell him about Paul, who would also be delighted at the idea. It is her way of punishing them both for not giving her enough time, for not loving her. Her small rebellion. She won't allow them such a treat and they will never know that she could. She wants Lionel alone. And she doesn't want to find out if they could both easily make space in their crowded diaries for such an event when their time with her is so limited.

Her therapy group want to know why she keeps choosing married men. She is baffled by the idea of choice; she can't remember when last she met anyone single. She is forty. In her age group most people are married. But they insist it means she is afraid of commitment. Maybe she is, and after two divorces it seems like a sensible fear.

She works by night, in a casino. Every night she watches men lose (or, much less often, win) in an evening more than she earns in a year. Who would want to go out with a man like that, even if they were not forbidden to fraternise with the punters? But it is only money, whereas she is gambling with her heart. Everyone else who works with her is married or much too young. Besides, married men are house-trained: they carry used glasses back into the kitchen and leave the lavatory seat down. And it is touching, the way they speak lovingly of their children.

With Lionel she explores the mutual pleasures of violence and the tenderness that follows. Sometimes the marks take a week or ten days to fade and when he telephones he asks if she would like some more. She always says yes.

She doesn't tell her therapy group about this: she doesn't think they could handle it. But she does try to explain to them that sex is magic, that she needs the reassurance of touch, penetration, ejaculation, to take her out of her head, to keep her in touch with life. They say they understand but she doesn't see understanding in their faces. Some of them are married, some celibate. One of them is both. They think she needs to have her consciousness raised. They think she doesn't value herself. They ask her to talk about her dead father.

She tries to explain what it's like out there in the jungle at her age. 'It's a seller's market,' she says. 'And I'm buying.' They have all got flats or houses, so surely they will understand that. They still insist she could find somebody single, somebody with time for her, somebody who would put her first. They don't tell her where this miraculous person may be found, or why, since he is so wonderful, he is not already attached to someone else. She knows he doesn't exist. Single men of her age are a little dusty and unkempt; rusted through lack of use; obsessed with the past. She has eaten enough dinners while listening to their bitter tales of what went wrong. Occasionally she has been asked to analyse their lost wives. 'What do you think is the matter with Wendy? Why did she behave like that?' Sometimes they say after a few hours of this that they shouldn't be talking about the past when they're with her; then they go on doing it. They are often quite surprised when she doesn't want to take her clothes off at the end of an evening, her head still full of Wendy's problems so that she feels like a nanny or a shrink. Undressing in these circumstances would surely be gross professional misconduct.

The AIDS horror goes public during her affair with Lionel but he is unperturbed. 'It's too late,' he says, 'we've already mingled our juices. Besides, I've got a very strong immune system.' She wants to believe him. It would be unbearable to have nothing of him left behind in her body. But it is something extra to worry about. He is an old sixties swinger, if he is to be believed, with a legacy of lovers, threesomes, foursomes, orgies. It would be ironic, she thinks, if this love affair should turn out to be not merely heart-breaking but also lethal.

Paul prefers to use sheaths, out of respect for his wife. He is adept with them, so that they are hardly noticeable, but she thinks how sad it is to be back to such primitive technology after all the years of freedom. Once, at Christmas, he doesn't bother, and it is like a gift.

Then without warning Lionel leaves her. He says on the phone, 'I suppose I've been putting off ringing you because I seem to have got involved with someone.'

She isn't surprised but she's stunned. 'My God, what a shock,' she says.

'Yes,' he says, 'it was for me too.'

The pain in her heart grows till she feels it will choke her: it was on the phone too that she heard of the death of her father. 'How long have you known her?' she asks.

'Three weeks,' he says.

'Are you trying to say goodbye?' she asks, very brave now, with nothing more to lose.

'I think I'm saying you may find I'm going to be a bit preoccupied for a while,' he says.

She digests that in silence: it is like swallowing a stone. She wonders if the new woman is preferred because she is married and shares the pressures of family life or because she is willing to enact all his fantasies or simply because she is new and her very newness can revitalise him. She doesn't ask: she doesn't want to know.

'I do actually love you,' she says for the first time, free to say it now it can't threaten him. 'Can we keep in touch?'

'I don't see why not,' he says, 'but you may not want to.'

'This is almost the first real conversation we've had,' she says.

'Oh,' he says, 'that's not quite fair.' And then: 'Well, I must go, I've got people waiting to see me.'

'Keep in touch,' she says again, heavy with loss. Touch was all they had.

'I'll give you a buzz,' he says, an expression she hates. She puts down the phone and picks up the pain, a huge burden of emptiness inside her.

Her therapy group, when she narrates this conversation, stare at her incredulously and ask how she feels. 'Sad,' she says.

'And how do we want her to feel?' the leader asks.

'Angry,' they chorus, almost shouting.

But she can't find the anger. It is not as if he has broken any promise.

The next time Paul makes love to her she weeps after she comes. She has done this before but out of pleasure not grief. She can't tell him Lionel has gone because he has always said it would be a burden to have anyone wholly dependent on him. Anyone except his wife, presumably. But he is warm and affectionate with her as usual. After he has gone she notices that instead of throwing away the used condom in a tissue, he has left it on the floor, its neck knotted like a tiny balloon, so the precious contents can't escape. She stares at it, this magic elixir, these few pale drops that there is so much fuss about. There must be some spell she could cast, if she were a witch and knew what to do. But she is only human and so she sleeps with it under her pillow to comfort herself, like a child with a teddy bear, and it soothes her, taking the edge off the pain, her little souvenir of life.

# Bliss on Wheels

The supermarket was crowded but she noticed him at once because he was her type. Not much taller than she was but heavily built, with dark hair curling over his collar and out of his open-neck shirt. He had a sulky, voluptuous mouth and the sort of olive skin that looked tanned even when it wasn't; he moved with an easy, confident swagger, very sure of himself, very comfortable inside his jeans and leather jacket, as if he owned the world, but didn't need to boast about it. And he wore dark glasses, like a film star. He must be foreign, she decided: he looked dangerous and self-contained, like a prowling animal.

Her husband had looked rather like that once, long ago, before all his glamour got submerged in mortgages and children and washing up, though he had never gone so far as to wear sunglasses in Safeways. That was definitely an affectation: she ought to despise the short dark stranger for that. Instead she found it perversely exciting. She ought to be long past fancying strangers in supermarkets, too, she thought, but she clearly wasn't: she felt definite stirrings of lust.

She had noticed all these details in a flash, of course, and turned away at once. God forbid he should think she was staring at him, or comparing the carefree bachelor look of his light wire basket, containing only smoked salmon and a lemon, with her own vast trolley loaded up with detergent and potatoes and disposable nappies and biscuits. And she wasn't wearing any make-up. She was the one, she thought, who really needed the dark glasses. He wouldn't look twice at her, would he, or if he did, he'd only think she was just another drab boring housewife.

She turned into the next aisle and added cat food, sausages, orange juice and loo paper to her trolley, moving dreamily, aware of a disturbing warm wet tightness between her legs, a longing to have the short dark stranger's cock forcing its way deep inside her and making her come. She was surprised: she hadn't fancied anyone new that strongly for a very long time. She really wanted him: she longed to have him fill her up, to feel him on top of her, heavy like a fallen tree, pinning her to the ground so that she was helpless, unable to prevent him from shooting his juice into her body. She never knew what to call that part of her that wanted sex: cunt was too often used as a term of abuse and vagina reminded her of a visit to the clinic. Neither was very erotic. There ought to be a new, completely different name for something so precious: perhaps she should make one up. It felt like her innermost self, dark and hot and secret, suddenly awake, it seemed, after years of drowsiness. It didn't know or care about respectability and rules, fidelity and marriage. A zipless fuck was what it wanted, like the one she had read about on her honeymoon in one of Erica Jong's books (*Fear of Flying*, just the thing to read on an aircraft), making her joyfully aware that other women felt as she did, that it wasn't only men who could separate sex from love and take pleasure in both.

By then it was too late, of course, because they were already married, but for a few days they had had fun pretending to be strangers: picking each other up on the beach or takes turns to knock on the door of their room as call girl or gigolo. She had enjoyed it. But she had always known it was a safe game, far removed from the real thing. Then he had bought her a copy of *The Story of O* for her birthday and she had read it, sickened but entranced, as a whole new world of bondage and sado-masochism opened up to her, things they had previously joked about, which she suddenly found turned her on. She used to read a few pages at night before he came to bed and they were both surprised and delighted to find her hot and wet and ready for him, begging him to fuck her, hit her, kill her.

Afterwards they always felt a bit silly, a bit embarrassed, but they slept particularly well and were in a specially good mood for days afterwards.

Oh well, all that was a long time ago, and the children had put a stop to most of it. It wasn't easy to have a sexy fantasy life with milk dripping from your tits, or when you ached with exhaustion rather than desire, or when the baby cried just as you thought you might be about to come at last. She loved her husband, of course she did, and she knew he loved her, and they both adored the children, but those early days of fun had gone for ever. They knew each other too well now and they were too tired. Now when they made love it was more affection than lust.

The next time she saw the stranger he had two large peaches in his wire basket and he was reaching for a bottle of champagne. She was furious with envy for the unknown lucky woman (or man, of course, he might be gay, for all she knew) who was going to share this feast with him. If only she had the nerve to chat him up at the check-out and invite him home. But she hadn't, and her next-door neighbour Rosie, who was baby-sitting for her while she shopped, would be shocked if she did, and there was always the chance that her husband might come home unexpectedly, although he had said he was working late. No, she couldn't risk it, and besides, she might be rejected and then she'd feel foolish and ashamed.

She turned her back on the stranger and pushed her trolley to the check-out with the shortest queue. As she unloaded her shopping on to the conveyor belt she heard footsteps behind her but she didn't look round. Then out of the corner of her eye she saw the wire basket containing peaches and champagne, smoked salmon and a lemon. The hand that held it had a few dark hairs curling out of a leather jacket and down the fingers. Her heart banged with excitement so that she was almost afraid he would hear it. If only she were brave enough to turn around and speak to him, make some light-hearted, joking remark, even ask him to help with her shopping. He was standing close to her: she was so strongly aware of his physical presence that she almost forgot to breathe.

She paid for her shopping, her hands shaking as she piled it into two carrier bags, aware of a tight feeling in her chest and a wet feeling between her legs. How ironic that he was right there behind her – she could have touched him, God, how she wanted to – and he'd never know the effect he'd had on her. She walked away, loaded down with her purchases, and took her usual short cut through the car park, excitement and tension ebbing away, replaced with sharp disappointment that it was all over, she'd never see him again except by chance if he lived locally and often went shopping there. Nothing had happened. It was all in her head. What a fool she was not to have had the guts to speak.

Sudden footsteps behind her, then a voice. 'Can I give you a hand?' Not foreign after all. She knew who it was before she turned round, because it was such a sexy voice it couldn't belong to anyone else. And she knew where she wanted the hand.

'Thank you,' she managed to say, trying to sound casual, surprised her voice came out more or less normal. She'd been afraid of a pathetic squeak or croak. He strolled up to her then, removing the sunglasses, and she saw that he had dark brown eyes, almost black. His nose was a bit squashed, as if it had once been flattened in a fight and never quite recovered. He looked good enough to eat. He had a smile that made her feel like the only woman in the world.

'Where are you parked?' he asked her, taking the carrier bags out of her hands. Their fingers touched as he did so and she felt as though an electric current shot up her arm and down to her stomach.

'I'm not,' she said. 'My husband's got the car.' Well, that was not only true but an easy way of letting him know she was married.

'Then you must let me give you a lift home,' he said. 'I'm over there.' She imagined something glamorous and sporty, but he pointed to an estate car attached to a caravan. 'I've just collected it. I'm taking the family on holiday tomorrow.'

So he was married too. Well, that was all right; better really, it made them more equal. But surely he wasn't buying all that luxury food and drink for his wife? She said without thinking, 'God, how lovely, aren't they lucky?' because she had badgered her parents for years to take her on a caravan holiday and they never had and the disappointed little girl was still inside her.

'It's all we can afford this year,' he said simply, not apologising, just stating a fact.

'But it's what I've always wanted,' she said, thinking he probably wouldn't believe her, he'd think she was just trying to make a good impression.

'Come and have a look,' he said, as if he knew she wanted him.

She followed him, knees shaking, across the car park to the caravan, but all the curtains were drawn.

'I can't see in,' she said stupidly.

'Then you'll have to get in, won't you?' he said, undressing her with his eyes. Her inside contracted as if he had already entered her and she was trying to squeeze his cock by practising her pelvic floor exercises. She ought to run away; he might be a dangerous maniac. Would anyone hear if she screamed? Instead, when he opened the caravan door, she climbed in.

Instantly they were in another world where everything was scaled down, like children playing house, like *Alice in Wonderland* or *Through the Looking Glass*. He said,

'God, I want to fuck you so much,' and she said, 'Yes please oh yes please.' They fell upon each other, kissing as if they wanted to devour one another alive, pausing only when they desperately needed to breathe. His skin had the most wonderful smell and she felt his cock pressing big and hard against her through his tight jeans.

'Take your clothes off,' he said. 'I want to look at you.'

She undressed slowly, watching the desire in his face as he watched her. Outside cars parked or drove away; there were voices and people. She stood naked in front of him, feeling suddenly shy and vulnerable.

'Now you,' she said, but instead he came across to her and knelt in front of her as if worshipping her body, burying his face in her pubic hair, finding her clitoris with his tongue and seeking out the magic spot, gently, slowly, quickly, roughly, stopping and starting and pausing to tease her. She sank her fingers into his hair to guide him, even to force him into her rhythm when she wanted to, and he glanced up at her and she stared into the dark, dark eyes and let herself fantasise about unspeakable things that she didn't approve of in real life until she knew she was going to come and nothing could stop her; it was like falling over the edge of a cliff and she screamed with the joy of it, not caring who heard her, and he stopped just before it began to hurt, knowing the moment, and smiled up at her, before doing it again and again until she was sobbing with exhaustion and each time she thought she couldn't come again but somehow she did.

'You taste wonderful,' he said eventually and stood up to kiss her so that she could taste herself on his lips. And it was true, she did taste wonderful, like some fresh delicacy from the sea.

She tugged at his clothes, ripping buttons from his shirt in her haste, but he had to help her unbuckle his belt while she unzipped his jeans. His whole body was covered with black fur and his cock was the right length for her and wonderfully thick, slightly curved at the end, and circumcised, which she liked. It looked so beautiful, so ready for her. She sucked it and played with it and scratched his balls with her nails, while he moved and moaned with pleasure and caressed her hair, saying, 'Oh God, that's good, that's so good, but I've got to come inside you.'

They lay on the caravan carpet and he eased himself into her, a tight fit at first, pleasantly painful, then sliding blissfully because she was so wet from all the sucking and coming. 'What a lovely cunt,' he said, making it sound like a term of endearment, his cock striking some unfamiliar glorious place inside her, perhaps the G spot at last that she had read about. Then he drew her legs up on to his shoulders, turning his head from side to side to kiss her ankles, and that was a painful position, but so exciting, letting him go so deep inside her, that she loved the pain and didn't want it to stop, until he rolled over and pulled her on top of him so that she was riding him and coming in great waves over and over again and crying out while he smiled up at her, playing with her breasts, looking pleased with himself and proud of her.

Eventually she collapsed on top of him, sobbing with pleasure, both of them soaked in sweat, and he kissed her and held her for a while before making her kneel and entering her again, telling her to play with herself and guiding her hand or letting her guide his hand until she hardly knew which hand was which, only that she was coming again, and then he was tugging on her hips and thrusting harder and faster until she thought she might burst and he came with several loud cries and she felt the pulse of his cock deep inside her and his semen flooding her, and she came again with the sheer bliss of feeling it, and then they both collapsed on the carpet and she was crushed by his weight, under her fallen tree at long last.

She had never been so completely satisfied before, floating back from some far off magical place in outer space, and she tried to hang on to him as long as she could, but presently she felt him shrinking and sliding out of her.

They rolled round to face each other, smiling with absolute goodwill, totally at peace, like friends, kissing and hugging each other. She wanted to stay like that for ever but eventually they had to wrench themselves apart, sticky as they were, and get back on their unsteady legs, groggy with pleasure; and get dressed. They did not speak or arrange to meet again. It seemed to be perfect as it was. He picked up his shopping and got into his car; she picked up her shopping and walked down the road to her house. She felt renewed, as if the inside of her head as well as her body had been completely rearranged.

Rosie gave her a funny look when she came in but was in a hurry to leave and didn't ask any questions. The children were mercifully asleep. She stood in the kitchen, dreamily unpacking her shopping, feeling an amazing orgasmic echo reverberating inside her, knowing she should have a bath before her husband came in but not wanting to wash the stranger away. Then it was suddenly too late. She heard her husband's key in the lock and there he was, strolling into the kitchen with a carrier bag in his hand, from which he took smoked salmon and a lemon, peaches and champagne. 'I thought you might fancy a little something special before the holiday,' he said.

'What a good idea,' she said, staring at him. 'Did you know you've lost a button off your shirt?' Then they both started to laugh.